Postscript to Poison

DOROTHY BOWERS

 Moonstone Press

This edition published in 2019 by Moonstone Press
www.moonstonepress.co.uk

Originally published in 1938 by Hodder & Stoughton

ISBN 978-1-899000-08-1
eISBN 978-1-899000-17-3

A CIP catalogue record for this book is available from the British Library

Text designed and typeset by Tetragon, London
Cover illustration by Jason Anscomb
Printed and bound by in Great Britain by TJ International, Padstow, Cornwall

Contents

Introduction

Postscript to Poison was Dorothy Bowers' first novel, originally published by Houghton & Stoddard in 1938. It delighted reviewers. Critic Maurice Richardson of *The Observer* wrote: "Miss Bowers is new this term. Let me be the first member of the staff to extend her a hearty welcome. She has been coached in our traditions, and is likely to settle down quickly. *Postscript to Poison* is a thoroughly satisfying piece of family narcotising... A double bluff by Miss Bowers effectively conceals who did it. This pupil has little to learn and should go far."

In *Postscript to Poison*, Bower introduces us to Chief Inspector Dan Pardoe of Scotland Yard and his colleague Sergeant Salt, who investigate the death of elderly Cornelia Lackland. The haughty and malicious widow of a wealthy man, she had made the lives of his granddaughters miserable. Before her death, the town doctor had received anonymous letters accusing him of poisoning her. But as Pardoe investigates, he finds motives for murder much broader than first anticipated. This is a town where everybody's business is known by everyone else. Pardoe is a satisfying and likeable creation, described by Milward Kennedy, crime writer and *Sunday Times* reviewer, as having "humanity and common sense as impressive as his intelligence".

Bowers was an advocate of the "fair play" school of detective novels, and displayed great ingenuity in piecing together the necessary elements of a baffling mystery, with clues shared freely with the reader. When Inspector Pardoe indicates he knows who the murderer is, the reader knows virtually everything he does. Bowers' skill in obscuring her characters' motives allows her to hide the identity of the murderer until exactly the right moment. However, what raises Bowers above contemporary fair play plodders is the perceptive description of her characters, no matter how small their part, and a keen eye for place unusual in a genre dominated by plot. For example, a description of the night of the murder: "Lights winked, went out, came on in some other room. Blinds shut out the deep-blue night that pressed against the windows. A few bats flitted and chased each other like a company of dark, undefined thoughts, and from one of the shrubberies an owl quavered low crooning notes. A cat darted noiselessly from one side of the square to the other."

Dorothy Violet Bowers was born in Leominster on 11 June 1902, the daughter of a confectioner. In 1903, the family moved to Monmouth, where Albert Edwards Bowers ran his own bakery until he retired in 1936. Educated at the Monmouth High School for Girls, Bowers received a scholarship to Oxford and, displaying the dogged tenacity evident throughout her short life, sat the Latin entrance exam three times before she was finally accepted. Though women had only recently been able to take degrees at Oxford, Bowers' sister Evelyn joined her there, which suggests a familial focus on education. In 1926, Bowers graduated from the Society of Oxford Home-Students (now St Anne's College) with a third-class honours degree in Modern History, and spent the next few years pursuing a career as a history teacher. Subsequent letters to her college principal documented her worries about family finances ("my father... our university careers have been a heavy expense to him"), and her desire to break away from Monmouth ("I have a dread of finding work in a small pleasant county-town such as this. The temptation to crystallize would be too great"). Temporary jobs teaching history and English did not inspire her and she turned to writing; letters to friends documented the "slow, uphill" battle to get published. During this time, she supplemented her income by compiling crossword puzzles for *John O'London's Weekly* under the pseudonym "Daedalus". With the success of *Postscript to Poison*, Bowers published three further Inspector Pardoe novels in rapid succession: *Shadows Before* (1939), *A Deed*

Without a Name (1940) and *Fear for Miss Betony* (1941). *The Times* heralded *Fear for Miss Betony* as the best mystery of 1941, stating: "Every page bears witness to a brain of uncommon powers." The outbreak of war brought Bowers to London, where she worked in the European News Service of the BBC. Her final book, *The Bells at Old Bailey*, was published in 1947, with Pardoe replaced by another Scotland Yard detective, Raikes. Never of robust health, Bowers contracted tuberculosis during this period and eventually succumbed to the disease on 29 August 1948. She died knowing that she had been inducted into the prestigious Detection Club, the only writer selected for membership in 1948. Moonstone Press is delighted to reissue the works of Dorothy Bowers for a new generation to enjoy.

For

GWEN

who did not read it

Chapter I

——AND TOMORROW

How does your patient, Doctor?

Macbeth

D r. Tom Faithful closed the door quietly and came downstairs with characteristically light tread. Well-controlled muscles lent to his movements a grace oddly at variance with his bulk. The hall was empty, still as the summer afternoon outside that sent a shaft of sunlight through the transom of the front door. From the servants' quarters came now and again tones he recognized for those of Hennessy, the butler, and from not far away the sound of somebody washing a car.

For a moment the doctor hesitated, then went purposefully towards a room on the left. Through the closed door came a murmur of voices, cut once by an impatient laugh which seemed suddenly caught back as Dr. Faithful, rapping perfunctorily, turned the knob and came in.

It was a small room he entered, high-ceilinged, its pleasant proportions rather sparely furnished in excellent taste. A girl who had been standing by the front window running the silk tassel of the blind cord through her fingers almost spun round, lips parted like a runner's, her eyes suddenly bright and concentrated, till seeing it was the doctor she composed herself and gave him a cool little smile.

"Well, Doc, and what is dear Grandmama's last decision?"

The doctor smiled good-naturedly. It was hard to do otherwise at the charming little blonde who confronted him, her hair beautifully coiffured in a style that gave piquancy to the half-shrewd, half-childish eagerness of her face. The sleeveless frock she wore, of extreme simplicity and vaguely suggestive of longer wear than its owner might care to remember, made all the brighter her challenging personality.

"So you think your grandmother's routed me, eh, Carol?" His voice like his step was easy and attractive. "Not a bit of it. But isn't Jenny here?"

"Yes," came a lazy voice from a deep chair beside a window facing the door. The chair grumbled a bit on its castors, and an untidy newspaper that had effectively screened its occupant was dropped. The girl called Jenny, dark, slim, deeply tanned, in a white-collared blue frock that set off her skin, got slowly to her feet and met the doctor's glance hopefully.

"What's that?" she asked. "You mean you're not letting Gran have her own way? You don't think she's well enough?"

"On the contrary. Mrs. Lackland, in spite of the disappointment she gave me on Saturday, is a highly satisfactory patient."

"But you said—" began Carol with unnecessary violence.

"What?" asked Faithful sharply. Hands in pockets he strolled to the fireplace, turned his back on it, and looked from one girl to the other with a faint lift of his brows.

"That she hadn't got what she wanted," Carol finished more quietly.

"I did not. You implied she'd got it in face of my opposition. She hasn't, because I'm in entire agreement with her. There's no reason whatever why your grandmother shouldn't come down tomorrow, and none at all against her seeing Rennie. In fact, the state she'll be in if she doesn't is likely to produce more harm than any interview with a lawyer can do."

"Traitor," said Carol briefly. Jenny began arranging the disordered paper without a glance for either.

"Don't be ridiculous, child," Faithful replied unhurriedly. "I'm not likely to insist upon Mrs. Lackland's stopping in bed and seeing nobody just because life's a bit more comfortable for you when she's upstairs. Now am I?"

"I think you might," said Carol shamelessly. "Anyhow, you could express yourself less brutally." For all the flippancy of her reply some agitation, hardly suppressed, seemed rising within her, but before she could say any more Jenny remarked calmly: "But you don't know, Doctor, that the interview with her lawyer won't excite her."

Faithful looked at her quickly, but before he could answer, Carol, eager to endorse the last statement, struck in with: "No, of course not. It all depends on what she wants him for, and for days now she's been all worked up at the thought of having him here."

The doctor made a brusque gesture.

"Then the best treatment for her nerves is his visit."

He turned abruptly to Jenny, who was gazing out of the side window against which a laburnum, its flowers withered long ago, hung soft sprays of leaves.

"Have you any reason for supposing that Mrs. Lackland's business with her lawyer will be upsetting?"

Jenny shrugged. "Plenty. But so would you if you were one of us. But, oh, what's the use——" She broke off and, sensing the doctor's impatience, adopted a mood of acquiescence which cleared the air.

"She'd like me to make an appointment then for tomorrow afternoon, I suppose?" she asked quietly.

"Probably. But I fancy by Mrs. Lackland's remarks that she'd already arranged the interview with Rennie, and that he's simply waiting for a medical verdict to confirm it. Well, that's how it stands," he added. "I was bound to tell her that I was pleased with her at last, and that there could be no real objection to an occasional visitor or two provided she knows when to part with them and goes on observing early-to-bed. Apart from the surprising sickness last weekend which seems to have been due to her disregard of the diet I've emphatically insisted upon, Mrs. Lackland has made astonishing progress in the last month, and though she had to be sent back to bed the other day it isn't necessary to keep her there now."

"No. Well," sighed Carol, perching herself with delicate caution upon a small table by the window and swinging one leg in dreamy fashion, "it's simply the old case of devil and deep sea. Keep Gran upstairs and increase her wrath. Let her come down and increase ours."

"Not exactly," observed Jenny curtly. "It's just as irritating whether she's in bed or out of it."

"That's out of my sphere," said Faithful thankfully. "All I can answer for is Mrs. Lackland's bodily improvement. If she pays reasonable attention to what she eats and when, it's unlikely she'll have a recurrence of last week's trouble. Miss Bullen too, who sees her more constantly perhaps than anybody else, says her spirits have picked up wonderfully in the past few days."

"Naturally," said Carol quickly, "'malice aforethought.' Grannie's, I mean, not Emily's—this time!" Then as the doctor looked steadily at her she added: "Oh you needn't make eyes at me like that! She's feeling vile to Jenny because of her young man, and that's what made her spirits go up with a bang and why she wants to talk to Rennie, I expect!"

Jenny coloured and made as if to speak, but Faithful had turned to Carol.

"And who, pray, is Jenny's young man? The film star?"

"Yes. Carnowski. It's been a heavenly thrill, but Grandma found out everything."

"With Emily's help," added Jenny, with finality. The colour burned brightly through the brown of her cheeks. She looked suddenly taut.

"Having revealed so much," said Carol lightly, "you'd better learn our deadly secret. Emily goes out tonight—to disport herself, we're pretty sure, at the pictures, where Jan Carnowski 'Continues to Draw Great Houses to *Black Arches*, the Super Film of Our Age,'" she giggled, "and Jan himself steps out of the picture and has supper here with Jenny! Now would you call that dramatic irony?"

"I'd say it was an unnecessary piece of melodrama," the doctor retorted grimly. "Isn't that mere unwise bravado?" He turned to Jenny.

"No, not really. Jan would much rather take me out somewhere, but I've got to spend my evenings in while Gran's in her room because from teatime onwards she's apt to want me at any moment."

"And it's hell," Carol added simply, "if you're not there."

"I see." The doctor's comment was brief, his expression merely professional. He turned to go. "I'll drop in by the end of the week," he said briskly, "to make my farewells. The locum comes in on Monday."

"Scotland, isn't it?" inquired Jenny, rather indifferently. "How long did you say?"

"A fortnight. Sure to go fast, but mountain streams and a spot of fishing will be a blessed oasis in this heat."

As he moved away his eye was caught by the whiteness of Carol's cheeks. She was twisting into little tubes the dropped petals of some large pink roses on the table.

"You look as if a tonic mightn't come amiss, Carol. Like me to shake you up something?"

The girl shook her head sharply.

"It's this grilling weather," she said, shortly. "The sort we always get in Minsterbridge when the sun shines for more than a week. I'm all right really."

As if to emphasize her vigour she ran swiftly the yard or so to the door and swept it wide open before the doctor could do so.

"Oh, miss," a small chubby maid standing very close to it gasped and swayed forward a little. Faithful, with an amused glance at her distress, went out into the hall and took his hat.

He heard Carol's angry "Hetty!" and the beginning of over-hasty assurances from the culprit, then lingering no further directed a wordless goodbye of raised eyebrows to Jenny in the background and let himself out.

On the short flight of steps, flanked by little brick pillars at the bottom, Dr. Faithful stood for some seconds looking thoughtfully down the familiar sun-baked path to the severe iron gate set in the wall on the road. In the mature warmth of the July day, the tea hour approaching, house and road and even the jaded grass of the lawn had the somnolent charm of a sleeping cat. Despite the strain visible in his face it was with satisfaction that the doctor surveyed the scene and looked back reflectively to the end of an exhausting piece of work. When he came down the short path and out into the square where the light lay shadowless on ripe old brick, and plane trees, formally spaced, stood breathless in the quivering heat, the tantalizing vision of his Scottish burn and the folding mists above it seemed a mirage unlikely to assume reality, so wide a gulf lay between this world and that.

In visiting Lacklands on foot the doctor had followed his usual custom. His own house was a bare ten minutes' away, and unless he had a round of visits at the same time it wasn't worth taking the car out. A short cut by the cool paths of St. Michael's churchyard would bring him almost to his own doorstep. He enjoyed walking, and walking in Minsterbridge gave an edge to his enjoyment. He was what the ladies of that small cathedral city liked to call a fine figure of a man, and he was conscious of it.

Six years ago Dr. Faithful had succeeded to his father's practice, following a five year's partnership of father and son. At twenty-five he had had the mental and physical poise of a man in his thirties, and now at thirty-eight he retained the lithe precision of carriage that had adorned his youth. It was true that he had put on weight, that his handsome, large-featured face bore a weariness unexpected in a man of his years, but his smile, the easy dominance of his personality, the pronounced histrionic eyebrows above the full dark eyes of Latin brilliance remained unimpaired and continued to make him the most sexually attractive man in the city, and a force to be reckoned with. Oddly enough, perhaps, his own interest in women was limited to the professional, which may have accentuated his charm for them. In spite of a fair amount of complicity to rescue him from such a condition, he remained a bachelor; though it could not be said that he showed any marked affection for them, his manner with children, whom he treated like adults, amounted to genius. Whatever the precise reason, Tom Faithful was the most popular doctor with the best practice in Minsterbridge, and this in the face of a large proportion of masculine indifference easily developing into hostility when the womenfolk expressed their admiration with rather less tact than usual.

There was too a disarming bluntness in his manner which was not discourtesy, so that rebuffed ladies invariably rose to a second onslaught, partly it is true because the wish was father to the thought and they could believe neither that the doctor despised them nor that he would not in time succumb to their charms.

After crossing the square and greeting a pram or two in the quiet walled road skirting the High School girls' playing field, the doctor mounted two shallow steps and entered St. Michael's graveyard through the tall gate which stood constantly open. Here you were suddenly in a grateful shaft of coolness, beneath the laced boughs of limes, with dark, secret laurels on the other side of the railings, sharp leaf-tips aglitter with light, and trim little cypresses managing to look perfectly at home in the Mediterranean sunshine.

From the south porch of the church a figure was slowly emerging, which, perceiving Dr. Faithful at a few yards' distance, shed its piety completely and rushed him with a determination it would have been impossible to withstand.

"Oh, Doctor," cried Mrs. Makin, a tall bouncing woman with a commanding bust and a good deal of youthful makeup on her face, "the very man I was praying to meet!"

The doctor glanced wickedly at the church door. "St. Michael was good to you then."

"Now, now," the lady reproved, with what she believed was a pout. "No, what I mean is, I'm going to send you an invitation, of course, but I do like to see my special people as well and get them to promise to come. It gives me confidence to carry on. It's my garden party next Wednesday week, oh, today fortnight, I mean," she hurried on, "in aid of the local branch of the League of Nations, you know, because in the autumn we hope to get down a really good set of people to lecture us on world affairs and try, as Mr. Whatley says—he *is* so good—to attract more members by running something lively and intellectual that will attract highbrows and lowbrows—you know the kind of thing—and Mr. Whatley gets so *little* encouragement and appreciation—"

"Yes, yes, a pity," said Dr. Faithful, in anything but a compassionate voice, "but I'm afraid—"

"Oh, now it's not much I'm asking you to do, but we're getting an excellent programme—well, for one thing, we're doing *She Stoops to Conquer* on the tennis court, and—"

"But, my dear lady," the doctor interrupted in a desperate attempt to stem the flood, and barely checking a burst of ribald laughter at a picture his mind presented to him, "forgive me, I shan't—"

"Oh, yes, you *will*!" exclaimed Mrs. Makin, with cheerful determination, her voice rising to clinch the certainty. "I just want you to do some of your famous conjuring—you know how successful you were last year at Lady Bilcox's 'At Home,' and it isn't much to ask and yet it will give *enormous* pleasure and swell our funds *tremendously* if I can tell people that's a feature of the entertainment. Now, Doctor," her voice sank to the gushing wheedle she practised on impaled victims like the doctor, "we know you enjoy telling us you can't come to grace our little efforts, because it makes us want you all the more, but this time—"

"Yes, this time," said the doctor, believing the affirmative opening would allow him to say what he wanted, "I shan't be in Minsterbridge on the date of your party. Alas, my dear Mrs. Makin," he held up a hand in face of what he saw coming, "a poor G.P. must take a holiday now and again, and I'm really looking forward to this one. So on Monday my locum comes in and I go out. I'm sorry, you know, to have arranged things so badly."

"Oh, but Doctor," wailed Mrs. Makin, disregarding the hint of sardonic humour in his eyes, "I was counting on you! Yes, it is badly arranged. Now, it isn't going to be for long, is it?"

"A mere two weeks," Faithful replied. "Thank you for wanting me. I'd be delighted to balance my biscuit, of course, but perhaps Dr. Riley will know some tricks."

He raised his hat and moved off. Mrs. Makin gave a deprecatory titter, intended to convey her appreciation of the proffered consolation and at the same time her own inconsolable sense of loss. Dr. Faithful, however, might have experienced some astonishment had he intercepted the look of sheer malevolence she gave him on parting.

"Stuffed cat," thought the doctor, without rancour, and exchanged a knowing look with an eighteenth-century cherub that leered at him between the bushes. He followed a path skirting the west side of the nave and came out in a minute through a modest gate overhung by a chestnut whose branches leaned half across the road. On the other side half a dozen Victorian houses stood in unpretentious comfort, their plain fronts sheer to the pavement. As the doctor approached the second of these the teatime postman was just leaving his door.

"Good afternoon, Walters," said Dr. Faithful.

"Good afternoon, sir," responded Walters cheerfully. He liked the doctor, not himself possessing womenfolk to cry him up vehemently. "Very 'ot." He plodded on up the street.

Dr. Faithful entered his house quietly. As he closed the door he turned to the cumbrous wooden letterbox inside and raised its lid. Before he had seen or touched the contents a sense keen as actual sight gave him infallible warning of what he should find there.

Only one letter lay within. With a single glance at it the doctor pushed it in his pocket, and after hanging up his hat went upstairs to wash his hands. When he came down it was unnecessary to ring for tea. Mrs. Bates, his bustling and efficient little housekeeper, had heard him come in, and brought in the tray as he entered his sitting room.

"A good cup of tea's the best medicine, isn't it?" she remarked. "I always do say being under thirty miles from London gives us the city heat." She threw out her observation, it seemed, as much to the room as to the doctor. She knew and respected his dislike of conversation when he came in to his meals.

Faithful assented absently, and she was struck by the intense weariness apparent in his face and attitude. Very unlike Dr. Tom, she thought. And much too soon. There were moments when he looked his father's age. But without saying anything more she went back to her own tea.

Left alone, the doctor deliberately set himself to follow his usual habits. He sat down in a low chair, the small table at his elbow, lit a cigarette, poured out a cup of tea, thrust his long legs out straight, crossed his ankles, and tilting back his head relaxed completely.

Not until his second cup did he take from his pocket the letter he had received. Then with a grim smile at his own patience he held it between his fingers for a few seconds, reading as with almost bored familiarity his name and address executed in what looked like painfully formed but quite legible block letters.

Picking up a knife he slit the thick white envelope and drew out a single sheet of cheap azure notepaper twice folded. Spread out it appeared at first sight to be almost blank, till in the centre you saw two lines inscribed in the same somewhat pinched capitals as the address. The message ran: "*Do you think it is a secret that you are slowly poisoning Mrs. Lackland?*"

The doctor read it with no visible alteration of expression on his face. With equal composure he returned it to his pocket, finished his tea with at least a show of appetite, then getting up crossed the hall to his study, a small book-crowded place not tidy enough to be uncomfortable nor sufficiently untidy to cause its owner any anxiety. Here he went straight to his desk and, pushing the chair back a little, took some keys from his pocket and inserted one in a drawer on the left. From it he took two envelopes, then closing the door sat down at his desk and placed these letters together with today's in front of him.

The writing was the same in each case. The only difference was that the earlier letters were contained in envelopes of the same common brand as the paper on which they were written. The doctor took out these old communications and reread each thoughtfully, comparing them with the new letter. For a few minutes afterwards he sat motionless, eyes half-lidded meditatively. Then he smiled.

Faithful returned the letters to their envelopes more briskly than he had withdrawn them. He locked them again in the drawer. With fresh assurance and a virility of movement Mrs. Bates would have approved, he turned to the telephone and picked up the receiver.

"Give me the police," said Dr. Faithful to exchange.

Chapter II

TWILIGHT OF A GODDESS

MACBETH: What is the night?
LADY M.: Almost at odds with morning which is which.

Macbeth

M rs. Cornelia Lackland sat up in bed and watched Emily Bullen knitting in a low chair. The very sight of wool in the kind of July they were getting was intolerable, she thought, but Emily was like that, imbued with the sort of irritating prevision normally regarded as the prerogative of scouts and guides, so that she was acutely conscious of autumn in the midst of raging summer and prepared for winter's worst rigours when the first leaves dropped in a windless fall.

By closing her eyes Mrs. Lackland was able to exclude Emily and her jumper, but that meant shutting out as well all the pleasant features of her bedroom, of which convalescence was making her increasingly aware; so, as there were things to look at other than her companion, she turned her head towards the window a foot or two away on the right and contemplated the empty, sunlit garden terraces, the line of the alder-fringed river, itself shallow and invisible, and far away between the top-heavy elms the great tower of the cathedral. Her room, which was at the back of the house and had to have its blinds drawn against the dazzling morning heat, was beautifully cool at this hour of the afternoon when the shadow of the house slipped gradually a little closer to the terraces.

Mrs. Lackland's thoughts ran hither and thither. What was it Dr. Tom had said? Not a doubt that she could see Rennie tomorrow. She savoured with slow relish the recollection, recalling the very inflections of his voice as he gave the coveted assurance. Get up, go out, please herself within bounds. No particular hurry either about renewing her tonic when this bottle was gone. Well, she'd show them. She'd take up things where she'd left off. She'd seen and heard enough downstairs last week to know that it was time she was about again. The thought of Saturday's horrible sickness made her shudder a little and shy away from the memory, too near to be comfortable. That was what had sent her back to bed when she thought she was down again for good. But there would be nothing like that this time. And once let her see Rennie she'd again be entire mistress of the whole situation.

She frowned slightly at thought of the solicitor's visit. A pity the scope of what he could do for her was actually so limited. But, after all, these upstart grandchildren-by-marriage were ignorant of the precise extent of that life interest provision which circumscribed her so narrowly. She could bluff them. She'd done it before and would do it again. Dangle the shadow before their eyes and pretend it was the substance. Besides, it was true that she had an actual power to wield. She was well too, feeling better than she'd felt all the year, better than for long before her illness indeed. Recovered health—that in itself was power.

Turning a little on her back, she stretched out her left arm to take up a hand mirror from the bedside table. Holding it frankly before her face she considered the image the glass threw back. Who would suppose she was seventy-eight? She admired with an almost detached pleasure the haughty poise of the head with its smooth strands of shining silver hair, the fine soft skin touched with a faint flush and the high-bridged, masterful nose. The colour of the eyes had faded perhaps, but there was no sag about the sharply defined jaw. In a gentle light, she knew, she would pass for barely more than sixty. She was good for long enough yet. She, the once lovely Cornelia Crown, notorious beauty and courtesan, who had wrestled with life and beaten it over and over again, would beat it once more.

Her marriage to John Lackland may have been a mistake in some ways. But looked at from another angle, what could have been more successful? It was a legalized union, at least, that had put at her command the security that money alone could bring. Homage, kisses, the dazzling triumphs of beauty were as ephemeral as dreams beside the solid fact of money. They had served their turn, and served it well. But money—she loved it, she had it. A barrage against the years when it wasn't possible to grapple with life and win with the same weapons as before. Money would conquer for her. She had had no children, she had known a trick worth two of that. So those bulwarks against the future were not for her. She neither gave nor expected loving kindness. But with money she had the whip hand of these grandchildren of John's, and when she cracked the whip she could make them jump which way she liked.

She looked across at her companion again.

"Bullen, put that horrible garment away. It makes me hot all over to see you. A wintry touch may be welcome, perhaps, but yards of wool don't make me feel it, and you'll never manage to look kittenish playing with the stuff!"

Emily Bullen flushed unbecomingly as she laid aside her knitting neatly and got up. She was a pale woman of medium height and indefinite age, rather plump, with brown hair and eyes. Her face bore a more or less constant expression of artificial brightness.

"I'm sorry, Mrs. Lackland. Shall I read to you?"

"No. I don't want to go to sleep. Come over here and sit by me."

Emily Bullen drew a small chair at the foot of the bed close to the table and seated herself obediently, her glance resting almost complacently on the arrogant old eyes regarding her.

Mrs. Lackland sighed. She wondered, not for the first time, why spinsters however sweet and compliant always leave an acidulated flavour. Bullen may as well have been an inhabitant of Mars for all the common meeting ground that was theirs. Cornelia Lackland would have understood a prostitute, but between her and the virtuous acquiescence of her companion a great gulf spread. However, Bullen knew her job, she was somebody to talk to, and she could be a source of malicious amusement.

"You heard what the doctor said, Emily? I get up again tomorrow and see Rennie. And I stay up this time."

"Yes, Mrs. Lackland. May I say that the medical decision only confirms what I have myself been saying the last day or two? With God's help you have made wonderful strides back to health."

"You're always right," sighed Mrs. Lackland. "But I wouldn't let Dr. Faithful hear me lay it to the charge of the Deity, if I were you. The good man takes an exalted view of his own skill. But he isn't what his father was," she added, with something of Queen Elizabeth's disparagement of the younger Cecil.

"Well, of course, he has reason to be proud of himself," Emily magnanimously admitted, "after a three months' fight for you against tremendous odds."

Mrs. Lackland clucked impatiently. "I wish you wouldn't make me sound like one of those Lays of Ancient Rome," she snapped pettishly. All at once her manner changed. "How long have you been with me, Bullen?" she asked abruptly.

"Twelve years, Mrs. Lackland." If she felt any surprise the companion, attuned to her employer's ways, showed none.

"Twelve years. Carol and Jenny were at school. You must be getting on."

Emily flushed again, the awkward red staining her sallow cheeks.

"None of us grow younger," she said sententiously.

"No, I'm seventy-eight and look fifty-five when I like. You're about forty, I suppose, and look fifty, so there's only five years between us." She chuckled spitefully.

Emily had recovered herself by now.

"I'm nearly forty-five," was her prim rejoinder.

"Good gracious. Whatever are you going to do when I'm dead?"

There was an uncomfortable pause.

"I said, what are you going to do when I'm dead?"

"My services, I hope, will still be acceptable to someone," Emily replied, her eyes slightly downcast. "But dear me," she added brightly, "you ought not to be considering that contingency, Mrs. Lackland, today of all days!"

"I don't. But you'll have to sometime. And don't tell me you've never speculated about what I might consider your twelve years' labour was worth!"

Emily's staidness was perceptibly shaken at that. "I'm sure——" she began as indignantly as she dared.

"Well, I'm not at all sure," Mrs. Lackland retorted with palpable relish. "However, when Rennie and I put our heads together tomorrow, who knows?" she added with deliberate ambiguity.

Emily was silent. It seemed the best escape from an embarrassing situation.

Mrs. Lackland fussed with the sheets for a minute or two. Emily looked steadily across the bed at the window which, set too high above her low seat, presented her merely with sky. Her employer spoke first.

"This is Wednesday, isn't it?" she asked suspiciously. "Then you'll be taking yourself off this evening, I suppose? Where?"

"To a violin recital at the high school," answered Emily smoothly.

"Didn't know you knew a thing about music," Mrs. Lackland said, with an air which defied contradiction. "Well, I shan't want you any longer. But I'm hungry. When you go down see that Edith brings my tea sharp at four, and tell Carol I want to see her."

Emily Bullen took her dismissal at once. She moved her chair neatly back to position, picked up her knitting from the further one, and was preparing to go, when Mrs. Lackland suddenly sat up straighter and stared at her with a hard brilliance in her eyes that was almost hypnotic.

"Wait, Bullen. I've something to ask you. Is it you who likes roaming these passages in the small hours, either in a somnambulistic condition or otherwise? Whichever it is, stop it." She kept her gaze unblinkingly on her companion's face, waiting for an answer.

Emily had halted near the door when Mrs. Lackland addressed her. She remained there now, perfectly still, looking at her interlocutor with frank bewilderment on her rather pudgy features.

"No, indeed, Mrs. Lackland, I—I'm a very sound sleeper—"

"Too sound perhaps," the old lady cut in tartly. "Who knows what you may get up to in your sleep? I won't have it. If it wasn't you it was somebody else, so it's all the same. I've been a very light sleeper since I got well enough to sleep at all, and all the rustles and whisperings at some ungodly hour last night woke me up. Yes, of course… there must have been two of you at it, unless you talk in your sleep as well as walk about. Well, if you don't know anything about it, don't stand there staring at me like a stuck pig! Bullen, you forget yourself!" Mrs. Lackland, who was beginning to feel a discomfort she could not define at the sight of the fear which had succeeded astonishment on the face before her, raised her voice to a pitch that jerked Emily back to reality. Muttering an apparent apology she made an exit which had about it nothing of her customary gentility.

The old lady directed a look of supreme contempt touched with surprise at the door.

Left alone she loosened the light shawl she had been wearing and lay back against the mountain of pillows to wait for her tea. Presently a mellow chime from the hall struck four, from across the water-meadows the cathedral too gave voice, and a tinkle on the stairs announced Edith with her tray. Mrs. Lackland stirred comfortably at the appetizing sound. Food, like money, had become precious now that life had withdrawn its flimsier blessings.

She looked up as the maid came in.

"Has Miss Carol had her tea yet?"

Edith, a tall, self-possessed girl with an expression of trained blankness, placed the tray on the table beside the bed after moving aside one or two things, and hesitated for a second before replying.

"No, madam." Her eyes were on the tray.

"Very well. When she has done so, ask her to come here. Thank you, I can pour out for myself. I'll ring if I want anything."

The maid went out, and for half an hour Mrs. Lackland solaced herself greedily. She was just about to pull the bellrope at the head of her bed when she heard light footsteps outside, a tap on the door, and Carol came in. She had changed into a green frock that lent seductiveness to her milk and gold beauty. Beneath skilful makeup her cheeks were still white.

Mrs. Lackland regarded her with undisguised hostility.

"Come on in, shut the door, and don't get any closer to me than the foot of the bed. You haven't a rudimentary notion of how to apply lipstick, and—in your wretched film jargon—I can't stand a closeup!"

As the girl approached, she added with a coarsely triumphant note: "I'm seventy-eight, but I could still teach you a thing or two in that line!"

Carol, remembering her grandmother's occasional practice in makeup, shuddered inwardly, but seating herself promptly on the end of the bed she gave a chilly little smile and waited for business to be broached.

"Why I sent for you was to ask about Hennessy. How is he taking his dismissal?"

Carol looked faintly surprised, as though she had expected something quite different.

"It doesn't seem to have made much noticeable change in him," she said unconcernedly, hoping to disappoint her grandmother.

The old lady, however, chuckled. "Not noticeable. Quite so. But he's sore enough inside, mark me. Oh yes. And when he's read the testimonial I shall give him he'll be even sorer! I'll make him notice!"

"Well, Grandma," said Carol, as if tired of the whole business, "you know Hennessy admitted he'd been slack, but he couldn't help it really if Jenny let Mr. Carnowski in by the garden door as she said she did."

Mrs. Lackland's face was unpleasantly flushed. "Couldn't help it! Couldn't help it!" she mocked. "And what, pray, is a butler for but to admit *gentlemen* at the front door and prevent guttersnipes from sneaking in all ways? He knew I had expressly forbidden that rascally fortune-hunter my house, yet he lets him come in after I've gone to bed. It was that upset of course that made me so ill on Saturday. The man's as good as a murderer—Carnowski, I mean, or whatever heathenish name he gives himself—his father never did, I'll warrant—sweepings of a Polish ghetto that he is! I'm not at all sure I can't charge him—and Jenny with him too—with housebreaking, forcible entry, and whatnot! I'll put it to Rennie tomorrow."

Mention of her solicitor quelled the old lady's rising anger and restored a measure of complacency.

"Don't get so excited, Grandma," Carol admonished. "Especially if you think it was that which made you so sick last week."

"Thank you—I can always keep my excitement, as you call it, in proper control. It remains to be seen whether you and your cousin can do the same after tomorrow!"

She scrutinized Carol's features with malicious intentness, then went on disagreeably: "How white you are! I hate whey-faced people about me, like you and that moony Bullen. You can go now. Take my tray with you, tidy up and give me my library book."

Carol got up without any betrayal of feeling at these injunctions. She placed the tray on the floor and obediently arranged the things on the bedside table within easy reach of her grandmother. There wasn't much, a small shopping-list and pencil, a few charcoal biscuits on a saucer, a bottle of tonic almost finished and a medicine glass, and a woman's magazine which Mrs. Lackland pushed impatiently aside.

"You can give that to Edith. I prefer more meaty stuff. Now pass me *Forty Years of Footlights*—those people could act, not posture in front of a camera and hunt heiresses for their money... While they've got it," she added after consideration.

Carol put the book beside her. Her lack of verbal response to these sallies made her submission distasteful to Mrs. Lackland, who seemed anxious for her to go.

"Hurry up. I want to read. Oh, and tell Jenny I must have my dinner not a minute after seven, and she is to bring it. I won't have anybody else, mind. She shan't go out tonight, I'll see to that, and tomorrow I'll be downstairs and seeing to it properly!"

"All right, Grandma. Neither of us had thought about going out. Jenny knew you wanted her to bring up your supper. That's why you let Bullen out oftener lately, isn't it?"

Mrs. Lackland looked at her sharply. "No impertinence from you, Carol. Unless you would like to be a beggar tomorrow."

Carol took up the tea things wordlessly and went over to the door. There, balancing the tray so as to turn the knob, she looked back and deliberately encountered her grandmother's gaze. Mrs. Lackland, noting the girl's head limned radiantly against the white panelling, her blue eyes wide open and cold in the pallor of her face, the mouth too red, suddenly hated because she could not defeat her.

"What an odious way you have of doing what I tell you," she said softly. "But you have to do it all the same."

Day melted reluctantly into a night almost as warm, which, with the generous luminosity of high summer, folded Minsterbridge in a veil that could scarcely be called deeper than dusk. Creeping vapours from the river promised again a sun-steeped world tomorrow. Sound gradually declined to the long hush that is never soundless. Now and again from the pastures came the desolate cry of a sheep, emphasizing the silence it broke like the ripples of a flung stone which shatters the mirror of a pond.

In St. Michael's Square the shadows welled and melted into one shadow. A thin breeze rose all at once and stirred the planes to stealthy life. Lights winked, went out, came on in some other room. Blinds shut out the deep-blue night that pressed against the windows. A few bats flitted and chased each other like a company of dark, undefined thoughts, and from one of the shrubberies an owl quavered low crooning notes. A cat darted noiselessly from one side of the square to the other as a piece of blown paper grated harshly on somebody's gate. At about twelve a policeman passed slowly by, out of one pool of lamplight into the next. There was nothing for him to do.

On the other side of the churchyard the houses settled down to the same truce between sunset and dawn. The same nocturnal secrecy had invaded the streets and given them a kind of invisible business charged with urgency.

Here, farther from river and dewy grass, the day's heat faded more slowly. Outside and in it stifled the proper coolness of night and thrust sleep from the bedrooms.

Dr. Faithful got to bed soon after eleven, to sleep hardly at all. After undressing he switched on his reading lamp, turning out the other lights. Then drawing the sheet over him and pushing back the other coverings, he pulled from beneath his pillow a current copy of a medical journal and resumed reading an article by an eminent pathologist, which he had begun earlier. Something to hold and cast an eye over in the heatless glare of electricity might provide a measure of relief till sleep came; but he had not counted on the great thick-bodied moths that, discovering a passage between his curtains an inch or two wide, came in to beat impotently at his lamp. Half an hour of this turned his interest in the paper to exasperation with the wretched creatures that presumed on his privacy, so that before midnight he had snapped off his light and was lying in the dark, exercising his mind upon the problem of the anonymous letter he had received that afternoon. He was amused to find that his imagination would play only about a faceless being—a woman, of course—as the author of it. No amount of mental research on his part would give her personality and features. Instead he fell into a light, dream-vexed doze, from which he was at once, it seemed, abruptly roused by the loud shrilling of his night telephone.

The doctor struggled up in bed to the accompaniment of its peals, lighted his lamp, and taking the receiver could make no sense for a minute or two of the message that seemed to ebb and advance like the snatches of his dreams.

He fancied that more than one person strove for a hearing at the end of the line, that a confused palaver was coming over and not a word of it directly addressed to himself.

"Hello... hello," he repeated. "Dr. Faithful speaking. Hold on... Dr. Faithful. What is it?"

Then a single voice broke through, muffled and almost unrecognizable because of the fear that whispered in it.

"Doctor—Doctor Tom—"

"Yes, yes. What's the matter?"

"It's I, Carol. Come at once. Come quickly. Grandma's dying!"

Sound trailed off into complete silence. The line was dead. He wasted no more time on it, but getting out of bed glanced at his watch. It was ten minutes to two.

Chapter III

THE LATE MRS. LACKLAND

'Tis neither as you think, nor as you think.

The Spanish Tragedy

The hardly audible shallow breathings that had succeeded the dreadful sounds of the last couple of hours had ceased now. Dr. Faithful stood up straight and looking down at the bedewed face of the dead woman wiped his own brow with a large handkerchief which he alternately dangled and gripped in his hand. Between the warmth of the room and the strain of this night's business he had to bring it into frequent use.

Beside the open window, half-turned towards the bed, Jenny stood, a coat over her pyjamas, watching the pearly morning flow smoothly from the east to the zenith and the surrounding horizons, spreading like a gentle tide over the dim reaches of the garden and terraced lawns. At the doctor's movement she turned her head without shifting her position and met his gaze across the still surface of the bed.

"Your grandmother is dead," he said in a low voice, appraising the cold level gaze and self-control.

"I know."

He noticed that she did not spare a glance for the dead. Nor was she pretending a grief it was plain she could never feel. But behind the almost audacious calm the doctor thought he detected an uneasiness too deeply grounded for hysterical expression. He felt suddenly anxious to give her something practical to do.

"See how Miss Bullen is and take her downstairs, will you? I'll join you in a minute. We can do nothing else now. And there's something I must say to you and Carol."

Jenny walked over to the armchair where Emily Bullen had been huddled for the last hour and more. She was hugging round her half-clad body a graceless pink dressing gown, and while she rocked herself in the chair uttered from time to time little whimpering moans. Even this was an improvement on her earlier condition. When the doctor had arrived, admitted by a shirt-sleeved Hennessy, shaken out of his usual equanimity, he had passed her in the hall and been struck by the almost gibbering terror of her eyes and mouth. Unable to attend to her then he had gone straight upstairs, where she had joined him and the girls in Mrs. Lackland's bedroom and added to the confusion by fainting as ostentatiously as possible. On recovery she had given vent to a storm of weeping, frightful to hear and to behold in so constantly self-effacing a creature, but, singular as it would have seemed to anybody in circumstances other than these, had resisted all persuasion to go downstairs and seek the company of the cook and maids. Force alone would have availed to remove her, and as time and place forbade that, she was left to subdue her fears in the chair where twelve hours earlier she had knitted under her employer's disapproving regard.

As Jenny looked down at her now, noting the untidy, lustreless hair and tear-smudged profile, a slow bitter distaste possessed her and was only with difficulty banished from face and voice before she spoke.

"Do you think you can come down now, Emily?" she asked quietly, laying a hand on her shoulder.

Anticipating refusal and wondering to what means they would have to resort to get her out of the room, she was surprised when the other instantly complied. She stood up submissively, with what was almost a return of her habitual eagerness to please, the only active sign of distress being the grip of her fingers on Jenny's wrist.

Jenny drew her towards the door.

"Come on," she whispered. "You'll feel better when we get down."

She had intercepted the long vague glance Emily Bullen was directing to the bed, and though she seemed exhausted at the moment Jenny feared a fresh onset of hysteria if she stayed a minute longer in that room. She was moving now with an almost mechanical jerkiness that alarmed Jenny, her eyes still upon the bed, so that the girl too looked in that direction.

Dr. Faithful had busied himself in putting his things away in their bag with the objective precision of a man who knows that for the time being at least his work is finished. At the moment Jenny turned towards him he was engaged in delicately holding between finger and thumb Mrs. Lackland's empty medicine bottle, from which he had removed the cork. While she watched he smelt it carefully, then in a moment recorked it with the same minimum of handling and put it back on the table. He met Jenny's eyes, his own face set in harsh lines and strangely mask-like, she thought, in the incongruous light.

Day was fully abroad but nobody had thought to switch off the electric glare that struggled with it, till the doctor remembering turned off the light at the head of the bed. He picked up his bag and without a word joined Jenny and Bullen at the door, which he opened for them, snapping up the switch that controlled the central bulbs in the room. Behind them the bedchamber, familiar for hours in a blaze of light only, withdrew at once into a chill ghostliness and silence that appalled after the life and death struggle that had recently racked it.

Out in the passage the doctor motioned Jenny on, and she, drawing the now quiescent woman along with her, heard as they walked away the unmistakable sound of a key being turned in the lock.

Carol was in the dining room, on the right of the stairs as you descended. There the blinds were still down and the light lit against the day. With her was Mrs. Beadle, the cook, an elderly woman who had once been both stout and comely. Her big frame had lost flesh sadly, however, and over-anxiety about trifles planted lines in her plump cheeks and greyed her still abundant hair. Faced with sudden calamity she appeared speechless, smoothing her hands again and again down the front of her person, as if reassuring herself as to her own substantiality. Habit, which had acquired an almost religious force, had forbidden her to appear anyhow but completely dressed.

As Jenny and Bullen came in, followed by the doctor, Carol, wrapped in a dressing gown with slippers on her naked feet, her hair bright and unruly beneath the chandelier, rose from a chair beside the hearth and came impulsively to meet them, stopping abruptly as she caught sight of the doctor's face.

"You needn't say it. Grandma's dead."

She whirled round, her back to the group, from which Emily Bullen now detached herself to join the cook at the sideboard. Carol put up both hands to her hair, thrusting her curls into untidy crests. Then she dropped her arms as though exhausted and slowly returned to her place, sitting down with a sagging movement.

She did not look white any longer. Red patches burned in her cheeks as her eyes roved from one to the other; she drooped forward a little so that her chest was hollow, while the fingers of her left hand beat an uneven, childish tattoo on the arm of her chair. She looked so young and bewildered that Mrs. Beadle moved instinctively towards her.

Carol took no notice. "I——" she began loudly, then immediately dropped her voice. "Well, I——don't understand," she concluded lamely.

Dr. Faithful alone disregarded her. He approached the cook who, almost standing over Carol, was tossing her head slowly in deprecatory fashion as if the entire upset ought to be judged as a catastrophic breach of culinary routine.

"Mrs. Beadle," said the doctor, in the tone which took command of situations, "Miss Bullen is far from well. I shall be grateful if you will take her along with you and give her a warm drink, and make her rest somewhere, preferably in bed. I want to talk to Miss Jenny and Miss Carol."

"Very well, sir." Mrs. Beadle, like the majority of her sex, was gratified at being singled out for the doctor's attention. She gave Carol a final solicitous look which was not returned, and going up to Emily

Bullen and passing an arm round her, marched her obediently to the door. As they passed Jenny, who had been standing aloof, the girl saw that cook's eyes were puffy with weeping. But not with grief, she thought. Trivial things imprinted themselves sharply on her mind. Her eyes were caught and fascinated by the ponderous imitation mother-of-pearl brooch that seemed almost to support Mrs. Beadle's chin, and left her marvelling that in the midst of chaos a woman could pay such meticulous attention to her own standards of propriety. She noted the involuntary twitching of Emily's lips. Then they went out and left her with Carol and the doctor.

Jenny looked round the brilliant room, at the highlights thrown back by the gleaming furniture, at the tall spires of the few lupins on the sideboard, their pastel shades unkindly quenched by the glitter, and shivered slightly.

"Can't we put these out?" she said in a sharp voice. "It's morning now. Oh, the blinds—of course—I forgot—"

Dr. Faithful took her arm in a kindly grip.

"Sit down there, opposite Carol. I've something to say to you both."

She took the chair he indicated, still self-possessed but glad to accept an order which robbed her of volition.

The doctor stood silent between them, looking down at the rug. Carol's thoughts involuntarily returned to a similar situation in the other room this afternoon. No, what was she thinking of? That was yesterday. It couldn't be. But Dr. Faithful was speaking, very quietly, and as if he were measuring words he had clearly prepared in the silence.

"Just now," he said, without looking at either girl, his hands clasped behind him, "Carol said that she did not understand. I think that is what we all want to say. For myself, I tell you both quite plainly, I don't understand—" He looked at each in turn, in response to two swiftly raised pairs of eyes and checked with a glance the words on their lips. "I left Mrs. Lackland this afternoon in a better condition of health than she has enjoyed since last March, that is to say, for several weeks before the onset of her illness. No grave illness could have brought after it a more successful convalescence than your grandmother's, and yet when I come tonight she is past hope of recovery."

He made a deliberate pause. Nobody spoke. Carol gripped her hands together tightly.

"In such circumstances," he added, "I'm bound to say I can't give a certificate of death."

He had tried on the last words to make his voice as impersonal and level as possible, nor did he look at either girl for whom he had so long been as much friend as doctor.

A brief, deadly silence was at first the sole answer to his words, disturbed only by the stately beat of the clock and the quarrel of sparrows outside somewhere close at hand.

Carol jumped up. Jenny did not move, but the doctor felt her eyes upon his face, although it was at her cousin that he looked.

"You can't mean what you say!" Carol cried foolishly. "To have come here every day for months, seeing Gran so ill that each time she rallied it was almost a shock, and now that it happens you pretend you don't know what it means!" Her hands were tightly clenched, her breathing laboured, as she faced the doctor, body and voice vibrant with a passion she could no longer control.

Jenny looked at her with the cool curiosity she might have accorded the antics of a stranger. Dr. Faithful's expression was unchanged. He put one hand towards the angry girl.

"My dear, I'm not here to bandy words with anybody who has had your and Jenny's experience tonight. But I'm not here to mince the truth either. Your grandmother's death has *not* been caused by the complaint from which she has been suffering, or rather from which she had recovered. I know enough to state that firmly. That being the case, I must withhold a certificate. I've no choice in the matter. No matter how sorry I am for you both, sympathy and regret don't alter facts—"

"And what do you mean to do next?" Carol broke in harshly.

"I shall notify the coroner, and it will then, I'm afraid, be a matter out of my control."

"It's unspeakable—"

"Carol, you don't know what you're talking about," Jenny said calmly. In the few minutes in which the doctor and her cousin had been engaged in riposte she seemed to have recovered strength and poise. "Dr. Tom's absolutely right. It's horrible, but what else can he do? You were the first to say Gran's death was inexplicable—"

"I didn't—"

"Well," Jenny wearily gestured her into silence, "you implied it then, if you must split hairs. It's pretty obvious that none of these last symptoms were like Gran's other bad bouts. She wasn't sick at all this time."

The doctor looked at her thoughtfully. Her eyes were shining, from lack of sleep perhaps. Her composure, superficially at least, was remarkable.

Carol made an impatient sound and tossed her head violently. "The whole thing's preposterous!" she cried. Suddenly she ran across to the switch and turned the lights out furiously. Day filtered through the blinds, giving a grey luminosity to the room which looked all at once a different place.

"Just supposing she didn't have exactly the same symptoms as before, what does that prove? Just nothing at all! She may have had heart trouble, probably did, after all these months of—"

"Your grandmother's heart was particularly sound," said Dr. Faithful, as though stating long familiar facts to a wilfully obtuse child. "It was simply that which gave her the strength to resist over and over again, and which pulled her through to the condition which pleased me so much in the last week."

"I think we should have a second opinion before that can be considered a fact," Carol said rudely. She was regarding the doctor, not a muscle of whose face moved at her last remark, with undisguised hostility.

"You will have a second opinion," he replied with grim courtesy. Jenny was surprised at his patience, as he went on gently: "Do you suppose, Carol, that any doctor in his senses would seek for himself, as well as for the family, the publicity of an inquest unless he had proper grounds for demanding one? Believe me, there isn't any course so repugnant."

"Well, I don't think you are in your senses. That explains it. Directly Grandma's gone you're ready to expose us to an odious publicity and yourself to ridicule, when everybody knows that if she hadn't had a marvellous constitution and a will of iron she'd have died months ago!"

"Exactly. If you think over what you've just said and relate it to Mrs. Lackland's recent state of health you'll have a partial answer to the question why I shouldn't give a certificate."

Jenny drew in her breath sharply. "But if it's only that," she said still calmly but with an utter fatigue expressed in her voice and lift of the head, "I mean that Granny after being so well lately now has this awful collapse—well, is it enough—"

"To justify an inquiry?" the doctor helped her. "I think so. But that isn't all in her case. I have very strong reasons for believing that your grandmother died from swallowing a heavy dose of some narcotic."

Jenny was pale. Her mouth quivered. "You were smelling the medicine bottle," she said faintly.

"Yes," said Dr. Faithful gravely.

"Oh, but it's impossible! It is, it is!" Carol urged, her anger subdued but in its place a kind of hysterical insistence upon the falsity of the doctor's conjectures, as if by repetition she might establish what was actually true. "How can you imagine that an accident like that could happen—"

Jenny looked up abruptly, as if stung.

Dr. Faithful had picked up his bag. He had merely looked at Carol, but something in the unresponsive gravity of his face seemed answer enough, for a complete silence fell almost uncannily upon her tumbling words. In that silence both girls regarded one another. Jenny was the first to lower her eyes. She started smoothing with exaggerated care a bit of frayed cloth close to a button of the coat she was wearing.

The doctor went to the door. When he spoke it was in toneless fashion.

"Please leave things to me. I will do what is necessary. Nobody," he looked keenly at each, "nobody may enter Mrs. Lackland's room until authorized to do so. It is locked, and for the present I have the key. None of this is needless pantomime, Carol, as I'm sure you realize. And I promise you you won't be kept long in suspense. My advice now is that you have something to eat and drink and go to bed for a couple of hours. I hope Miss Bullen's there now. I'll send her along a pick-me-up. If you won't go to bed, get a good breakfast as soon as you can. Don't come—I'll let myself out," he added with a sort of hasty gentleness.

When he left them it seemed to both girls as if the familiar figure of Dr. Tom Faithful had already receded to a remote distance, while the shadow of the Law he was about to invoke had become dimly visible.

Chapter IV

QUESTION AND ANSWER

Not telling all the Truth is hiding it,
and that is comforting or abetting a lie.

Marquis of Halifax: *Moral Thoughts and Reflections*

Superintendent Littlejohn and the City of Minsterbridge would, had inquiry been made of each, confessed to mutual satisfaction. The superintendent enjoyed the highly respectable, slightly pedantic, orderly flavour of the place, where even the small snobberies and fuss over trifles seemed nothing worse than the rather superfluous trimmings you more or less expected to find in a cathedral city without industrial life of any kind. For its own part Minsterbridge readily admitted its appreciation of the superintendent's tact and habitual effacement of himself and his men. It was as if he said, you must have a police force, I am afraid, but I will keep the fact quiet as far as possible. That suited the citizens admirably. They felt too much obtrusion of uniforms as a sad blackening of blameless characters. They were prepared to lend their unequivocal support to an efficiency that was never on parade. To do them justice they had not hitherto seriously let down the superintendent's faith in them. Petty traffic fines, and those chiefly on account of bicycles, constituted the main vexations within the city purlieus. Occasionally some malefactor belonging to the metropolis aroused the indignation of Minsterbridge by selecting the city for the continued exercise of his misdoings and got himself arrested within its boundaries, but such alien sinners could hardly be said to leave their stigma on a resentful neighbourhood. The only local upset of any importance during the superintendent's decade of office had been the absconding of a grocery store manager with the week's takings on the eve of the Derby three years ago. Local colour had been lent to the affair by the fact that the culprit had been a chorister of the cathedral treasured by the ladies.

It might then be easily understood that news of the death at Lacklands and the necessity for an inquest must have disturbed Superintendent Littlejohn in any case. Coming as it did, however, not much more than twelve hours after he had learned of the anonymous letters Dr. Faithful had been receiving, it filled him with consternation. What was happening to the place all at once? The superintendent had not as a rule sufficient imagination to impair his self-confidence. His tactful reluctance to do any mental probing into the conduct of people who habitually behaved themselves in the eyes of the law, his promptness in fair weather to accept superficialities as the whole truth, would have made him discredit the suggestion that perhaps an undercurrent ran strongly beneath the placid surface of life in Minsterbridge.

He stood now at eleven o'clock with Sergeant Vale in the morning room at Lacklands, where he had been shown by Hennessy, waiting to see Miss Quentin, for whom he had asked. They had seen the body and inspected the room, following on the visit an hour or so earlier of the divisional surgeon, who had been accompanied by Dr. Faithful. With as little fuss as possible the remains of Mrs. Lackland had been removed, and articles found on the bedside table confiscated by the police. Certain of the dead woman's organs were to be sent to Sir Lewis Blayne.

While the front of the house was heavily shrouded in deference to the conventions, the morning sunlight, comfortably modified by half-drawn curtains, came warmly in from the garden to the room where the policemen waited. Superintendent Littlejohn cast an eye over his surroundings to keep his mind off a distasteful job, noting the fine taste in the furnishings, the delicate curves of the Louis Quinze clock on the mantel, and the unpretentious beauty of a homely interior by Chardin that hung above it. There's money here, he thought. The sergeant, on the other hand, kept his back to the room while his eyes rested thoughtfully on the golden July landscape that stretched between the house and the distant cathedral. He was a fair young fellow, with plenty of intelligent ambition beneath a quiet, courteous exterior, and a personality which had marked him out in the Minsterbridge force as a man likely to rise.

The house was extraordinarily still, after the passage of the strange footsteps that had so recently intruded there. At a sound outside both men turned. The door opened and Carol came in.

She was wearing a thin black frock that looked faintly shabby, with shoes and stockings to match. Her pale face was unpowdered, her lips not rouged. Yesterday's very close little bangs of curls seemed less trim, and in the sombre dress she looked very small and childish. Her eyes rested immediately on the superintendent.

Littlejohn came forward. "Good morning—Miss Quentin, isn't it?" He spoke quietly. "I needn't say how sorry I am for what has happened, and for the inquiries I must make." He cleared his throat rather awkwardly and pulling an armchair forward and so placing it that the light from between the curtains would fall on the sitter, added: "There are a few questions I have to ask."

Carol nodded. "I understand," she said briefly. Sergeant Vale observed with a certain admiration that before seating herself she deftly turned the chair from the window. Nor did she attempt to ignore her own manoeuvre.

"I find the perpetual glare of this heat wave very trying, don't you?" she said almost brightly, but with a shaky smile. "Please sit down."

They had no choice but to do so. Carol, who had never bothered to notice Superintendent Littlejohn in the years that he and she had lived in Minsterbridge, saw a spare man with grizzled hair and deep, mild eyes regarding her with sympathy and apparent simplicity.

Sergeant Vale sat very quietly outside her range of vision, with his notebook ready.

Littlejohn did not intend to prolong the initial silence.

"It will be more straightforward, Miss Quentin," he said, "to begin at the beginning, so to speak. Will you please tell me when you last saw Mrs. Lackland in her usual health—I mean the usual health she has enjoyed lately since she appeared to be getting better?"

Carol considered a moment. "Just after tea. She wanted to see me, and I brought her tray down. I don't think I was in the room more than ten minutes. It must have been about five o'clock when I left her."

The superintendent nodded. "What were her spirits like then? Did she impress you as being happy, depressed, or what?"

Carol gave a slight smile in which the superintendent detected a touch of bitterness. He had noticed that there was no trace of recent tears upon her face.

All she said, however, was: "Her spirits were very bright. She was looking forward to getting up." She added voluntarily: "She merely wanted to speak to me about little matters relating to the servants, and I was with her a very short time, as I said."

"Her cheerfulness is important." The superintendent looked at her closely. "And she was to have got up—?"

"Today."

The superintendent made no comment, but in the little pause before he went on Sergeant Vale caught his chief's eye.

"Mrs. Lackland was your grandmother?" Littlejohn inquired casually.

"In a way. I mean," Carol explained, "she was my grandfather's second wife. Actually she was no blood relation of myself or my cousin."

"I see. How long had Mrs. Lackland been ill?"

"Oh, all the spring and summer. Well, nearly. She wasn't well in March, and then at the beginning of April Dr. Faithful sent her to bed and she was very ill indeed for over two months." A wistful note crept into Carol's voice. "We thought she was dying early in May."

The superintendent wore his best look of commiseration. "But she made a very good convalescence, didn't she?"

"Yes. When she started to mend at the end of last month she got rapidly better. The doctor was very pleased with her."

"And she was to start coming down today?"

"Oh, but she'd been down before. Yes," added Carol in reply to Littlejohn's unspoken surprise, "more than a week ago Dr. Faithful had said my grandmother was well enough to get up a little. So she came down and seemed to be getting on nicely."

"Then she had to go back to bed? Why was that?"

"She was sick in the weekend. Last Saturday. The doctor thought it wouldn't be safe for her to get about for a day or two, so she was staying in her room for the best part of this week."

"Was any particular cause assigned for the sickness, Miss Quentin?"

"No-o. Well, yes, perhaps. The doctor thought she may have been eating unwisely. She had had severe gastritis, you see, and had to be very careful."

"Yes." The superintendent made a mental note to see Dr. Faithful about this as soon as possible. "Well, to return to yesterday. After you left your grandmother how did you spend the evening, Miss Quentin?"

Carol raised her eyebrows faintly. "Here," she replied coolly. "In the house, I mean. None of us went out except Miss Bullen."

The superintendent looked his query.

"My grandmother's companion," Carol explained. "She had Wednesday evenings from tea till bedtime to do as she liked."

Littlejohn nodded. "Then that left you and your cousin in the house, and the servants."

Carol remained silent, and a flicker of hesitation in her eyes prompted him to ask: "Was there anybody else, Miss Quentin?"

The girl smiled, almost happily. "You would have to know, of course, Superintendent. Besides, there was nobody but Grandma who objected... We had a guest to supper, my cousin's friend, Mr. Carnowski, the film actor."

"Oh, yes. What time did he come?"

"A little after seven, it must have been."

"And when go?"

"I think it was about ten."

"Now why did Mrs. Lackland object?" inquired the superintendent with casual geniality.

Carol hesitated again. "Well," she evaded, "she didn't last night, if that's what you mean, because she didn't know he came. But," she continued impulsively, at sight of Littlejohn's surprise, "this has nothing to do with my grandmother's death, and if you want to know anything about Mr. Carnowski I would so much rather you asked my cousin."

"Why, Miss Quentin?"

"Well, he's her friend, really. In any case it's not important."

"I'm the best judge of that, you know," said the superintendent good-humouredly. "I don't want to appear to pry into things which to you seem quite irrelevant, but I should be glad to have your own opinion of your grandmother's objection to this gentleman. Besides," he added, "don't you think that by telling me you might be doing your cousin a service—you would spare her the telling?"

"I expect you'll ask her just the same," said Carol shrewdly. "Well, if I don't tell you you'll only attach much more importance to it than it's worth. It's really very petty. My grandmother disapproved of our friendship with Mr. Carnowski because she used to be an actress, you see, and he was on the films, and she despised the pictures. She was very old, and—opinionated."

"And that was all?" The superintendent did not conceal his astonishment.

"Well, no, not quite, perhaps. Mrs. Lackland was our guardian. By the terms of my grandfather's will we could not marry without her consent. She was very suspicious of any masculine friends we had."

There was a rather heavy silence.

The superintendent broke it by remarking as half-statement, half-question: "The suggestion was that male friends might—?"

"Be fortune-hunters," Carol finished for him. "Yes. It was odious, and quite untrue."

The superintendent made no answer for a few seconds. Then: "Will you please give me Mr. Carnowski's address?" he asked.

"Oh, but you can't think it necessary to bring him into this! It's absurd." Carol spoke with the first indignation and apparent alarm she had yet shown.

"As mere routine, Miss Quentin, I am obliged to question everybody who was in the house at the time of Mrs. Lackland's death."

"I don't know exactly where he lives. Chelsea way, but that's not very helpful, I'm afraid."

"Thank you," said Littlejohn, "I can find out. Now," his voice held a brisker note, "I want to know at what time your grandmother had her supper."

"At seven o'clock. Precise to the minute."

"Which of the maids took it to her?"

Carol smiled slightly again, and again with a just noticeable bitterness. "None. My cousin took it."

The superintendent did not seek an explanation. "About the medicine," he pursued. "We have taken the empty bottle to be examined. Now, Dr. Faithful says he gave Mrs. Lackland a dose when he visited her in the afternoon. How much was then left in the bottle, Miss Quentin?"

"I'm not sure. But why not ask the doctor himself?"

The superintendent looked rather stern.

"That wasn't the point of my question," he replied frankly. "I wanted your own observation. But if you're not sure we'll leave it. Was your grandmother supposed to take a dose at night also?"

"Yes. But the doctor said yesterday that when this bottle was finished she needn't continue the tonic. I don't know whether that may have made her careless about taking the last doses."

"Didn't she take it regularly?"

"Yes. But she didn't like it much, and she had to be reminded."

"I see. Well now, Miss Quentin, I should be obliged if you'd tell me exactly what happened from dinnertime on to the time when you discovered your grandmother was dying, as you thought, and you sent for the doctor. Just tell me everything you can remember, no matter how trifling it may seem to you. First of all, what was the usual proceeding with Mrs. Lackland after she had had her supper?"

Carol frowned. "You mean what did we do other nights? Oh, she used to ring for somebody to talk to, or perhaps she'd just read—when she was well enough, of course. Then at nine o'clock Mrs. Beadle—that's the cook—would take her up a glass of hot milk and fetch down the tray, and that would be the signal for whichever one of us happened to be looking after her that evening to go up and see that she was comfortable for the night."

"There were no general good nights to her?"

"Oh no. She didn't bother to see anybody unless she had something to tell them."

"No. Well, go on, please, Miss Quentin. What happened after dinner?"

Carol considered a few moments. "We had ours usually at seven-fifteen, after my grandmother was served. Last night it was a little later because of Mr. Carnowski coming, and we didn't finish till eight o'clock. After that we talked and then went into the drawing room and turned on the wireless, and—"

"One moment, please. Did any one of you leave the other two during the time you were all in the drawing room?"

"Why, yes. I certainly did. I thought Jenny would be glad of a few words with Jan alone, so I went out. After all, I'd been with them every minute since he came, and it was very decent of Jenny to put up with me on the few occasions they were able to meet here. So when there was a sort of silence I said I was going to speak to Mrs. Beadle about Hetty—the housemaid who is under notice to go—only first I went upstairs to get a handkerchief. If you want the time I should say that would be about twenty minutes past eight. Then I went down to the kitchen and stayed talking to cook for some time. I don't know when it was I left her. Mr. Carnowski and my cousin were still talking together when I joined them again, and it was soon after that—I don't know how soon, though—that Jenny said she was going up to see if Grandma was ready for her milk."

"Was it usual to inquire first?" asked the superintendent quickly.

"No. But when Jenny had taken up my grandmother's dinner last night and was going as usual to pour out a dose of medicine ready for her to take afterwards, Gran had told her to leave it alone and said that she'd do it herself. Jenny got the idea that she was going to shirk finishing the bottle, now that she'd been told she'd not have to take any more. So she went to see if she had taken a dose before the milk was brought up. When Jenny came down she said Grandma was asleep, and she'd let cook know not to take the milk."

"Then what happened?" Littlejohn prompted, as Carol paused.

"About an hour after that, I suppose, Mr. Carnowski left. And less than ten minutes after he'd gone Emily Bullen, my grandmother's companion, came in, and went into the dining room, where cook had left her some cold supper."

"Did nobody else go up to see if Mrs. Lackland was awake and wanting her milk?"

"No. You see, she was always very quick to ring if she wanted anything, and it was absolutely undreamed of to disturb her if she was sleeping. Besides, she had gone to sleep a few times before about that time and failed to have her milk."

"Yes. When did you go to bed, Miss Quentin?"

"Jenny and I went just before eleven. Miss Bullen had already gone. It was Hennessy's duty to lock up at ten. He had done so, and the servants were all gone to their rooms. It was Jenny who let Jan out and opened the door to Emily a few minutes later."

"That is very clear. Now, I want you to answer this carefully, please: what sent you to your grandmother's room in the night, when you made the discovery which caused you to summon the doctor?"

"I knew you would ask that. Dr. Faithful asked me the same thing last night. But I'm afraid I can't give you an answer you'll think is satisfactory. It was nothing but fancy. I suppose you might call it intuition, though I've never claimed to have much of that."

"You were worried about Mrs. Lackland?"

"Not exactly. But I did feel that it was a long time since anybody had seen her, and wondered if she might have been wakened by our going to bed, and whether I oughtn't after all to have looked in on her on my way there."

"But you said that Mrs. Lackland had fallen asleep in this way on previous occasions."

"Yes, I know. But those were some time ago, when the nurse was here, and she has been gone over a month now. After last Saturday's bad sickness too we were all more or less on the alert, I think. I was worried, I know, and it was very hot. So I just lay awake with nothing much to think about but the ordinary, trivial things that will keep bothering one's wakefulness and magnifying themselves. And it was then that I thought of the pillows, and wondered if Gran had been too sleepy to put them away before she settled down."

"What about the pillows, Miss Quentin?"

"She always sat up in bed with a lot piled behind her, but they had to be reduced to one before she went to sleep, and I remembered how once she'd fallen asleep before she could be made comfortable and how very cross she'd been about it next day."

"So you went to see if it had happened this time?"

"Yes. I didn't think of it till I'd been in bed a long while. Then I turned on my light and saw it was half-past one, and even then I didn't go at once because I knew how she hated to be disturbed if she was all right. I simply didn't know which to do, and everything seems more of a worry at that hour in the morning than in the middle of the day."

The superintendent nodded without comment. He was genuinely interested in the girl's own appraisal of her motives in visiting Mrs. Lackland's room at an unusual hour, and he did not want to hurry her. She looked paler than when she had first come in, and kept her eyes on a point of the room somewhere beyond Littlejohn's shoulder, while her voice that had run on with crisp spontaneity faltered a little as she continued:

"So after a bit more hesitation I made up my mind to go along quietly to Grandma's room and see for myself. I sleep in the front, you know, looking out on the square, and had to slip along the main passage, past my cousin's room, and down a shorter one to hers."

Carol stopped abruptly. Her eyes went quickly to the superintendent's face, and he saw that she was frightened.

"I am sorry you should have to go over this," he said gently. "Give me just the facts and it will soon be done with. Did you knock?"

"No. It was horrible. Directly I reached the door I could hear what I thought was somebody talking or singing. I was scared. I went straight in. I think I said: 'Grandma, are you all right?' That's what I *meant* to say, but perhaps I didn't speak. She was groaning... though it wasn't exactly that, either. I turned on the light at once—"

Her voice had risen a little. Suddenly she got up, moving so hastily to the window that both men were taken by surprise. There she stood, back to the room, her hands gripped behind her, staring out at the hot, calm garden between the half-pulled curtains, while she fought down a mastering fear.

When she turned to the room again it was with as little warning as she had turned away. Littlejohn and Vale were about to get up, not knowing whether she would be seated again, but she came swiftly to her chair and though her cheeks were white smiled at them both.

"That was stupid of me. I'm sorry. But putting it into words somehow sent me back there. I'll be sensible now. But I've lost what I was saying. What did you want to know next, Superintendent?"

"You had turned on the light, Miss Quentin," Littlejohn replied quietly.

"Oh yes." Her tones matched his own. Sergeant Vale cocked a still more attentive ear to catch all she was saying.

"I saw immediately that something was dreadfully wrong. Grandma had fallen sideways in the bed. One of the pillows was on the floor and the rest were slipping. But, it was—oh, it was my grandmother's look that was so frightening. She was a very red colour, dark and high, not a bit like her. She seemed to be waving her hands about, lifting her arms restlessly, and moaning all the time. I—I didn't know what to do. I think I ran out calling for Jenny. She and Bullen roused up soon, and came with me, and then I ran downstairs to the telephone to get Dr. Faithful. I think Emily went to call cook and Hennessy, and Jenny stayed with Grandma—"

"Can you remember what you did until the doctor came?" Littlejohn asked.

"He was here very quickly. He lives only about five minutes away, you know. But we tried to quieten her. We moved some of the pillows. We didn't know what was the matter, and we were afraid of doing the wrong thing. Then the doctor came."

Carol sighed on the last words, as much in remembrance of that arrival as in relief at having reached the end of her story.

"Thank you, Miss Quentin." The superintendent contrived admirably to convey sympathy in a firm, practical voice. "It was a very distressing time for you all. Now I'm not going to keep you much longer, but I've just three questions to put to you which you may answer as briefly as you please."

Carol was now looking straight into his eyes. "Yes?"

"First, who is Mrs. Lackland's solicitor?"

"Mr. Archibald Rennie, of Rennie and Chaplin, you know. Their offices are behind the cathedral."

The superintendent nodded. "I know Mr. Rennie."

He paused as if considering his next words.

"Now," he said gravely, "I would like you to tell me whether to your knowledge Mrs. Lackland had ever at any time spoken of taking her own life."

"Never," Carol replied in a firm and slightly more frigid tone than she had used at all. "If any such suggestion has been made it's cruel and preposterous. My grandmother was the last—the very *last* person to commit suicide."

The superintendent slowly bent his head. "I believe you, Miss Quentin," he said, and before she could perceive the implications of his remark, added more lightly: "And now my last question: have you ever received an anonymous letter?"

This time there was no mistaking the look which came to the girl's face for anything but the frank astonishment it was.

"An anonymous letter?" she repeated, rather haughtily, Sergeant Vale thought, and looked from Littlejohn to him and back again. "No, certainly, I haven't. Why, what's—"

The superintendent smiled a little. "That's all then, Miss Quentin," he put in. "When you go out I'd be glad if you would ask Miss Hernshaw if she could spare me a few minutes."

Carol got up, and so did the police. Sergeant Vale opened the door for her. She did not spare him a glance as she went out, and her face bore an expression that was no longer fear or fatigue, but a sort of contemplative bewilderment.

Chapter V

THE LAST DOSE

I will have my Doors lock'd up—
I'll punish you, not a Man shall enter My House.

Congreve: *Love for Love*

N o sooner had Jenny Hernshaw been admitted and seated herself quietly in the chair Littlejohn drew forward, without, Sergeant Vale observed, any consideration for the light, than the superintendent noted that here was different material from that which he had had to work upon in her cousin's case.

Carol's bright, shrewd loquacity would here, he knew, be replaced by reticence; where the other girl's natural fear and repulsion had been openly displayed this one's emotions would be subdued with caution. The superintendent inwardly sighed at the recognition of a type whose examination meant as a rule uphill work for the police. Thank heaven, though, he thought, there's compensation in everything: she's not the kind to conceal evidence behind a screen of hysteria, real or affected. As for the laborious part of his job he determined, at this stage, at any rate, to ease it by not prolonging his initial inquiry.

He began with the conventional opening of regret and assurances. Jenny disregarded completely the murmured formalities and was palpably waiting for whatever questions he had to put. Perceiving this, Littlejohn readily cut the cackle and came to the point.

"I understand, Miss Hernshaw," he said in the businesslike tone he reserved for those who expected it, "that it was your duty last night to take up your grandmother's supper?" Directly he had spoken it occurred to him that he might have phrased his query less humiliatingly. Jenny, however, appeared not to notice.

"Yes," she replied.

The superintendent waited a second or two for a possible supplementary remark, but she added nothing.

"That was at what time?" he inquired.

"At seven o'clock."

"Did she begin to eat it while you were with her?"

"No."

Littlejohn sighed shortly at the unilluminating monosyllable. He leaned forward a little.

"Did she take her medicine while you were there?"

"No," said Jenny without a moment's hesitation.

"Wasn't it usual for her to have the tonic before her last meal?"

"Yes, it was."

This was no good, thought the superintendent. He plunged resolutely.

"Miss Hernshaw," he said firmly, "you're not being very helpful, are you? My job isn't a particularly pleasant one for either of us, but you could help to curtail it by telling me a little more."

He saw a quick flush warm her brown cheeks. She came to life then, and he noticed all at once what a contrast she was to her cousin. Almost plain, you might have called this one on superficial acquaintance, with her dark hair uncompromisingly shingled, the rather high cheekbones and direct grey eyes under unplucked brows; yet there was something in the very austerity and lack of trimmings, so to speak, that might be beautiful when you thought about it.

"I'm sorry," she said, and added without a hint of sarcasm, "you asked and I answered. What more do you want me to do?"

Her words may have appeared sulky, but there was nothing sullen in the tone in which they were spoken. It was a genuine enough inquiry and Littlejohn replied to it in the same spirit.

"I want you to tell me in your own words," he said, "how and why Mrs. Lackland refused to take her medicine last night."

"I can tell you how, but I don't know why. I picked up the bottle after putting down my grandmother's tray, and was just going to uncork it when she said: 'Put that down. I can take my own medicine, thank you, and I'll take it when I please.' I was a bit surprised at the tone she used, which was as if we had been arguing whether she should take it or not, and we hadn't. I did as she said, and that was all."

The superintendent nodded, his eyes on the girl's face.

"Now, Miss Hernshaw, can you tell me how much medicine was left in the bottle when you were about to pour out a dose for your grandmother?"

"Yes. Only one dose was left."

That confirmed what the doctor had told him, thought Littlejohn. Seeing that Jenny had thawed, as he termed it, he pressed his advantage and questioned her closely about the evening's activities, careful at the moment to avoid any direct inquiries about Carnowski.

Jenny's replies agreed with Carol's story. She seemed vaguer than her cousin as to precise times, but thought, yes, that it would be about a quarter-past eight when Carol had gone from the room and left her talking to Mr. Carnowski. She had forgotten when it was she returned, but she herself had gone upstairs at five minutes to nine to see if her grandmother had taken her medicine yet before having her milk.

"I meant to go earlier," she added, "but we were talking and time slipped by."

"Was it so important then that Mrs. Lackland should take this last dose?" the superintendent asked.

"No, if you put it like that, I don't think it was especially important. But Dr. Faithful had been very particular about my grandmother taking her tonic regularly—she was inclined to be erratic about it—and it was important that she should be in good trim for next day."

"Because she was coming down again?"

"Not only that. She had arranged to see her solicitor, and was very excited at the prospect."

The superintendent woke up. A lawyer's visit, eh? He wondered why the other girl, by nature so much more informative than this one, had not referred to it.

"Do you know the purpose of the solicitor's visit, Miss Hernshaw?"

He thought he detected some hesitation in her manner as she replied: "I—we believed my grandmother intended making a fresh will."

Now we seem to be getting somewhere, thought Littlejohn. Sergeant Vale looked discreetly at his superior, but the superintendent was watching Jenny.

"Can you tell me," was his next question, "if Mrs. Lackland had entire control of all that your grandfather left? Was she at liberty, for instance, to make you and your cousin her heirs or to leave the estate elsewhere?"

Jenny's hesitation was plain this time.

"Those are difficult questions," she said. "You see, my cousin and I have always been uncertain as to our position. The financial side of my grandfather's will has never been made clear to us. Mr. Rennie was not allowed to tell us, though the terms of my grandmother's guardianship"—here was an edge to her voice—"were very fully explained."

"Didn't your grandmother ever enlighten you, even indirectly?"

Jenny shook her head. "She implied sometimes one thing, sometimes another. I know that some years ago we were led to think that hers was only a life interest and that we were bound to inherit when she died. But since then she's talked so often about her will that we don't really know how much is under her full control, nor whether she couldn't make us beggars if she liked." Her voice trembled. "Lately I've thought that her earlier hints that we were Grandpa's heirs were simply made to deceive, so that she could give us a shock by cutting us right out at the last."

The superintendent certainly received a shock at the suggestion. His eyebrows shot up.

"That is crediting Mrs. Lackland with a good deal of malice," he ventured boldly.

"Yes," said Jenny with finality.

Littlejohn sighed. "Well, you will learn the exact provisions of the will very shortly now," he remarked.

Jenny did not reply, and the superintendent, resuming his questions, returned to her nine o'clock visit to Mrs. Lackland's room. She had just gone inside when she realized that the old lady was asleep. Yes, she had noticed the pillows, but knew that her grandmother would be very vexed if she were waked up, as was inevitable if she moved them. Besides she felt pretty sure she would wake later and ring for one of them. No, she did not go near enough to the bed to notice whether or not the last dose of tonic was still in the bottle.

"How was your grandmother sleeping?" asked the superintendent.

"She was half-sitting and snoring rather loudly."

"What did you do then?"

"I went downstairs and told cook not to disturb her by taking the milk."

Littlejohn accepted her replies without comment, and passed smoothly on to the crisis of the night, the summoning of the doctor and Mrs. Lackland's death. She was, she said, in a sound sleep when her cousin came in to rouse her, but was quickly awake at the agitation in Carol's voice. The flurry in the corridor and their half-whispered conversation must have disturbed Miss Bullen, who came out of her room across the passage and as soon as she had joined them and learned what was the matter went to rouse Mrs. Beadle. Jenny hurried with her cousin to their grandmother's room, where she was left while Carol ran downstairs to telephone the doctor. Her grandmother died rather more than two hours after he got there. Yes, she was in the room at the time, and so was Miss Bullen, who had collapsed and was incapable of doing anything from the moment the doctor arrived.

"How is she now?" the superintendent inquired.

"She's in bed. The doctor gave her a bromide and advised her to stay there today," said Jenny. "I don't think she's at all well. Neither does Carol," she added, half to herself.

"I'd like to talk to Miss Bullen later," Littlejohn observed. "Just now, Miss Hernshaw," he went on casually, "I'd be grateful if you would give me Mr. Carnowski's address. In an inquiry of this sort it's my duty to question everyone who was in the house at the time, as a matter of form."

He saw the girl stiffen. "Mr. Carnowski had left the house before my grandmother was taken ill," she said curtly.

"You mean hours before it was discovered that she was ill," he corrected her mildly.

Jenny subjected him to a searching look. "How do you know that what I said isn't right too?" she asked.

"Because, Miss Hernshaw, in the joint opinion of Dr. Faithful and the police surgeon Mrs. Lackland died from the effects of an overdose of some narcotic which must have been administered hours before she arrived at the condition in which the doctor found her. When the analyst's report comes in we shall, I hope, know the drug and quantity taken, and can then be more precise, perhaps, as to time."

Jenny sat in a strained attitude, one leg crossed upon the other, hands tightly clasped about her raised knee. She shrugged her shoulders in a manner which Sergeant Vale, considering the matter under discussion, was compelled to think rather callous.

"Mr. Carnowski's address," she said with sudden defiance, "is 110, Tite Square, Chelsea, where he has a flat."

The superintendent made a note of it.

"Thank you, Miss Hernshaw. I can assure you that I shall trouble him as little as possible. Since we are on the subject I must tell you that your cousin, on being questioned, reluctantly admitted that Mrs. Lackland had objected to Mr. Carnowski's presence in the house. Will you give me your own opinion as to why she should have done so?"

Jenny laughed, undisguisedly and without mirth, regardless of the fact that superintendent Littlejohn immediately looked down his nose at the improper sound of it.

"There isn't an opinion about it. There's simply facts. It was not so much that my grandmother feared Jan and I would get married without her consent—she knew that I knew I stood to lose everything by doing that, and would probably have the common sense to wait—but that she knew I was happy when I was with him." The colour burned suddenly in Jenny's face. Her eyes filled with a rush of tears for which the superintendent was wholly unprepared. He looked confused, while Sergeant Vale, feeling oddly enough more comfortable at the sight of "proper emotion," as he privately called it, stared down at his notebook.

Jenny added simply: "She made it her business to see that Carol and I were never happy—but we were, sometimes."

Littlejohn noticed that just as she had laughed without attempt at concealment she was now unashamedly wiping away her tears. Before he could put his next question into form she went on speaking rather fast:

"It will be better, I think, if I tell you at once that Hennessy, the butler, is under a month's notice to leave because I let Mr. Carnowski in by the garden door one evening last week after Hennessy had been forbidden to admit him to the house. It was horribly unjust and, of course, if the property is ours now, we shall see that Hennessy is kept on. I tell you this now because I don't want you to find out afterwards and think that we were trying to hide anything."

"Quite right," said the superintendent. "It is, as you say, Miss Hernshaw, much more sensible to tell everything clearly at first. It's merely evasions which help to magnify so many things trifling in themselves." He seemed to dismiss the matter, and after considering for a minute with a slight frown, said: "That reminds me of something, though. Didn't your cousin tell me a maid had also been dismissed?"

"Oh, that's Hetty. Nothing to do with what I just told you. She was caught listening at doors, and Carol told cook last night, I think, that she would have to go."

"I see. I'd be glad if you'd tell me just who the servants are, and their position in the house."

"There are five. Hennessy, whom you saw when you came, the cook, Mrs. Beadle, and two maids indoors. They all live here. Then there's a chauffeur named Francis who sleeps at his home in the town. When the car isn't needed at night he goes home at seven o'clock. He's been doing that all the summer while my grandmother was ill."

"And what is the other maid's name?"

"You mean besides Hetty? That's the parlourmaid, Edith Dawes."

"Have they all been here a good time?" the superintendent asked carelessly.

"All except Hetty. She came just after last Christmas. Hennessy was with my grandfather before I was born, and cook must have been here about fifteen years and Edith five, I should say."

"Thank you. I needn't keep you much longer, Miss Hernshaw. I only want answers to a couple more questions." He paused, then added quietly: "Have you any reason for supposing that Mrs. Lackland may have contemplated taking her own life?"

Jenny lifted her head higher and stared at Littlejohn. "Good gracious, no," she said candidly. "That's absolutely impossible."

The superintendent looked interested. "Why do you say that?"

"Well, if you'd known my grandmother. It's so ridiculous to imagine that she could have done so," she went on hastily, "that I find it hard to say why she couldn't. But surely a suicidal bent means a— an inferiority complex, doesn't it? The very opposite to whatever complexes Grandma cherished!"

"I'm inclined to agree with what you say, Miss Hernshaw," said the superintendent gravely, and did not remind her that in this case there was only one alternative.

"Then I have only one more thing to ask you." His voice was

as indifferent as he could make it, but his eyes were keen all at once. "Have you received an anonymous letter at any time lately?"

As he finished speaking he noted a peculiarity in the girl's attitude. Instead of the natural shades of expression, suggestive of movement and life, which might have been expected to succeed one another on her face, she sat quite motionless while he was framing the question, regarding him with a disconcerting fixity of gaze, yet without anything responsive or comprehending in the veiled eyes. Like a dead person, he thought, or, to choose a less gruesome simile, like a being whose spirit and thoughts are transported far from the range of his material vision. He noticed out of the corner of his eye that Vale was observing her closely.

He was about to repeat his inquiry when Jenny seemed suddenly to come to life. She continued to look at him, it is true, while her posture remained practically unaltered, yet so entire was the change in her it was as if a different individual confronted him.

"An anonymous letter?" She repeated Carol's words brightly, but with far less amazement, both men thought. "No, I've never had one." She sighed a little and stood up before Littlejohn could indicate the close of the interview.

"That was all, I think you said," she remarked bluntly.

The superintendent rose. "That was all, Miss Hernshaw, thank you. I should like a few words with Mrs. Beadle please, if I might trouble you to ask her to come here."

"Certainly," said Jenny, equally polite, as she went out slowly.

Sergeant Vale had strolled to the window. In the brief time that they had the room to themselves, Littlejohn attempted no conversation with his colleague; instead he approached a small bookcase in a diagonal corner of the room and regarded with a satisfaction inspired more by their comeliness than by their contents: the volumes of a mid-eighteenth-century diary bound in golden calf, which bore evidence of having grown old beautifully. Only the liquid notes of the clock made the silence incomplete.

It was a mere minute or two, however, before a flat, hasty step was heard, and after a hurried knock Mrs. Beadle entered. She was a little breathless, and the superintendent saw that her heavy features wore an expression that was at once doleful and anticipatory. Her eyes were red with recent tears, but after a minute or two Littlejohn put her down rightly to be a woman who wept dutifully on occasions without personal experience of grief.

As she came in both men turned in her direction, and the superintendent with an eye to her print frock and apron and rolled sleeves remarked cheerfully: "I'm sorry to fetch you from your kitchen, Mrs. Beadle, at such an hour of the morning, but I can promise you it won't be above many minutes before you're back again."

He drew forward the low chair the girls had occupied, but the cook shook her head and seizing a small, high-legged, firm-bottomed one seated herself squarely and looked at the superintendent.

"I'm not partial to those so near the floor," she explained, "me being none too good of breath. Well, there, it's right what you say. I *am* busy, for live or die, folks must eat, and it's going on for lunchtime. So I'll be glad if you'll make it short."

"That I will," said Littlejohn with sincere resolution, for he had no desire to prolong his examination of the staff at this stage. The police were standing now, and Mrs. Beadle, to whom both were familiar enough sights, looked from one to the other without alarm.

"This has been a sad shock for you, I'm sure, Mrs. Beadle," the superintendent began rather hurriedly, for he did not want to renew the tears he guessed might easily flow again, "and all I want to know now is what your late mistress had for her supper last night?"

"Little enough, I can tell you. She was a hearty feeder, meaning no offence, when she could be downstairs, but being in bed so much took her appetite. Just a small piece of breast of chicken, a bit of cauliflower and potato, and afterwards some trifle. Oh dear, oh dear," she cried, remembering she ought to be flustered, "and to think I never knew it was to be the poor dear's last meal! And her so full of pleasure, so I'm told, poor thing, at knowing she was to leave her bed today—"

"Yes, we none of us can see the future," the superintendent broke in sententiously, with a sudden nasty notion as he voiced the words that somebody may have foreseen Mrs. Lackland's future only too well. "Now at what time did you prepare Mrs. Lackland's milk last night?"

"I put it on to heat just before Miss Carol left me."

"Oh yes. What was it Miss Carol wanted to talk about?"

"*Well*," Mrs. Beadle invested her voice with as much scornful astonishment as she could at this display of sheer curiosity, "I don't see what that can have to do with poor Mrs. Lackland, that I don't, but if you *must* know such things she came to tell me as how Hetty was giving trouble and what with her never being much good at anything either, for all she's been here six months and more, it would be better to send her going. And so I think," she concluded emphatically.

"And that was all you talked about?"

"That was all," Mrs. Beadle replied with some satisfaction and a considerable muster of dignity.

"Very well," said the superintendent. "Now I wonder if you can remember what time it was that Miss Quentin came into the kitchen?"

"Well, I don't then. I can't keep looking at my clock every whip-stitch just because such matters are to be pried into later on. I'm sure I don't know at all when she came in, but it was ten to nine when she went because I was getting poor mistress's milk ready when she got up to go."

"That's something, at any rate," said Littlejohn in a determinedly hearty tone. "You can take it from me, Mrs. Beadle, I don't want to pry into anything which is off the track of my inquiry, but by checking up on times—comings and goings, you know—I hope to make things easier for everyone concerned." He was sanguine enough to believe that this ambiguous explanation would be more comprehensible, not to say acceptable, to Mrs. Beadle than it was to himself. It seemed to work, for after a rather woebegone stare she looked sufficiently mollified.

"Could you perhaps give a guess," asked Littlejohn in a friendly manner, "how long you and she were talking?"

"No, that I couldn't. I'm not much good at that sort of calkylatin'. It might have been ten minutes or it might have been twenty—there, you know how time is when you're talking."

"Yes, it doesn't matter." The superintendent spoke lightly. He did not want the cook or anybody else to start concentrating on a particular point of his investigation; as far as was possible he preferred not to leave a definite impression of any one subject behind him. "When was it Miss Hernshaw came to tell you that her grandmother was asleep?"

"Well, that was a funny thing. In a way, you know. I'd just poured the milk out and would have been going up with it next minute when Miss Jenny came in and said as how not to go up because her grandma were asleep and it were better she go without the milk than be disturbed."

"Did Miss Jenny look worried, or excited at all?"

"Excited?" Mrs. Beadle looked pityingly at the superintendent. "Miss Jenny? Not she. What was there to be excited about? She was just ordinary. Solemn like. She was always the quiet one."

"Not anxious, for instance?"

"Why no. Nobody knew then as how the poor old lady would be took bad in the night. To speak truth, there wasn't one of us sorry to know Mrs. Lackland was asleep. Let them sleep as can, I say. Sleep's good for the temper."

Littlejohn had an idea that Mrs. Beadle had hurriedly rejected the obvious reference to dogs as being unsuitable to subject and occasion alike.

"Bit of a tartar, wasn't she?" he asked confidentially.

But the cook's primly resolute look to divulge nothing spoke volumes. "No doubt but many of us might be if we had all the power in our own hands." The reproof in her voice suggested that even dictators deserved charitable judgement from their critics.

"Quite so. Well, that's all, Mrs. Beadle. Thank you for your help. By the way, who took Mrs. Lackland's tea up yesterday?"

"At teatime, do you mean?"

"Yes."

"Oh, that was Edith—"

"And did Hetty ever attend on her mistress too?"

"No." Mrs. Beadle almost sighed her denial, in contempt for such ignorance of domestic proprieties. "All *she* did was to tidy up there mornings, and she wasn't too good at that, getting so flummoxed if the old lady spoke to her sharp like."

"I see. Well, when you go back, please ask Edith to step this way for a minute."

The superintendent graciously ushered her out, before the cook, as she indignantly recounted to Hennessy afterwards, had had time to ask him how he thought the mistress had come by her end, seeing they wouldn't allow it was her own illness had done for her, poor soul.

Edith Dawes gave the impression of resenting her inclusion in the police inquiry while enjoying the publicity it afforded her. An aura of crushing superiority to the whole uncalled-for situation clung about her as she listened to the superintendent's query as to when she had last seen Mrs. Lackland in her usual health.

"Well, of course," she said coldly, "if that's what you want to know, Mrs. Lackland hasn't been in her usual health for about four months."

"Then shall I say when did you last see your mistress alive?" was Littlejohn's patient amendment.

"At four o'clock yesterday afternoon when I took up her tea."

"Can you recall what were the things then on her bedside table?"

"Oh yes," said Edith, who was proud of her observation and memory, "a bottle of medicine, glass, charcoal biscuits—three, I think—a shopping pad and a magazine. I had to move them to one side to put down the tray."

"Do you remember how much medicine was in the bottle?"

"Well, it was right down at the bottom. One dose, I should say."

The superintendent considered her thoughtfully. "Have you been happy here, Edith?" he asked abruptly.

The pale, rather contemptuous face flushed suddenly. "Why not?" she asked in a hard tone. "I do my work and I'm paid my wages."

"All right." Littlejohn dismissed her at once, but as she turned to go he saw her regarding him with a frown between her eyes in which an absent, puzzled expression dwelt for a moment.

"It's funny," she said in a hesitating, vaguely interested manner that overcame the superiority and at once made her more human, "but when you asked me about the things on the table I thought there ought to be something else. But I can't remember... I don't know. Perhaps it was nothing."

Littlejohn ran through the articles again, but none stirred any response in the girl. He knew it was worse than useless to badger an elusive memory, so did not emphasize its importance.

"It'll come back most likely when you're not chasing it. Let me know when it does," he concluded with an encouraging smile.

The police left almost immediately. There remained only Emily Bullen, the butler and Hetty; the last two could wait a little, and in the case of the first the superintendent shrank from recalling hysteria by questioning her before she had regained proper control of herself.

Shown out by a silent Hennessy, Littlejohn and Vale returned to the police station at a moderately quick pace. The superintendent was anxious for the fingerprint report on the bottle, though having in the past had no special reason to put much faith in it he subdued his expectations.

The lunch hour was on Minsterbridge now and the warm streets practically deserted. Neither man felt particularly communicative; each was busy revolving his own thoughts. When they had covered about half the distance, however, Littlejohn turned to his companion and, lifting a brow, asked: "Anything strike you particularly, Jimmy?"

"One or two things, sir. What about the way Miss Hernshaw took your question about the anonymous letters?"

"'Mm." Littlejohn was preoccupied and noncommittal.

"What about yourself, sir?" Vale prompted after a minute, but the superintendent made no reply.

When they reached the station, however, he suddenly burst out with: "I wouldn't be sorry if the chief called in the Yard for this job if the doctors are proved O.K. Local family and all. Not overmuch to my taste."

The sergeant, while ready to agree in his heart that it might be interesting to watch Scotland Yard at work, was inclined to regret a probability that would clip his own ambitions.

The fingerprint report was awaiting them.

Only one set of prints had been discovered on the medicine bottle, and those, clearly marked, presumably belonged to Dr. Faithful, who had handled it last on the fatal night.

Chapter VI

POISON AND PENMANSHIP

The Gnat that sings his Summer's Song
Poison gets from Slander's tongue.

William Blake

C hief Inspector Dan Pardoe of New Scotland Yard had been looking forward to a holiday among the Cotswold uplands when the case on which he was engaged should be brought to a triumphant conclusion. Air that would be sweet even in August, generous spaces and aloof horizons that respected the hankerings of a man uncomfortably circumscribed by city life and the inconsiderate behaviour of its transgressors, presented him with a picture that had made this day's business seem extra worthwhile. Weeks of tedious work had tracked the murderer of the man whose torso had been found in the Wiltshire hayloft, grotesquely reclad in a shirt, and whose identity had seemed for a month as unlikely of solution as that of the Brighton trunk victim. Now all the ends of a particularly filthy business were tidied up, and Pardoe's patiently accumulated evidence had that morning effected the arrest of a highly respected member of the Partisan Club who had had at least a run for his money.

It would get him plenty of kudos, Pardoe knew. But he wanted a holiday most, and now, before the world had had a chance to gape at the announcement of the end of the Hayloft Case, they had showed him into this Minsterbridge business, "because," the Assistant Commissioner had explained half-apologetically, "with Gatty on the Hartlepool job, you're the best man we've got for this family jiggery-pokery."

Pardoe jibbed a bit at the Universal Uncle flavour of the testimonial, but accepted the inevitable with a good grace and even a show of interest. He was a man nearing forty, tall and lithe, with the long stride of the countryman. He had a finely shaped head, the lean, red, sensitive face of an out-of-doors man, and strong curly hair that was already almost white. His appearance carried none of the inanities that in a perverse world suggest cleverness. He looked what he was, an able imaginative man who in the course of his work maintained a pretty fair balance between reason and imagination, and despised nothing instrumental to his job. He was a widower of many years, for whom a short and searing honeymoon on the heels of front trench experience as a boy fresh from grammar school had been a nasty jolt, but too brief and immature to have left permanent embitterment.

Pardoe ran over the few facts of this Lacklands affair. So Blayne had found 2.8 grains of morphia in the old lady, eh? And the empty medicine bottle had been thoroughly wiped before the doctor had last handled it. On the face of it it looked a crude, silly business, whatever was at stake, in spite of the craft employed, as well as a bad one. That was no reason, of course, why it shouldn't continue crude and silly all through. Contrary to the dicta of the crime novelists, things were not frequently in fact opposite to what their superficialities suggested. Family affairs were usually the very devil. The Chief Constable had patently thought so. Well, they could wait till he'd had his lunch.

As a rule Pardoe preferred the train service to a car, and Minsterbridge even by a slow train was little more than an hour away. Catching a fast one from Paddington just after two, accompanied by Detective-Sergeant Salt, a sound officer of disarmingly homely appearance, the inspector was in Littlejohn's office before three on the Friday afternoon.

Together they went carefully through the report up-to-date. Fingerprints of each member of the household as well as those of Dr. Faithful had been taken, without official enthusiasm, it is true, but as a means at any rate of checking up on that almost virgin bottle. The prints on the latter were, as was supposed, the doctor's. Sergeant Vale had seen Hennessy and the housemaid that morning. The butler's contribution to the general information had dealt almost wholly with the question of his dismissal by Mrs. Lackland nearly a week ago, after twenty-six years' service in the family.

"He was pretty frank about it," Littlejohn explained. "Said he knew perfectly well it was his job to keep Carnowski out of the house, but that he didn't see why the girls shouldn't have their fun while they could get it. It would mighty soon come to an end, he said, when the old lady took things over again. So when Miss Jenny pointed out how he could keep the letter of the law, so to speak, by just leaving the garden door unfastened, he agreed, and the other fellow let himself in that way."

"When was this?" Pardoe asked.

"Last Friday. After the old lady had gone to bed."

The inspector looked thoughtful. "And she was taken ill next day?"

"'Mm. About teatime. After she'd found out and sacked Hennessy."

"Any particulars of the illness?"

"No-o. Not beyond pretty bad sickness, which Miss Quentin, the younger granddaughter, puts down to a too hearty appetite. I meant to see the doctor about it."

"We will." Pardoe made a brief note. After considering the typed report for a minute or two, he looked up and inquired: "Hennessy's alibi for Wednesday night? Has he got one?"

"It seems sound enough," the superintendent admitted, "unless the servants are all in it together, which is unlikely, to say the least of it. The four of them corroborated each other's statements about being downstairs in their own quarters at the crucial period—"

"Now, look here," Pardoe interrupted good-humouredly, "what are you calling the crucial period in this business? No, wait a minute. It was silly of me to ask for Hennessy's alibi. The medical report, I know, says that in view of the fact that Mrs. Lackland talked with Miss Hernshaw at seven o'clock and ate her dinner immediately afterwards the stuff couldn't have been drunk earlier than that, and since she was found presumably in a drugged sleep at nine o'clock, the time at which she must have taken it is pretty well narrowed down for us. But that isn't the only time which concerns us, nor, if it comes to that, the most important. Somebody put that morphia in the medicine—in the bottle, not the glass, and"—he consulted the report for a moment—"that could have happened any time after the doctor gave her the previous dose, which was at about two-thirty in the afternoon."

Pardoe paused, but before Littlejohn could speak he went on: "That's not all. Somebody else wiped off any fingerprints there must have been on the bottle before Dr. Faithful arrived in the early hours of Thursday morning, but we don't know when. He came just after two A.M. So," the inspector grinned faintly as he encountered the superintendent's gaze, "there goes your 'crucial' period. Poisoning the tonic, drinking it, the destruction of evidence—which shall it be?"

"No, well, when it's put like that," Littlejohn sighed, "there's a spread-over of twelve hours. Oh Lord!"

"Exactly. Instead of two. Twelve hours of unchecked comings and goings in and out of rooms, and ample time for the murderer or murderers to get to work."

"D'you think," Sergeant Salt asked, "the old lady poured out her own medicine and drank it unsuspectingly when she was alone?"

"But for one thing. If that had been so wouldn't it have suited her murderer to leave her prints on the bottle? Suggestion of suicide strengthened a little. Anyway there wouldn't have been much point in taking the trouble to rub 'em off."

"Unless," the superintendent put in shrewdly, "the idea was to make it look at first sight as if the doctor had done it."

Pardoe frowned. "At first sight, perhaps. But that would be pretty clumsy and wouldn't work. The doctor left the house before four that day, and since she couldn't have had the stuff till three hours later at the very earliest—well, think of it. What sense, anyway, is there in one set of prints only, when for all we know and all the murderer knew any number of people may have shifted and handled that bottle before night? You've got the maid's evidence for one that she touched it when she put down the tray."

"Yes, it doesn't make sense," Littlejohn admitted, "unless the murderer panicked and got stupid at that point, and didn't reason things out."

"Easily might have." The inspector looked at him keenly. "When you hinted just now that somebody might be trying to implicate the doctor, you were thinking of those anonymous letters?"

"Yes." The superintendent half rose. "Like to see them now?"

"In a minute. I shall want to see Dr. Faithful too as soon as I can catch him."

Littlejohn glanced at the clock.

"He takes his tea early, I believe, if he's not on a case," said the superintendent. "He'll be at it now, I should say."

"Then in half an hour or so," the inspector replied and got up. "Meantime, come and have a cup with us, and let's finish over there."

The superintendent, feeling that the hospitality should have come from him, reddened slightly, and said awkwardly: "I ought to be asking you—"

"We're nearly next door," Pardoe retorted. "Come on. I left my bags at the Swan and Ferry. Seems a nice little place."

It was, and is. Of an unobtrusive, you might say unconscious antiquity, this moderate-sized hostelry stands in a quiet little bay of Minsterbridge High Street. It lays no undue emphasis upon either tradition, dating as it does at least to the middle years of Henry VIII, or prices, which have a comfortable range, and scorns no decent and acceptable modernities. Originally, as the superintendent explained, the name had been the Swan of Ferris, "a big family hereabouts hundreds of years ago, but not of much account, they say, after the Wars of the Roses, so bit by bit the meaning was lost till it got to be what you see today." Indeed, as Pardoe observed, no ferry figured on the sign, where a lonely swan floated placidly in the middle of a faded azure shield.

They had tea in the small sitting room assigned to New Scotland Yard during its stay, a homely if rather airless place.

Over the meal they tidied up the remaining evidence by discussing the examination of Hetty, the housemaid. Littlejohn admitted that Sergeant Vale had been able to make no headway with her.

"Something funny there," he went on guardedly. "Vale couldn't get anything coherent out of her because she's in floods of tears all the time. It seems as if being told to go on account of the eavesdropping had completely thrown her off her balance. Not that I think she could tell anything of much use. It wasn't her job to wait on the old lady at all, and it seems she only saw her for a bit in the mornings when she tidied the room, and then was usually scared stiff of her. But there it is. However it stands we'd better leave her alone till she's pulled herself together, or even if she's got anything material to say we shan't hear it."

Pardoe listened without comment. "What about the other woman—companion, isn't she?"

The superintendent grimaced. "Name of Bullen. There's another who's been throwing hysterics about the place. She did a faint soon after the doctor arrived that night, and was in bed yesterday and today—medical orders. I'm not in a position to say how far she was faking so as to get out of being questioned. I haven't seen her at all since it happened, but I had a minute with Faithful this morning when he called at the house and he says she ought to be up and fit for an interview tomorrow."

"All right. Then the next thing is to see the doctor."

Sergeant Salt, who had the qualities of a magnet for picking up valuable information, sometimes from out-of-the-way sources, stayed behind, both to settle in and sound the possibilities of the Swan and Ferry.

Inspector Pardoe and Superintendent Littlejohn left the inn, and after the latter had collected from his office the poison-pen letters Dr. Faithful had committed to him they walked together along the streets that in the brilliance of the afternoon were sharply sliced into contrasting light and shadow. Pardoe was always acutely alive to his environment, and was beginning to appreciate the apparently tranquil backwash of life in Minsterbridge. That it might actually have no such tranquillity only added to his relish of its charms.

When they came to the quiet house opposite the great chestnut, Dr. Faithful was in and would see them. They were shown into his sitting room, a cool room at the back of the house, low-ceilinged and comfortable with books and well-sprung chairs and some pieces of good china, with steel engravings of the town and cathedral in the early eighteen hundreds. Casement windows with small leaded panes and broad seats stood open to a narrow walled garden with espalier pear trees. It was like entering the refreshing shadow of a stone archway after the glare of the streets.

The doctor rose from a low chair by the hearth where he had been hastily writing a letter on his knee, and placed paper and pen on the mantelpiece before coming forward to greet them. The superintendent to whom he was a familiar figure thought, as he introduced the inspector, how tired Dr. Faithful was looking. Pardoe, seeing him for the first time, received the impression of an extremely handsome man of compelling personality who was running a bit to seed.

Formalities over, and smoke passed round, the inspector approached his subject.

"I'd like to know," he began, "whether Mrs. Lackland had a professional nurse at any time during her illness?"

"Oh yes. She came in May and left at the end of last month. She was practically driven off by the old lady." Faithful smiled. "Not for inefficiency. She was very capable. But from the first Mrs. Lackland protested against a nurse, who was absolutely necessary as much for the girls' sakes as her own. She only gave in about it because I got Jenny and Carol to oppose the idea!"

He thought for a moment, then took out a small notebook, tore a leaf from it, and scribbled a name and address, handing it to Pardoe. "If you need to get in touch," he said. "But there's nothing additional she can tell you."

"Thanks," said Pardoe, slipping it inside his own notebook. "Now forgive a layman's ignorance of what must have been obvious to you, Doctor, and tell me what it was that first suggested to your mind the need for an autopsy."

Dr. Faithful permitted himself a faint surprise.

"You've seen my evidence?" he inquired politely.

"Oh yes. And I've no intention of taking you through that again. I only want to hear from you your first reactions to Mrs. Lackland's death."

"I'll tell you. The whole shocking business was, and is, incredible to me. I have attended Mrs. Lackland, as you know, throughout a long and dangerous illness starting with influenza and developing into gastroenteritis of such severity that her death was expected at any time in May and early June. At the end of May a London specialist, Mr. Tuxtin, was consulted. He, I may say, wholly approved of my treatment, and with one or two suggestions from him I carried on and hoped for the best. Nothing more but the patient's own astonishing stamina was likely to pull her through, and that is what finally happened. After a life and death struggle of weeks she took the return towards recovery, and when once it was taken her convalescence was as swift and assured as her resistance had been amazing. She was a patient to be proud of."

The doctor paused a moment and delicately tipped off the ash of his cigarette. "That's why," he went on, in a voice which hinted at suppressed savagery, "her collapse and death the night before last was plainly more than questionable. It was the impossible happening. Why, man," he turned hotly towards Pardoe, "her heart was sound as a bell, she'd been in excellent spirits for days, and I myself had seen and chatted with her for an hour in the afternoon when she could do nothing but talk about her plans for next day. There's something damnable afoot."

The inspector, who had not anticipated this heat, observed the flush that had risen to the doctor's face, and noting the faint twitch of his nostrils considered that here was a man whose professional pride had been as severely stung as his solicitude by this untimely death of a promising patient.

In less than a minute, however, he had control of himself, his features relaxed, and the suggestion of a smile set lines about his mouth.

"I've been a bit on edge, I'm afraid," he said quietly, "having, as you know, through the kind offices of my unknown correspondent an additional personal interest of a highly unpleasant nature in this unhappy business. What's more, I've had to cancel a long cherished holiday due to begin next week, wire my locum who was coming down on Monday, and follow that up with an explanatory letter which I was writing when you came in. All very trivial, you'll say, and rightly, beside murder, but none the less annoying for all that." He smiled frankly at his own egotism.

Littlejohn murmured something vaguely sympathetic, while the inspector returned to the point with: "Then Mrs. Lackland's appearance immediately warned you that something was very wrong—in the sense that these were not natural symptoms?"

"Exactly. As I stated yesterday I could see from the start that it was quite hopeless. By then no stimulus could possibly have aroused the old lady. She must have been insensible hours before I was called in. With all her muscles relaxed, her pulse extremely feeble, the cold bluish pallor of her face and much contracted pupils, there could be no mistake, I'm afraid. Besides that, there was the faint odour suggestive of morphia, and a much stronger smell from the empty medicine bottle. Dr. Wylie, the police surgeon, confirmed my diagnosis and it only remained to find out if possible how much of the stuff the poor woman had swallowed."

Pardoe nodded. "That's what I wanted to know, Doctor—that you felt no hesitation in refusing a certificate."

"None whatever. That is, of course, on medical grounds. From the social angle and the fact that for some time I've enjoyed friendly relations with the family as distinct from professional, it was a wretched business. Thank God, it's rare enough a doctor's compelled to such a course."

"How long have you attended at Lacklands?"

"For six years. Before that I was partner in the practice with my father who was the family doctor for nine or ten years. It's been a smooth enough connection until now," he added.

"Well now, with regard to the bilious attack Mrs. Lackland had at the end of last week, Doctor. Will you give me your opinion of it, the symptoms and so on?"

Tom Faithful looked at the inspector sharply. "Are you inclined to link that up with the fatal attack? It's natural to do so, I suppose, but I may as well say at the outset that the two illnesses had nothing in common. Whatever Mrs. Lackland may have eaten on Saturday it was certainly not morphia that caused her sickness. I was called in a little before five. I think it was the butler who rang me up. Both girls were out playing tennis and taking tea at the pavilion. Only Miss Bullen was with the old lady, and I fancied she did not take the attack particularly seriously—at any rate, she wasn't frightened or beside herself, as this time. She had had the sense to get Mrs. Lackland to bed. I should have said that being thoroughly convalescent by then the old lady had been downstairs or sitting in the garden the greater part of each day that week. So with a mild emetic and hot-water bottles we soon made her more comfortable. But it was nasty while it lasted. She was violently sick several times, had shivering fits and a weak pulse, but there was definitely no drowsiness, stupor, or any other symptom suggestive of a drug like morphine. On the contrary, Mrs.

Lackland's mind was quite unclouded, and her remarks in between the bouts of sickness very apposite and biting!"

The doctor smiled reminiscently.

"Then you saw nothing that time," said the inspector, "to feel alarmed about?"

"Alarmed? No. I was puzzled, I must admit, because the onset was so sudden and, while it lasted, severe. But Mrs. Lackland had an imprudent appetite which she was prone to indulge whenever she felt well enough. She was very restive under a prescribed diet, which in her case was absolutely essential. I could only conclude she had had too much of the forbidden stuff—rich cake, for instance, to which she was partial. In fact she confessed as much."

"And that would account satisfactorily for her illness?"

"Yes. Gastric trouble is only too easily set in motion in those subject to it, and in Mrs. Lackland's case a prolonged illness had to be considered as well as the fact that she had a sensitive stomach she didn't properly respect."

"So you sent her back to bed for some days, Doctor?" the superintendent put in.

"Yes, but again I wasn't prepared for her to make such a complete recovery so rapidly. I told her on Saturday that she must stop in bed for a week, reminding her of the risk of a chill. Actually when I called on Sunday evening she was as fit as she'd been on the Friday and quite able to get about again. But I gave no hint of this until Wednesday when I told her she could get up next day."

Pardoe looked thoughtfully at the doctor. "Recalling that sickness, Dr. Faithful," he said, "in the light of what's followed, have you any reasons to suspect that somebody had designs on your patient a week ago?"

The doctor looked as though he would have preferred silence on that point. After hesitating he said reluctantly: "It is bound, of course, to look odder now that this horrible thing's happened. I wouldn't like to go further than that. If some irritant poison were used then Mrs.

Lackland succeeded in throwing it off entirely by the very severity of her sickness, and I, not suspecting anything at the time, never thought of examining any articles she'd used in connection with her meal."

"Of course not," Pardoe replied, and went on immediately: "Is it true that Mrs. Lackland had been very upset that day about Mr. Carnowski's visit the night before?"

The doctor hesitated again. Distaste of the direction inquiry was taking showed in his face when he answered.

"I think she was, Inspector. But there, I'm afraid, I can't be of much use to you. No confidences concerning Mr. Carnowski were placed in me, and if I might put in my oar without being impertinent, don't you think that in pursuing that line you may be mistaking shadow for substance?"

"In what way?"

"Why, girls' friendships and flirtations nowadays carry very little weight, and if, as I believe, Mrs. Lackland objected to entertaining young men, it was due to nothing else but the legal position in which she stood to Jenny and Carol. She was their guardian, you know."

"So I've gathered," said Pardoe, who could not for the life of him see that this illogical contribution to the discussion eliminated Carnowski as a substantial factor in the case. "You don't happen to know, I suppose, to what extent Mrs. Lackland controlled her husband's estate?"

"Not with any certainty. Only surmise, you know. Rennie, her solicitor, could put you right there. There was a lot of money at stake, I believe."

The doctor spoke cautiously and the inspector, marking his reserve, did not labour the point. As Faithful had said, he could get enlightenment on what he considered the all-important feature of the case from the lawyer himself. He tacked abruptly, and observed the relief on the other's face as domestic differences were abandoned for scientific fact.

"About the morphia that was used. We have to do our best to trace it to its source, and I'm told you've made a very helpful suggestion in that quarter, Doctor."

"Let's say I reminded the superintendent of a fact already in his possession," Faithful replied with a slight smile. "I reported the loss of my tablets to the police on a Monday early in June, the 7th I think it was. I'd made four visits between one-thirty and a quarter to three that afternoon and had left my car outside each of my calls. It was on my way to hospital after leaving the last of these that I suddenly missed my case from its usual place on the seat, and after stopping to make a search hooked it out at last from under the seat. It was unfastened, and at first glance nothing seemed to be missing. But later on at the hospital I found I couldn't account for about fourteen of the morphia sulphate tabloids I was carrying. I reported the theft, as it undoubtedly was, that evening."

"How much does one tablet contain?" Pardoe asked.

"Mine contained a quarter of a grain each. Smaller ones are made, but these are the commonest."

Pardoe made a rapid calculation. "Then about twelve were administered to the old lady?"

Faithful nodded. "Which leaves two unaccounted for, perhaps," he agreed.

"Now that Monday in June was an occasion you visited at Lacklands, Doctor?"

"Yes. At the time it happened I gave the police the addresses of those I visited. Lacklands was my third call, I know. I didn't take my bag into the house, though. In fact, it was outside in the car at each place except the first."

The superintendent cleared his throat. "That's right, sir. I have the addresses. But as I was telling the inspector, nothing came of our inquiries. We made 'em as tactfully as possible, with a house-to-house call. We didn't mention the tablets by name, only said casually the doctor fancied he may have left something behind. But nobody had seen anything, of course, and we didn't really think they would have, as the bag was outside most of the time."

"It doesn't get us very far," Pardoe admitted, "but it's something to know when and about where there was such a theft. When you left Lacklands that day, Doctor, can you remember if there was anybody in the path or on the road by your car?"

The doctor's brows lifted in an attempt to recall the occasion.

"I've a pretty bad visual memory, if you like to call it that," he confessed. "But wait a minute," he went on more quickly, and then looked faintly ashamed of his haste to retrieve this memory. "It wouldn't be of any help, though," he continued slowly, "but I fancy I met Jenny—Miss Hernshaw, you know, returning from wishing some visitor goodbye at the gate, and I'm afraid I've no idea who her visitor was, though she might remember if you think it worthwhile to ask."

Pardoe thanked him, and then asked in an interested voice: "Did you mention the loss of the morphia to anybody but the police, sir?"

"No, I've never spoken of it to anyone."

"Then I'll be glad if you won't do so from now on."

The doctor agreed, and Pardoe, as was his custom, dropped the subject without worrying it.

"While we're here, Doctor, I'd like to look over those letters you had. I haven't seen them yet, but the superintendent has brought them along."

The doctor hitched his chair a little closer and appeared glad of the introduction of a fresh theme, or at least of a new angle to an old one.

"Fetch 'em out," he said with grim joviality. "You don't know what it cost me to part with those endearments even temporarily!"

From an inside pocket Superintendent Littlejohn produced the letters, each in its respective envelope, clipped together with a rubber band. He handed them to the inspector, while the eyes of all three men were concentrated on the cheap flimsy envelopes.

Pardoe slipped off the band and studied the top one with the cold distaste he reserved for this particular type of self-indulgence. Then placing the two others on his knee he drew out the folded sheet of paper from the first envelope with a certain fastidious reluctance. Unfolding it he held it before him in such a way that its contents were visible to his companions.

In a quiet voice he read the message:

> *Dr. Faithful—Look out. Evil doing shall not prosper. There are those who watch.*

"Mm. Ill-formed block capitals, but looks as if the writer may have done them on purpose, the cheapest of scribbling-block paper with envelope to match, and rather washy ink, faded, watered or quickly blotted. Nasty ingredients altogether, and all mixed in with a slightly pious flavour, which makes it nastier still. I see there's no date, Doctor," he added, turning to Faithful. "Do you remember what day you received this?"

"Oh yes. I made a note of each, but I don't need to consult any memoranda to tell you about *that*. That's Number One letter, and it came by the early morning post on Saturday, June 12th. I believe the postmark is legible on the envelope."

It was. Marked full and square on a three-halfpenny stamp stuck on awry, they could read the hour six-thirty P.M., the date June 11th, and most of the name Minsterbridge.

Pardoe put it down and drew out Number Two. Envelope, paper and script were identical with those of the first, but here the faint and scrubby postmark was scarcely discernible. The doctor, however, could supply the information. The letter had come by the first delivery on July 2nd, "a Friday, I think," and ran:

> *Dear Dr. Faithful—Why does Mrs. Lackland's illness last so long? You know the answer. You will see that she does not get better. You beast.*

"A little more expansive, not to say expressive, this time," said the doctor in an equable voice, though Pardoe was quick to observe that a tightness round his mouth showed that the ease with which he spoke cost him something.

"And more malicious too," the superintendent remarked.

"Less controlled, at any rate," commented Pardoe. "Now for the third. A change of envelope here, I see. I understand you got this on Wednesday, Doctor? Hello, Minsterbridge wasn't the office of collection this time then?"

He peered at the stamp where the hour five-thirty showed plainly, the date not so well, and where the place was obliterated save for the four final letters, "*lham*".

"That would most likely be Bullham, a village eight miles away," Littlejohn said. "Not that it need exactly have been posted there. Bullham's sorting office serves two or three hamlets round, and the postmistress says their latest collection is five-thirty and that letters posted to catch that would be delivered in Minsterbridge teatime next day. It fits in. One of those near-and-not-so-near places," he explained, "with a rotten train service."

"That's useful," Pardoe said. He took out the letter from the thick white envelope which matched ill with its vulgar tint and texture, and gave his attention to the latest abuse.

Do you think it is a secret that you are slowly poisoning Mrs. Lackland?

The inspector lifted his eyebrows. "Concise and much more explicit," he said, almost softly. "God, what revolting methods the little ego has to adopt!"

He turned to the doctor. "Do you know of anybody in this town or near it likely to bear you a grudge, sir? Even if it's some trivial thing, let me have it. Anonymous letter-writers aren't to be accounted for by ordinary standards."

Seeing Faithful hesitate, he added: "Put aside scruples now, Doctor. We're investigating murder and have got to bandy names about, and nothing you say is going to get an innocent person into trouble. Besides," he tapped the sheets on his knee, "you've got a very personal interest in it, seeing you've been accused of the deed!"

The doctor relaxed into a bitter smile. He touched his heavy black eyebrows with a shapely forefinger. "It must be because I look the operatic villain," he murmured. "No, Inspector, I'd help you if I could. I don't need you to tell me to have no hesitation in naming names. After getting these poisonous squirts I've no tendernesses for the author. But the fact remains, I can't think of anybody."

"A pity," Pardoe said. "Think—isn't there anywhere some female patient perhaps whose attitude has changed towards you recently?"

The inspector was aware that he was treading risky ground. He was a good enough judge of human character to know that pride and even hauteur were fairly strong constituents of the doctor's. What he really wanted to suggest was that a change of medical man had been made lately by some woman patient, irate at a fancied or actual neglect.

But though the doctor appeared to show not the slightest offence at the implication, he still shook his head and disclaimed all knowledge of such resentment.

"It isn't vanity, Inspector," he urged, with sudden uncanny insight into Pardoe's mind, "it's simply that I don't know. There isn't a doctor, of course, who doesn't meet with some enmity, trifling or serious, in the course of his work. But when it comes to laying a finger on this man or that woman and saying: 'Here is the source of the hostility,' well," he shrugged slightly, "that's not such an easy matter."

"No. Well, it might have helped materially if you could have told us something, but then again it might not. Anonymous letter-writers aren't commonly the type that displays bad feeling. The author of these may very well be somebody who appears amiable in ordinary intercourse." Pardoe gave the doctor a brisk look as he added: "However, before we drop that side of it, sir, can you name any former patient of yours who has been calling in another doctor—say in the last year or so?"

"Not one, Inspector," Faithful replied immediately, almost rueful at his inability to oblige.

"All right," the inspector said, not in the least cast down, "then we must look elsewhere for our evidence. These letters will be sent to Brassey, the graphologist, who will give us indications of sex and age which will probably narrow the inquiry. Now just give me your own ideas of the writer. Never mind if you feel them to be unfounded. I'd like to hear your feelings even though there wasn't a tittle of evidence to support them."

Dr. Faithful hedged a bit. "Do you mean you want me to tell you suspicions of identity entirely on an imaginative basis?" he asked, a little indignantly.

Pardoe understood that whatever approach he made the doctor meant to remain reticent. He determined to be forthright. "Not exactly. But do you believe that the person who wrote those letters is the person who murdered Mrs. Lackland?"

The doctor sat up straight, and seemed pleased to fasten on something which avoided specific charges.

"That had occurred to me, of course. It's the natural conclusion, I think. But there's a good bit, it seems to me, that doesn't fit in with that theory. Why 'slowly poisoning'? That's an inaccuracy, if it wasn't deliberate on the part of the writer, for what is certain is that the old lady was killed by one heavy dose of morphia, and not by the cumulative effect of some unnamed poison administered over a long period, as the letter suggests."

The inspector nodded. "A good point, Doctor. Anything else strike you as odd about the theory?"

"Yes. Why was that third letter posted so as to arrive the very last day of Mrs. Lackland's life? It was bound to draw such attention to the writer as wouldn't have been given when the earlier letters came and the patient was mending. A different sort of attention, I mean, certainly the special kind a murderer would want at all costs to avoid. Or did he or she—shall we say It?—think that I, an innocent man, was going to lie down beneath these devilish accusations and never bring any of them to light?"

"What would the writer have gained if you had lain quiet?" Pardoe put in rather quickly. "Precisely nothing but the satisfaction of gloating over the delivery of the letters. Which seems to point to the poison-pen wielder, pure and simple. Sorry," he grinned amiably at Littlejohn, "impure and complex. What I mean is, it looks like an anonymous letter-writer of undivided allegiance, so to speak, not one who was necessarily giving more than half his mind to murder at the same time. Doesn't that agree with your own suggestion?"

He turned to Dr. Faithful, who nodded.

"It does." He added thoughtfully: "Then it seems to me to follow—" He paused.

"Yes?" Pardoe prompted.

"I was going to say that it follows that the writer had an inkling of something going on, perhaps even knew murder was planned, perhaps knows the murderer, and for reasons best known to Itself decided to try to throw suspicion on me."

"It might be," Pardoe said without actual agreement. "But this brings us back to your original objection: since Mrs. Lackland wasn't killed slowly, but at once, how much practical preparation could there have been which became apparent to an outsider at least as far back as June 11th?"

"That's a difficulty," the doctor agreed. "Unless—yes, suppose writer and murderer are together in this, and the letters were sent to me with the murderer's knowledge?"

"I'm afraid that won't get us far," said the inspector. "That would mean it was just as awkward for the murderer to have that letter posted somewhere about Bullham on Tuesday as though he'd written it himself. Again, in that case too why suggest slow poisoning?" He caught Littlejohn's eye. "What do you say, Superintendent?"

The superintendent assumed a thoughtful air. "Well, for my own part, I'd be inclined to say it was one and the same person, and that the things that don't fit were done deliberately by somebody pretty clever for a purpose we can't see at present."

"That's sure enough," said Pardoe, "that we can't see any of it now. Well, what you say may be right. We must consider 'em all, all the theories anybody can put forward. But if it's one person at the bottom of this there's some wrong psychology got in somewhere. And if it's two it's even more incomprehensible."

He got up, followed by Dr. Faithful and the superintendent.

"I shan't keep you any longer, sir," he said to Faithful. He quickly put the letters up, clipped the band round them and pushed them into an inner pocket. "Please let me know if you get another of these. I'll put an expert on to them. Now we must push along to the solicitor's."

The doctor was standing, his hands deep in his trousers pockets, his dark shining gaze on the inspector's face, and something so markedly hesitant in his manner that his expression arrested the attention of both police officers.

"Before you leave for Rennie's place," he said quietly, "there's something I think you should know. I didn't mean to mention it, because I'm well aware how unreliable a good many of Mrs. Lackland's declarations were, but," he gave a whimsical lift to his eyebrows, "better bring everything into the open as I'm supposed to have poisoned her, and at least this does if true supply a kind of immediate motive for somebody to kill her. And I'm inclined on the whole to think it was an unpremeditated murder?" There was a query in his voice as he looked at Pardoe.

The inspector said nothing, however, and the doctor continued: "When you asked me if I knew whether Mrs. Lackland had complete control of her husband's money, I said correctly that I didn't know. What I do know is that she had money of her own, quite independent of what came to her through marriage. She told me it amounted to about fifteen thousand pounds. With this sum she was always either pretending to play about, or—I don't know which—actually playing about, by making new wills and scrapping old ones. That's what I mean when I say I don't know how much reliance was to be placed at any time on what she said were her intentions. Because on Wednesday afternoon, the last time I ever saw her in good health, the old lady told me that she was only waiting for me to tell her she could see Rennie next day so as to get him to draw up a new will, in which the fifteen thousand which was hers to do with as she liked was to come to me on her death."

Whatever Inspector Pardoe and the superintendent had anticipated it was not this. Dr. Faithful was not displeased at the surprise he had evoked.

"She added," he went on, "that her lawyer already knew of her intention, so if that's so Rennie can confirm this. On the other hand, I was inclined at heart to be sceptical."

"This is news worth having, Doctor," said the inspector. "D'you suppose Mrs. Lackland spread it further, or was it confided to you alone?"

"I've no idea. She was certainly excited enough that day to have announced it, and it wasn't her habit to keep anything to herself if she thought she could provoke annoyance by telling it."

"Do you happen to know how the money was to be disposed before her final decision to leave it to you?"

"No. She'd occasionally spoken to me in the past about her money, but never of where she would leave it. She revelled in half-confidences and mysteries."

"I understand. How did you receive the news, Doctor? A bit embarrassing, wasn't it?"

"It would have been if I hadn't known Mrs. Lackland and her wilfulness so long. Oh, I took it half jestingly as I fancied it might be meant, told her I'd got no such claim on her kindness, that she still had a day in which to change her mind, and that in any case she was in good health now and was going to live long and enjoy it herself.

Poor old woman… of course she pooh-poohed any protest, said her mind was made up, and so on."

"Well, it looks, Doctor," said Pardoe, "as if somebody had a devilish grudge against you, depriving you of a fortune and trying to fasten a murder on you in one and the same breath!"

He and the superintendent took their leave, making for Mr. Rennie's house, which was situated behind the cathedral.

In the half-mile or so they had to cover the inspector showed no readiness to discuss immediate problems. Both men were preoccupied. Pardoe's thoughts revolved idly round the doctor, the only protagonist he had encountered as yet. He thought of the heavily built, handsome man, his large mobile face and full black eyes, the sudden passion that had shaken him at the thought that Death had snatched at the very last, when medical triumph seemed assured, a victim he could have had so easily months earlier; he thought of the anonymous letters, of the promised legacy, this last perhaps the real clue to the murder, leading to the doctor as the focal point of somebody's odium. Whose?

"Wonder who it is he reminds me of," said Pardoe aloud.

"Mussolini," retorted the superintendent with a burst of imagination, not questioning the inspector's train of thought.

Chapter VII

MR. RENNIE RECALLS——

We think our Children a Part of ourselves,
though as they grow up they might very well undeceive us.

Marquis of Halifax:
Miscellaneous Thoughts and Reflections

Mr. Rennie accepted a cigarette from Pardoe but did not light it immediately. He looked from him to the superintendent and back again with his customary air of giving a faint deliberation to the most trivial of actions.

"You are quite sure, gentlemen," he tentatively inquired, "that you think the early facts relevant enough to your problem to justify a start of, say, more than seventy years ago for my story?"

"We should like to hear everything you can tell us, Mr. Rennie," Pardoe replied. "So fire away."

"Very well," agreed Rennie. It was obvious that nothing really pleased him so much as being able to pay proper respect to the sequences of his story. Inspector Pardoe had perceived as much before five minutes had passed, and soon made up his mind to allow the old solicitor to impart the information they wanted in his own way. It made for mutual satisfaction by the promise of better results.

Mr. Archibald Rennie was a small neat gentleman of seventy-two years, made physically with the sort of precision and respect for logic that informed his attitude to life. He was all of a pattern, so to speak, displaying no incongruities save, perhaps, an impression of rotundity without actual stoutness. His beautiful white hair, bisected by an admirably drawn parting, matched perfectly the almost infantile

pink of his cheeks and the guileless blue eyes, evidence in the happy
blend of age and youth of the harmony existing between both ends
of life. He was an honest, charming, intelligent old gentleman, with
a reverence for the law he practised hovering this side of idolatry.
At present he had every need of the self-control which had become
second nature to him. Mrs. Lackland's death in such circumstances
and on the very threshold, it might be said, of employing his services
afresh, troubled him horribly.

He had received the inspector and the superintendent in his pleasant rooms behind the cathedral, looking on to the close and Deanery
and beyond these to a fine expanse which served Minsterbridge
as a public recreation ground for children. His manner had held
the inevitable misgiving at the entry of the police into a client's
affairs. Admitting that he had received a letter from Mrs. Lackland
on Thursday morning arranging an interview that afternoon, and
that within the same hour he was informed over the telephone of
her death, the old man had seemed in the first moments of their
arrival on the verge of breaking down. Pardoe, who wanted as
much information relating to the murdered woman's past as he
could obtain, as well as immediate details, put his difficulties frankly
before Rennie. He suggested that as the lawyer's knowledge of the
Lackland family was unrivalled in Minsterbridge it would clarify
matters considerably if he could supply them with a background
to the present situation.

"Give me the human side of it first," he said. "People, you know,
and how and why they did this, that and the other, so far as you
know. We'll lead up to the will and this week's doings that way, in
proper order."

This appealed to the old man, who was not averse to revealing
what he knew to further the ends of justice, but preferred to dignify
it in the guise of history. He now cleared his throat impressively,
and as far as such a metaphor can be applied to so cautious a being
plunged directly into his narrative.

"John Lackland, the grandfather of Miss Hernshaw and Miss Quentin, was born here in Minsterbridge in the fifties of last century. His father was a shoemaker, but his cobbling days did not last very long because of a wasting consumption that made an invalid of him in what should have been the prime of life, and of which he died when John was twelve. John was the only child, and after her husband's death Mrs. Lackland took in washing as a means of livelihood, work she had started when the shoemaking failed. She was a very competent laundress, I believe, and even after her son became a moneyed man and was anxious to set her up in luxury for the rest of her days, I am told that she preferred to take in a little washing or visit a few of her chosen patrons as in the old time, rather than live in what she considered idleness."

There was a slight impatience noticeable about Superintendent Littlejohn at this leisurely description of the activities of Mrs. Lackland, *mère*. He was amused to note that Pardoe, to whom everything apparently was grist, was listening with an expression as absorbed as if what he heard bore directly on last Wednesday night's events.

"Then," continued Mr. Rennie, "when John was nearly fourteen he left his odd jobs in Minsterbridge, newspaper selling, a bit of gardening now and again, and such casual work as came his way, and through the intermediary offices of some relatives of his mother who lived in Leicester, he got work in that city as assistant in a small clothier's establishment. That would be in 1871.

"He assisted, of course, in a very junior capacity, but from the first, I think, his business acumen must have developed quickly. Nothing else can account for his remarkable transition from poverty to wealth in so comparatively short a time."

As the old lawyer paused thoughtfully, Pardoe put in: "What about his mother's relatives? Were they able to help?"

"Not at all. By what he has told me they were themselves struggling tradespeople in a small way, with no influence whatever beyond sufficient acquaintance with the clothier to get Mrs. Lackland's boy the preference over any other. No, I think we may accept it as a fact that so far as friends could have a practical effect upon his career, John Lackland in Leicester during his teens was friendless."

Pardoe nodded. The superintendent, in a dutiful effort to keep his interest alive, began unobtrusively to make notes on the back of an envelope.

"Very soon as the years go," Rennie pursued, "the boy rose to manage the business and to relieve his master of the entire executive. Then, the clothier being childless, the shop passed finally to John while he was still in his twenties. Not long afterwards a branch shop was opened in another quarter of the city, and only a year or so later a third business sprang up and absorbed fresh employees—"

"When did his first marriage take place, sir?" inquired Littlejohn, anxious to arrive at this point.

"I am coming to that," said Mr. Rennie primly. He had a pronounced distaste for interruption and continued unhurriedly to relate things in his own fashion. The superintendent resumed his patient pencilling with a good grace as the lawyer went on.

"Then began what is so often termed the mushroom growth of John Lackland's shops in Leicester and the surrounding towns. But the stability and shrewd common sense which formed the basis of this commercial enterprise had nothing about it resembling the shallow growth of mushrooms. In Loughborough, Hinckley, Market Harborough, and in many smaller places the Lackland businesses sprang up. He soon stretched out into adjacent counties, absorbed his rivals' establishments, took over shops that were not paying and soon compelled them to be profitable, and in fact by 1890 was the controlling force in the clothing and hosiery trades in the Midlands.

"Meantime," Mr. Rennie glanced at the superintendent, "John Lackland had married. The marriage took place in 1885. His wife was a Leicestershire girl of good working-class family by name Basset. She made him an excellent partner for the eight years of their married life, and when she died during a smallpox epidemic about 1893 John Lackland suffered a harsh blow to his pride as well as to his affection. I am afraid," the old man's voice grew gentle, "he had grown to believe that nothing could interfere with his ambitions and his way of life, that not even death could be so presumptuous."

In the momentary silence which followed, the lawyer at last lighted the cigarette he held and gave one or two preliminary puffs before resuming more briskly.

"And now we come to the part which is of direct importance as bearing on John Lackland's will—the part concerning John Lackland's children. Though, dear me—" Mr. Rennie broke off rather confusedly.

"Why," said Pardoe, "that's right, isn't it? Marriage first, then children. The usual sequence, I believe."

"Yes. But in this case," Mr. Rennie explained with an almost apologetic air, "the widower remarried while his children were still very young—the youngest, you see, was only four when her mother died—and the really crucial period of their lives, and his, came years afterwards when the Mrs. Lackland into whose death you are inquiring had been his wife for at least fifteen years. Perhaps I ought to speak of her next?" he mildly suggested.

"It doesn't matter," remarked Pardoe politely. "Just tell us who the children were, and then we'll be ready to hear about Mrs. Cornelia."

"Well, there were three of them, a boy and two girls. Andrew was the eldest, then Jane, and a year younger than Jane came Charlotte. At the time of their father's second marriage Andrew was ten and the youngest girl about seven."

Pardoe raised his brows. "Not a widower long then?"

"No. You see," explained Mr. Rennie charitably, "John Lackland, as I said just now, had suffered a severe blow by the very untimely death of his first wife. I think it was his bewildered sense of loneliness that drove him in the first place to a hasty second marriage," he continued with some hesitation, blessing his own limited bachelor experience for raising a doubt as to John Lackland's second impulse to matrimony.

"Most probably," Pardoe confirmed. He warmed suddenly to the unexpected insight into humanity's patchwork motives that old Rennie had displayed. The superintendent on the other hand wondered why it was necessary to discuss the length of time old Lackland had let elapse before tying himself up again.

"What I gather puzzled people—I won't say his friends," went on Rennie, "for John Lackland had very few—was not so much why he married again, as whom he chose for his second wife." He began to look a little miserable and uncertain and added hastily: "Since Mrs. Lackland has just died in such dreadful circumstances it hardly seems correct—I mean, *de mortuis*, you know—" He looked to the inspector for guidance.

"Don't worry, Mr. Rennie," Pardoe said encouragingly. "The best service you can pay your late client is to tell us all you can about her, for only by learning everything available can we construct a true enough picture to make us understand her relations with those who lie now under suspicion. What you tell, remember, you tell as much in the interests of the living as of the dead, and both the superintendent and myself are good enough readers of human nature, I hope, not to believe that any criticism of Mrs. Lackland you find it necessary to make is actuated by malice." He smiled, and so did Littlejohn who added a few confirmatory noises.

Mr. Rennie relaxed too. "Then I suppose I mustn't mind what I say."

"Besides," added the inspector, "if what I hear of her is right, Mrs. Lackland would not have considered a little plain speaking amiss!"

"That is certainly correct," the old man was eager to agree. "One of the reasons, I am sure, for the increasing arrogance of her later years was that she met with so little opposition from those around her."

The superintendent was about to speak, but catching Pardoe's eye remained silent.

"Yes," the lawyer mused, "all that deference, one might almost say subservience, is bad for a proud self-centred nature. It creates a kind of megalomania that makes it worse by reacting upon itself. It wasn't as though the compliance Mrs. Lackland exacted was given agreeably, adoringly, as some such services are paid. Even then the idolatrous part of it is bad, but at least there is nothing poisonous about it as there was about the intense dislike in which this lady came to be held."

He paused, adding with a slight embarrassment and a touch of dry humour: "I am afraid 'poisonous' was scarcely a happy choice of word."

Then looking up brightly first at Pardoe, then at the superintendent, he said: "Both of you, I think, are too young to recall anything of Cornelia Crown of last century?"

"Wasn't she a famous actress, sir?" Littlejohn inquired. He had heard the old lady described as such.

"No," said Pardoe before the old man could reply. "She was on the stage, I believe, at one time?" He turned politely to Mr. Rennie. "But that is another matter."

The superintendent looked puzzled. But Rennie nodded.

"You are quite right. Cornelia Crown appeared occasionally on the West End stage during the 'eighties. But she made no pretensions to being an actress. To do her justice I don't think she ever laid claim in after years to histrionic ability. Her appearances in productions she graced from time to time were simply due to her extraordinary loveliness and the drawing power of her name, which had a magic effect that would be quite unimaginable to this generation."

"For all their Garbos and Gables." The superintendent grinned.

"Quite so," said Mr. Rennie. "I know very little about it, but I should suppose there was a good deal of difference between the kind of worship given to shadows on a screen and the homage that was paid to Cornelia Crown when I was a young man."

"I'm not so sure," remarked Pardoe quietly. "But go on, Mr. Rennie."

"Well, whatever the degree or quality of the adoration felt for Cornelia Crown, for six or seven years of her life, at least, she was all London's darling, as well as the idol of the provinces that take their cue from London. Nothing she did met with disapproval. Indeed there was a saying current of her in her heyday which used to provoke laughter—'the Crown can do no wrong.' But," continued Mr. Rennie somewhat primly, "I am afraid Cornelia did a good many things that were not exactly right."

"Where did she hail from?" asked Pardoe.

"I don't know. She was a girl of the people, you know, for all her patrician bearing. I often think it was the fact that they were both of plebeian stock which drew her and John Lackland together. They recognized a common ground of intercourse, and there's none firmer than equality of birth, so that their sudden union wasn't perhaps such a mingling of opposites as most people thought.

"To go back a little—Cornelia Crown was first heard of when she was a model to Frisk, the great portrait painter of late Victorian and Edwardian days. About 1880 it must have been when she burst on London in that year's Academy as the 'Girl with Primroses,' a picture of great distinction, full of charm and innocence, and yes, subtlety—because of that other charm of sophistication that the innocence somehow managed to suggest. Frisk was a great man."

"Who debased his art," Pardoe supplemented.

"Yes. He painted to please in this century." Mr. Rennie sighed. "Portraits of rich brokers and racecourse gadabouts and insipid society ladies with the greed and amoral qualities that characterized them and were their sole claim to interest very effectively eliminated. But he was still a long way from that unhappy stage when he painted Cornelia with the great basket of pale primroses on her arm and the light shining on her lustrous dark hair, and something in the eyes that the lips belied."

"I have seen it," said Pardoe simply.

"Of course. I need not describe that picture," the lawyer replied.

"I am glad you did, for now I have seen it twice." Pardoe smiled.

Mr. Rennie blushed with pleasure. "That is kind of you. When I recall certain things I fear I get carried away from the story you want to hear.

"They said Cornelia was Frisk's mistress. She may have been, I don't know. What is certain is the number of conquests she made in the few years of her real ascendancy. Peers, politicians, actors courted her, and jostled princelings for her favours. At one period when she was living under the protection of a foreign royal personage some wit gave her the name of 'Crown Imperial,' which clung to her persistently afterwards."

"Funny, isn't it," said Littlejohn respectfully, evincing something of awe at Mr. Rennie's superior knowledge, "that I should have lived nearly fifty years and spent the last ten of them in Minsterbridge and never knew half of this?"

He looked a trifle cast down, as if his failure to conduct inquiry into the late Mrs. Lackland's history reflected sadly upon his official position.

The old lawyer shook his head. "No, there's nothing strange in that, superintendent. Cornelia Crown's day was over a long time ago. You saw what everybody else saw, an old haughty lady reputed to have had a romantic history, who made her mark locally in very arbitrary fashion and could not keep her maidservants. She had, I think, the misfortune—for herself as for others—to live on into a period in which she didn't fit, in which all the colours of her background had faded even from the minds of those who might have recalled them."

He paused. Through the open window from the playground beyond the cathedral close floated the sharp, merry voices of children.

"From their first meeting," Mr. Rennie continued, "John Lackland intended to make Cornelia his wife. The qualities that ensure success in attaining one's ends were, I suppose, his in abundance. He was ruthless and acquisitive to a high degree. What he wanted he would possess, and that in as short a time as possible. By then too Cornelia

Crown was disposed, as she has told me herself, to relinquish past frivolities for the safety of marriage. She was approaching forty—they were married in 1896—and was shrewd enough to recognize the importance of some sort of stability in her life from then on. John Lackland could supply it. He was a very rich man, and wealth was the factor which counted most with Cornelia."

The inspector leaned forward. "Would you have described Mrs. Lackland as a mean woman, parsimonious, I mean?"

Mr. Rennie hesitated. "Not in her youth. But on her own admission she was always mercenary, even in the halcyon days when her lavish spending hardly kept pace with the gifts showered upon her. Such a trait is a pretty sure foundation for miserliness in later years, and Cornelia Crown had begun to change in the practical use she made of money some time before she married Lackland. About the time she was considering security the most desirable asset, in fact. After that the love of money for itself, the hoarding instinct, developed in her. Her egotism hardened too. The consequence was that in her old age you could not really have said that she was averse to spending—on occasions extravagantly—on herself. I think she really came to believe that whatever was spent should be spent only on herself. No, she was certainly never parsimonious when her own creature comforts were concerned. Her real meanness went hand in hand with her craving for power, and she practised a rigid thrift upon her dependants."

The lawyer spoke quietly, almost as though to himself, with a rueful expression that declared reluctance to make this exposure of an unfortunate lady's failings.

"But all that came afterwards," he went on more firmly. "When she became John Lackland's wife his children were very young. I have no idea what their relations were with their stepmother at the start. Probably she troubled herself little with them, their father was absorbed in business and the unresting search for more and more wealth, and I expect their young lives centred mainly around nurses and preparatory schooling.

"But when the children grew up the trouble began. John Lackland has told me, with an injured pride that nothing ever healed, the facts of their escapades over and over again. But the children's part I never heard... and I don't want to do Mrs. Lackland an injustice by the suggestion that her own part in those dissensions was any greater than that of her husband or her stepchildren."

"The boy died early on, didn't he, sir?" Littlejohn asked.

"Yes. That didn't make life easier for the others. His death darkened his father's outlook, enraged him afresh against the destiny which had first presumed to deprive him of his wife, and turned that earlier grief sour because of the disappointment as well as the loss he suffered in his son. Andrew was a bright engaging boy of some promise. He was his father's special favourite. The girls counted for much less. It may be his gifts were always of a superficial kind, or perhaps John Lackland, who had had no education to speak of, was prone to exaggerate his children's abilities. Whatever it was, Andrew's talents quickly ran to seed. At nineteen he went up to Cambridge with a history scholarship, and was barely twenty when he was killed in a drunken brawl with some toughs at a riverside brothel. Before that there had been minor upsets, money fines for misdemeanours of a more or less serious nature, and one rather nastier business connected with a young girl of good family, which caused his father a lot of trouble to smooth over and which might not have been allowed to rest at that if it hadn't been for Andrew's death."

"Going the pace in one year," Pardoe remarked. "Where were they living then?"

"In London. They didn't come to Minsterbridge, you know—but you will have inquired on that point—until John Lackland retired from active business fifteen years ago."

"I suppose all this pretty well broke up the old man, sir?" the superintendent put in.

"No." Mr. Rennie considered. "That wouldn't be a correct description of the effect on John Lackland. Andrew's dying in those circumstances didn't 'break' him. It made him more than ever determined that nothing should break him. Nothing now should deflect him from what purposes were left. In his embittered mind was born the idea from which so much trouble has arisen for a later generation. He made up his mind that he would keep his remaining children, his two daughters, constantly under his paternal care so that they at any rate should escape the corruption that had snared Andrew.

"It didn't work, of course. Even before the war the ponderous patriarchal business was declining. John Lackland's children, voteless, unemancipated young women as this generation would regard them, were not at all disposed to consider themselves chattels. The bondage lasted five years in the elder girl's case. For five years, I have John Lackland's word for it, neither girl had an hour in the day unaccounted for, not a visitor uncensored by their father, not the merest suggestion of a young man's company. He was liable at any moment to demand to see their correspondence, infrequent as it was. What began as stern supervision ended as sheer tyranny, and in—let me see, 1911—Jane revolted to some effect. She made a runaway match with a penniless actor named Will Hernshaw."

The superintendent brightened visibly as a familiar name turned up.

"Her father," the lawyer went on, "cast her off with, I'm afraid, proverbial thoroughness. So far as I have been able to gather she never saw him again nor he her. She didn't live long enough, though, poor soul, to bring about a reconciliation had any been possible. The unsettled, undernourished life she'd elected to follow was too sharp a contrast to the oversheltered home, prison as it was, she'd left. Jane died when her little girl was four years old—during the war—and for reasons we can only guess at John Lackland sent for the child."

"What about Hernshaw? Was he quite willing to give his daughter up?" Pardoe inquired.

"I don't know anything about Jane's husband except for the few, very few remarks John Lackland has made to me concerning him. Those, as you can suppose, were highly derogatory. He was described as a feckless, thoroughly selfish scamp who had married Miss Lackland in, we might say, the expectation of plenty, and finding the marriage to be unprofitable was only too ready to renounce any responsibility arising from it. So that's how Miss Jenny came to the Lackland home."

The inspector frowned slightly. "Is Hernshaw still alive?"

Mr. Rennie looked a little surprised. "I don't know. He was always, so to speak, dead to the Lacklands, and since he apparently never made the least attempt to communicate with anyone in his wife's family there's no saying what might have happened to him. I believe I heard he was in the army in the war years, but I could not say with certainty."

"So Miss Quentin is the other daughter's child, sir?" Littlejohn inquired.

"That is so. Charlotte, John's younger girl, must have found home still less tolerable after Jane's flight. At any rate, only about two years later, she went shopping one morning, and instead of returning to the house sent a letter posted in Brighton to say that she was being married at the registry office there to a young fellow her own age named Maurice Quentin."

"Ah, yes," put in the superintendent, "now haven't I heard that Miss Carol was connected with the Quentins of Loadwains, the big people over the Bucks border?"

"You probably have." Mr. Rennie turned to Pardoe. "A county family," he explained. "Maurice was the youngest son then—he'd be brother to the present lord of the manor, and his runaway match broke his relations with his own family as completely as Charlotte's were broken with hers."

"When these girls finally asserted themselves," Pardoe remarked, "they appear to have been very definite about it."

"Yes. One of the unhappiest features of the whole unhappy business was the indifference with which the children treated the chances of reconciliation with their father—"

"Mere acceptance perhaps of a situation they knew couldn't be mended," the inspector said.

"Perhaps. Charlotte's marriage was more of a failure in some respects even than her sister's. Hernshaw at least wasn't accused in my hearing of ill-treating his wife. Quentin was a brutal wastrel who wreaked his vengeance on Charlotte for being, as he chose to consider himself, cheated of his own and the Lackland thousands. It seems that the only service he ever did her was that of dying suddenly while still young from excessive drinking."

The old lawyer's face wore a stern expression. "It is evident, I think, that he reduced poor Charlotte to a spiritless creature prepared to accept any humiliation in exchange for a home. Else she would not have returned as she did to John Lackland, though her baby must have been a strong persuasion to that course."

Pardoe raised his eyebrows. "Surprising, wasn't it? Out of character, I mean, for him to relent so far as to have her back?"

"He didn't relent. He took her back, but he never spoke to her again. He told me so."

"Devilish," said Littlejohn.

"Yes. Well, Charlotte came home the same year that the first grandchild was 'rescued,' as Mrs. Lackland liked to put it. She saw something diabolically humorous in the coincidence of their arrivals. But her stepdaughter's presence did not burden them for long. Charlotte died about eighteen months after coming home." He hesitated. "They said it was her husband's treatment. She was a fragile girl. But physical cruelty's not the only sort. One is forced to think that a little kindness at that time would have gone a long way to mend the poor child."

"So," said Pardoe in a hard voice, "now that both daughters were out of his reach, I suppose Lackland turned his attention to his grandchildren?"

"Yes," replied Mr. Rennie. "They were mere infants when Charlotte died, her own baby, Carol, less than three, and Jenny only two years older. Young enough to be malleable. So the grandfather planned for them a regime he had failed to enforce till his own children were practically adults. By those means he believed, honestly, I am sure, that he could retrieve the past and make these children's lives what he had wished his own children's to be."

Pardoe nodded. "You really mean," he suggested gently, "prevent their lives from becoming what his own children's had been, a more negative ambition."

"Yes, perhaps," agreed Mr. Rennie. "They lived in their cages, those little girls. But John Lackland—he did not live to see the fruits, ill or good, of his efforts. He came to Minsterbridge when they were ten and eight years old, bought and renamed the fine old house you know as Lacklands, and died when they were still schoolgirls, seven years ago."

"I remember it well," Littlejohn put in quickly, glad to be in a position to endorse some information. "Something of a sensation, wasn't it?"

"Yes. He had a pompous funeral. Ostentation of that kind, and a parade of grief, was in the old lady's blood."

"Of course," Pardoe concurred. "The theatrical side had to be satisfied, and it was necessary to impress Minsterbridge with the importance of John Lackland, dead as well as alive, and the importance of his widow. What happened to the children then?"

"Jenny had left school more than a year before her grandfather's death. Carol was still there, in her last term, a convent boarding school north of London, but she was brought home in the middle of the term to attend the funeral, and never went back."

"And John Lackland's will?" asked the superintendent, unable to restrain himself any longer. "Their grandmother was left sole guardian, I suppose?"

"I am coming to that," Mr. Rennie replied primly. "If you will excuse me a moment." He got up hastily and went into a little room across the passage.

Chapter VIII

I, JOHN LACKLAND

I have no heir but thee,—
And yet not thee, if with a wayward spirit
Thou start from the true bias of my love.

Thomas Dekker: *The Shoemaker's Holiday*

The will itself was locked up at the office. Mr. Rennie, however, with a view to subsequent questioning by the police, had prepared a synopsis that afternoon to supplement an already perfect memory.

He came back, the paper in his hand, and sitting down again produced the particulars which the superintendent at least had been impatient to hear. When they were at last expounded they proved surprisingly few, but as valuable as Inspector Pardoe had anticipated. John Lackland had conceived his disastrous will on broad and simple lines.

"He didn't relish complexities or elaboration," the lawyer explained, adding with a faint sigh: "I'm afraid he had no appreciation for the niceties of legal procedure. However, his business shrewdness stood him in good stead, and a liking for the most direct method didn't make his instructions any more open to error."

Pardoe smiled to himself.

"When he retired from business," Mr. Rennie continued, "he sold all his shares in it and made a clean break. It was characteristic of the man that he made a will which underwent no modification or addition. Once it was done it was in its final form.

"Everything of which he died possessed was left to his widow, who was to enjoy a life interest on the capital amount. From his death seven years ago until now she has had at her disposal the income from a sum amounting to roughly £435,000. Yes, a very pleasant sum," Mr. Rennie agreed in response to the inspector's expression, "for even at the reduced rates it has placed at her service annually something like the sum of £16,000.

"Now, as I was saying, the income only was in the hands of Mrs. Lackland. She had no control whatever over the capital, reversionary interest in which belonged to the granddaughters, Miss Hernshaw and Miss Quentin. They are joint heirs on the decease of their grandfather's widow, but their inheritance is subject to two provisions."

The lawyer paused to allow his listeners time to appreciate the position.

"And the provisions?" asked Pardoe.

"They were not to marry without consent of Mrs. Lackland. They were not to obtain employment without her consent."

"Wasn't a time limit imposed on Mrs. Lackland's guardianship?" Pardoe inquired. "I mean when the girls reached a certain age, weren't they at liberty to do as they liked without jeopardizing their inheritance?"

"No. Those conditions held for the period of Mrs. Lackland's lifetime."

"Lord," Superintendent Littlejohn exclaimed, "what a man!" Inwardly he added: "It's tantamount to ensuring murder," but stopped himself in time from voicing what he felt was a highly prejudicial comment.

"So that virtually," Pardoe said, "these girls were subject to their grandmother's control entirely."

"Well, yes," Rennie conceded with a little hesitation, "that is to say, their actions were a good deal restrained by her wishes."

"I'd say they were. What about their own incomes during her lifetime? Was any such provision made for them?"

"I'm afraid not. John Lackland left them entirely to the 'discretion,' as the will states, of Mrs. Lackland. Remonstrance was quite useless on this as on any other point. He had made up his mind, as he told me, that his grandchildren should have 'no independence to misuse.'"

"And to what extent did Mrs. Lackland's discretion permit her to go?"

"Not very far, Inspector, I believe. But that lay in her hands, not mine, so I can't say with certainty. The old lady on several occasions referred to their individual allowances as 'pocket money.' I believe the sums varied according to her mood."

"I see." Pardoe considered for a minute or two. "Then it amounts to this: that Miss Hernshaw and Miss Quentin stood to gain over £200,000 apiece at the death of the old lady, providing they hadn't in the meantime flouted her wishes regarding marriage and employment. Now what I want to know is, did these girls know exactly how the will stood? The superintendent is under the impression that they didn't."

Mr. Rennie shook his head. "They didn't. Their grandfather stipulated with a good deal of emphasis that they were not to be told they were reversionary beneficiaries. I think"—his palpable hesitation gave a deprecatory note to the words—"he was not averse to the likelihood that in ignorance of the facts they would believe themselves entirely dependent on Mrs. Lackland's charity. Not," he added, "that John Lackland lied to them himself. They were children when he died, and it is extremely unlikely that any mention of his will was made in their hearing in his lifetime. No, all that he wished was that they should know nothing certainly until Mrs. Lackland's death."

"So he preferred a living—or, shall we say, a dying lie to a spoken one?" Pardoe's face and voice were hard.

Mr. Rennie reddened slightly. "I don't defend the morality of it, Inspector. That has nothing to do with me. The fact remains that the old man believed his grandchildren would be more amenable to his widow's guardianship if they did not know that eventual independence would certainly be theirs."

"And did neither girl ever approach you on the subject?" the inspector asked bluntly.

Mr. Rennie appeared a little put out. "It was hardly a matter likely to be discussed, Inspector," he replied primly.

"Oh come, Mr. Rennie," said the inspector lightly, but nevertheless rejecting evasion, "you don't mean to tell me that two girls in circumstances such as these could grow to womanhood without speculating about their future. They were old enough to know that their grandfather at his death was a very rich man, weren't they?"

"Yes, certainly they knew that." The old man's tone carried a hint of indignation. "Well, Inspector, I can recall nothing in the nature of a discussion. Miss Quentin, I can assure you, has never mentioned one word to me of any possible expectations she may have had, and I can only recall one occasion when Miss Hernshaw touched on the matter."

"That's something," said Pardoe. "When was that, and what, please, did Miss Hernshaw say?"

"It would be about a year ago," the lawyer replied reluctantly. "I was in the garden at Lacklands with both girls, and Miss Carol made some jesting remark, I forget what, about making her will. We had been enjoying a very light conversation. I noticed that Miss Jenny grew quiet, and after a minute she turned to me and asked, as far as I remember, how they would stand in the future. That was all."

"I see." Pardoe sounded uninterested. "Can you recall her exact words?"

"That is doubtful," said Mr. Rennie. He thought for a few moments. "I think her question was: 'Talking of wills, do you know what is likely to happen to us when Grandma dies?' It was rather bluntly put, I know, but that has always been Jenny's way. I replied to the effect that she needn't trouble her head about that, as some provision would certainly be made. It was as far as I could go."

"Thanks," said Pardoe, "what you have told us is helpful. Not," he added, catching sight of the lawyer's expression, "that it necessarily gives me any opinion one way or another about Miss Jenny herself, but it gives an insight into the extent of these girls' igno-rance of the will. How did Miss Carol behave on that occasion?" he finished abruptly.

"She looked surprised, I thought. Then she laughed and said something about expecting they would have to look to the ravens for sustenance. But she pressed for no information, which of course I wasn't prepared to give."

"Of course not." Pardoe spoke absently. His next words implied that the matter was dismissed. "To come to Mrs. Lackland's own personal property: I understand that she possessed capital of her own, and that as she intended seeing you about her will, this must have been the money in question."

"Yes," said Mr. Rennie. "Mrs. Lackland's own separate estate amounted to between fifteen and sixteen thousand pounds. This was hers to do as she pleased with, and," he added with a sigh, "she exercised her power fully and often."

"She made various wills?" Pardoe inquired.

"Five in as many years. Unfortunately she talked a great deal about the changes she proposed making, I believe, without ever specifying the amount at stake or drawing any distinction between this sum and the income she derived from her late husband's estate, so that there was bound to be confusion in the minds of those who shared her half-confidences."

"Exactly. Can you remember more or less the general provisions of these different wills?"

"A few years ago," the lawyer replied, "Mrs. Lackland had one drawn up bequeathing the entire amount to Jenny, who at that time, at any rate, was regarded as her favourite grandchild. Not long afterwards she destroyed it, and made another, dividing most of her wealth equally between the two girls, with a residue of about a thousand pounds to her companion, Miss Bullen. After this the changes that were made vacillated between leaving the whole sum to one person and dividing it between all three, accompanied by open threats to make some charity her sole legatee. The latter, I may add, she never put into force."

Superintendent Littlejohn looked alertly at Mr. Rennie. "And what are the provisions of the last will, sir?" he asked. "I mean the one in existence when Mrs. Lackland died."

"It is more or less a restoration of what she had previously drawn up in her second will, except that Miss Bullen's share now stands at £750, there are minor legacies to servants who have been at least seven years in her employ at the time of her death—which of course excludes all but the butler and cook—and the residue equally between Jenny and Carol, roughly about £7,000 each."

"And now, Mr. Rennie," the inspector put in, "have you any idea of Mrs. Lackland's final intentions with regard to the new will she proposed making this week?"

"Yes," the old man replied promptly. "That is, I know what she first mooted when I visited her nearly three weeks ago. She was much better then, you understand, though she had not as yet come downstairs. She told me positively, in the manner she always used, that directly she was able to get about again and 'see to things' properly for herself she intended cutting the entire household out of her will and making Dr. Faithful her sole heir."

Mr. Rennie did not secure the sensation he had anticipated.

"Were you surprised at her decision?" Pardoe inquired.

"I was. That is confessing a good deal, too," said the lawyer whimsically, "for Mrs. Lackland's caprices should by now have inured me to any new course upon which she might choose to embark. It wasn't that I was the least astonished she should want to recognize the doctor's skill and services in restoring her to health, nor even that Jenny and Carol were not to benefit by the fresh will, for Mrs. Lackland herself knew that they would inherit on her death. What surprised me was that she proposed leaving the entire sum to the doctor without the smallest consideration for her companion. With all her harshness and vagaries I had believed her to be a just woman at heart."

"Did you comment on the proposal at the time, Mr. Rennie?" the inspector asked.

"Very little. I reminded her that this would fail to make provision for Miss Bullen, thinking that she may have overlooked the omission, but she only laughed and said something to the effect that Miss Bullen knew quite well how to look after herself. I said nothing more then, because I believed that she would quickly change her mind again and apportion the money differently."

Pardoe nodded. "A reasonable conclusion, I should say. Well, it seems that this time, at least, the old lady stuck to her resolve, for on the last day of her life we have Dr. Faithful's word for it that she told him he was to inherit her money."

The lawyer raised his eyebrows and looked grave. "Ah, I did not know that," he said, and made as if to add more, but remained silent, his expression perturbed.

Chapter IX

STARSHINE IN CHELSEA

To vouch this is no proof.

Othello

Pardoe went alone to London next day to call on Jan Carnowski at his flat. There was plenty to occupy Salt at the home end of the case. The inquest was fixed for Monday, but it would be nothing more than a formal opening at which the police would ask for an adjournment.

Though Carnowski, at present disengaged, was not likely to be found at home at any given hour, the inspector preferred to chance his luck rather than give him warning in advance of a police visit. Before reaching Victoria this morning he had been cynically conjuring up the differences he would find between the film star off the set and the one invested with the meretricious glories of the screen. He was himself an infrequent patron of cinemas, but had ungrudgingly admired the art of Carnowski in the few pictures he had seen in which the Polish actor was starring. The latter's poise and skilled technique, the economy of gesture which could hint at latent unrestraint, appealed to Pardoe, who delighted in subtlety in any form. He had wondered too at the actor's gift for complete absorption in a role without the attendant sacrifice of his own personality, for repeated exhibition of which his public paid so eagerly. There had been the Lorenzo di Medici picture. While Carnowski's fans had never once lost sight of their idol, the historians had found nothing to quarrel with in his portrayal of the great Florentine. The Russian picture too—its name escaped Pardoe—was a recent noteworthy triumph, for in spite of its besmirched story and obvious insincerities it had won for the Pole praise from all the more exacting critics.

With this in his mind Pardoe was eager for the meeting, while fairly certain that he would find the man beneath the skin of the artist, if not a disappointment, at least quite another proposition.

At Victoria the inspector took a taxi to Tite Square. Even the intense heat which hung almost palpably between earth and sky could not quell the delicious breeze trickling along the Embankment and making the narrow entry into the square almost a draughty alley. Here it lay, within stone's-throw of Oakley Street, a dim quadrangle of lanky iron-railinged houses, solid, pleasant, comfortable in their very discomfort, eloquent only of stability, a final stronghold of Victorianism which the invaders had neither spared nor conquered.

Number 110 was halfway down the east side of the square, a naked-looking house with shining brass and trim appointments. Like many of its fellows it had surrendered its character as a family home by undergoing uneasy conversion into flats. Carnowski occupied one of these on the second floor. There was of course no lift, but a short flight of stairs brought Pardoe into a hall of minute dimensions off which the actor's rooms led. He rang the bell and was not kept waiting long. A short manservant with the puckish solemnity of a Cockney took Pardoe's card and disappeared for about half a minute. The inspector's luck was in. Mr. Carnowski was at home, and would Mr. Pardoe please come in?

Pardoe walked into a long drawing room of surprising proportions after the Lilliputian hall. It was coolly panelled in stippled grey and though, except for a luxurious carpet, furnished with modesty and restraint, carried that inviting air of masculinity which prefers comfort to affectation. A fine landscape by Matthew Smith caught his eye, but before he had time to feel pleased with his surroundings the mirror above a small desk of modern design gave him the reflection of Carnowski coming into the room.

The two men faced each other, height matching height. There was mutual appraisal. Pardoe at least was quick to recognize that there was no substance in his doubts. This man's strength, perhaps subtlety, lay in himself at all seasons. It was no cloak donned and discarded by a clever actor.

"Please be seated, Inspector Pardoe," Carnowski said. He spoke slowly with a marked accent, giving each syllable an emphasized value. But without the evidence of the voice and in spite of his English tailoring he was unmistakably a foreigner. The inspector, noting the finely modelled head, the depth of forehead, the harsh yet sensitive lines of face and mouth and steady regard of the dark clever eyes, understood without cynicism the enchantment a man so endowed had been able to cast over his world.

Carnowski waited quietly for the inspector's opening.

"I have called," Pardoe began, "in connection with the death of Mrs. Lackland, of Lacklands, Minsterbridge." He paused a moment, but the actor was considering him with an untroubled expression which did not change at his words. "She died, as I expect you know, early on Thursday morning."

Carnowski looked grave. "But yes. I know that Mrs. Lackland die two days since. What then is wrong? Does she not die of her sickness?"

Pardoe replied bluntly: "Mrs. Lackland was poisoned."

At that it seemed to the inspector a flicker of interest passed over the actor's face. But he did not look astonished.

"Ah," he said gravely. Suddenly he stretched a hand out towards an electric bell. "You take coffee, Mr. Pardoe?" he inquired.

Pardoe shook his head with a brief smile. "No, thank you. I breakfasted late."

The actor accepted his refusal without comment, and before his visitor could make any further remark picked up the discussion at where it had broken off.

"So it was poison," he said in a careful voice from which Pardoe learned nothing. "That is bad. But why then do you come to me?"

"It's my job, Mr. Carnowski," the inspector replied, "to see everyone connected however remotely with the Lackland household at the time Mrs. Lackland was last taken ill. I understand you were a guest at the house the night before her death?"

"Yes," Carnowski answered promptly. "But I do not see Mrs. Lackland. And when I go, you understand, there is no thought that she is ill."

"I understand. All the same, I think what you can tell me may probably be useful. For instance, a check must be made on comings and goings so that we may be clear as to the times at which different members of the household were together. I should appreciate your help in this."

"I will tell you, of course, what I can. But I think I do not say anything to help. One moment, Inspector."

As Pardoe made to speak Carnowski slightly extended his hand as if to stop him. Pardoe remarked immediately what the screen so frequently displayed, the singular blend of strength and delicacy in the fingers, a sinewy grace that was somehow oddly disquieting.

"I do not know what you mean," the actor was saying. "'When different members of the household were together,'" he quoted carefully. "Is it then thought that somebody at Lacklands give poison to the old lady?"

"That," said Pardoe, "is exactly what the police have to find out." He saw the quiver of Carnowski's nostrils, a hint of fire in his gaze, and added: "And only by finding out can we hope to establish the innocence of the people at Lacklands. You see that?"

"Yes, I see that. But it is horrible. And suppose that you find out to put the guilt on the innocent person? But no, that does not happen in England?"

He smiled so suddenly and with such complete friendliness that Pardoe was baffled and did not know whether or not he was supposed to detect a sting in the query.

"We will trust not," he said, and went on: "Now, Mr. Carnowski. Please tell me at what time you arrived at Lacklands."

The actor considered for hardly a moment. "Dinner was at half-past seven. I came about ten minutes before that. So we say I come to the house at twenty minutes after seven."

Pardoe jotted down the hour in his notebook while Carnowski watched him idly.

"How did you come? I mean, was it by car or train you travelled down?"

"I come in my car."

"Did you drive up to the house in it?" Pardoe shot him a keen glance.

Carnowski's returning glance was equally keen, and a slight smile accompanied his words. "That is clever of you, Inspector. No, I do not drive to Lacklands. I go to River Street which is quite close, and put my car in Capper's Garage. Then I walk to the house."

Pardoe nodded, and noted the garage address for the mere routine job of checking Carnowski's statement. He had been pretty sure that the actor had not risked attracting the old lady's attention by bringing the car to the house and garaging it there.

"I thought it would be something like that," he said quietly. "What time did you leave Lacklands?"

"I do not know exactly the minute. It was after ten. But not long after, I think. The butler, he must lock all doors at ten o'clock. I know it is after ten because they unlock for me."

"That is quite clear. I don't want my questions to sound imperti-nent, Mr. Carnowski, but it will be a help if you can tell me how and in whose company you spent the time after dinner."

The actor's gaze was disconcertingly steady. "Your question, what shall I say—it goes very close. Do you then suspect me?"

The blunt *naïveté* of the query almost put Pardoe off his guard. Then he smiled frankly.

"It's no evasion to say that at this stage I suspect everyone, and therefore no one. You can be assured that nothing that has happened up till now has made me suspect you in particular. Only a refusal on your part to tell me what I want to know—and you can, of course, refuse if you like—might draw suspicious attention to the information you were keeping back."

Pardoe felt suddenly a certain meanness in this indirect compulsion of a man who, it was plain, did not easily comprehend the drift of all his remarks. Carnowski, however, seemed unaware of the mild threat the words carried, and said simply: "But I hide nothing. It was all very—ordinary."

It was, as he told it, all very ordinary. It bore out the evidence of the girls, a quiet evening spent in talk and listening in. But Pardoe was disappointed to find that Carnowski either could not or would not be definite as to the time Carol had left Jenny and himself to go upstairs, nor how long she had been away. At first it seemed that he was honestly trying to remember, then all at once he had given Pardoe one of his penetrating glances and become reticent. "I do not know. I cannot remember," was all he would say, and the inspector, quick to recognize failure, stopped worrying the point.

One interesting fact emerged in reply to Pardoe's inquiry whether the actor had spent any time out of the drawing room. But yes. At about half-past nine, or perhaps a little later, he had gone upstairs to the bathroom. He was away perhaps five minutes. Yes, he knew where the bathroom was, he had been there on a previous visit to Lacklands, but he was emphatic in denying that he knew Mrs. Lackland's bedroom was close to it.

"But I have not known ever which room Mrs. Lackland have," he protested so indignantly that a comic flavour of propriety was lent to his words. "I never see Mrs. Lackland. I never speak to her."

No wonder, thought Pardoe, the old lady had objected so furiously, if the girls had brought about no formal introductions. He took this up quickly.

"You never met Mrs. Lackland then?" he remarked, and did not try to keep the surprise out of his voice.

"Never. She would not. I know Miss Hernshaw and Miss Quentin since the New Year, before their grandmother is ill, but she will not speak to me. She will not even see me. Then when she was ill they cannot go out. Nor when she is better. So then I visit them here, but I do not see Mrs. Lackland. No, she will not," he repeated.

A rising excitement in his voice had made him a little incoherent. Pardoe was interested and awaited some further disclosures; but none came. Carnowski had either regained control of himself or he found the English tongue an unhandy vehicle for his emotion. He fell silent, and Pardoe took the opportunity to ask quietly: "Do you know, Mr. Carnowski, why Mrs. Lackland refused to see or speak to you?"

His calm tone was reciprocated. The actor who, Pardoe noticed, was as extraordinarily sparing of gesture off the screen as on, gave a slight but eloquent shrug of his shoulders.

"She was mad," he said with intensity, his voice pitched low. "She is for the—" he searched for a word and almost beckoned it to him—"for the mind doctors. Because she is not young now, she does not want her granddaughters to be young. Because she have money she want to make their whole lives, and then break their lives, so." With his hands he made the most eloquent gesture Pardoe had ever seen, a pattern of lustful creation and destruction as wanton. He looked at the inspector, his face as expressionless as the glowing eyes would allow.

"They must not meet with men. They must not meet with men because she herself is not young any more," he said cruelly, picking a deliberate way through the pitfalls of language.

"I see," said Pardoe gravely. "That would apply alike to all the friends Miss Hernshaw and Miss Quentin wanted to make. Can you think of any special reasons applicable only to yourself for Mrs. Lackland's behaviour towards you?"

Though he could not have said why he expected a negative reply. Instead, Carnowski seemed to brighten, and answered promptly: "But yes. There are very good reasons. Mrs. Lackland, she was a great actress"—Pardoe could not determine whether this was as guileless as it sounded—"and I, I play for the cinema." He smiled. "That is one cause why she push me from her door. But there is worse. I have married, and I am *divorcé*. The old, they become proper when they are old. So I must not talk to Miss Hernshaw."

This was the first Pardoe had heard of Carnowski as a married man. He did not see what bearing his matrimonial status could have upon his relations with the Lacklands, except of course as an additional factor in the dead woman's dislike of him. Not that she could have had much objection to his divorce on moral grounds, unless indeed she had reformed incredibly since her youth; it would serve, however, as a sufficiently strong handle for her purpose in denying him the house.

"There is certainly a reason there," Pardoe agreed, "with an old lady who showed herself so strict a guardian of her wards as Mrs. Lackland." He hesitated. "D'you mind telling me how long ago your marriage was dissolved, and whether your former wife is living in England?"

Carnowski did not mind, but he was much astonished that the inspector should want the information. It was plain that he found it hardly credible to encounter somebody who was unable to tell a film star more about his domestic difficulties than he knew himself. He looked pleased.

"You do not know it? No." He began patient explanation. "My wife, she was Fidela Luke. I think perhaps you know who that is?"

Pardoe did. She was still the most talked of screen actress in both the New World and the old, with the possible exception of Greta Garbo, whose reticences Fidela did not copy.

"We like each other," Carnowski was saying. "But to live together, no. We part one, two years since. She is never in England. Hollywood, New York, Paris, yes. Here, never." He denied her presence with fervent self-congratulation, Pardoe thought.

"Well," he said in reply, "I don't think your marriage can have any effect upon the inquiry I am making. All it has probably done has been, as you say, to harden Mrs. Lackland's resistance to your friendship with her grandchildren."

As he was speaking his thoughts ran in another, though tributary channel. If, as was practically certain, the old lady would have made his divorce grounds for persistent objection to his marriage with Jenny, here was a reasonably strong motive for murder. Other things might have been overcome, given a man of Carnowski's charm and determination, even with a character as obdurate as Mrs. Lackland's, but a dissolved marriage was a fact which could neither be modified nor eradicated, if she was resolved to take up her stand on that point. Pardoe wondered, not for the first time, what the actor's finances were like. Expensive furnishings and material evidence of well-being were often, he knew, deceitful guides to solvency. Carnowski's affairs would bear looking into.

He suddenly broke off his train of thought as he intercepted a shrewd look from the actor. Damn it all, the fellow must have some sixth sense, was his unspoken comment, as Carnowski exclaimed with an abrupt cut and thrust very unlike the parrying to which the Yard man was accustomed: "You think, do you not, that I cannot be sorry Mrs. Lackland die? That I am perhaps even glad? Well, it is true that I cannot wish her to live again."

The words were spoken without truculence, though with a calculated bitterness that robbed them of the impulse Pardoe would have found more excusable.

"The admission is yours, Mr. Carnowski," he remarked coolly. "It wasn't I who suggested you were glad." Before the actor could reply he went on: "Can you remember anything that happened or was said, or that even failed to happen, on Wednesday night that you think worth reporting? Don't think that what you may say will necessarily draw my suspicions to any particular person. You may just as easily succeed in drawing them away."

Carnowski heard him with a certain hauteur. It seemed to Pardoe as if he resented the scant heed the inspector had paid his frankness just now.

"I have told you all that I know. It was as other evenings."

"As last Friday, perhaps?" Pardoe inquired sharply.

The actor lifted his brows casually. "But yes. As last Friday, Inspector. It is only later I learn that Mrs. Lackland is very angry I come last Friday. She will not have me in the house, and she will not see me neither. I do not give up my friends, you understand, because one old lady hate me without seeing me."

"Couldn't you have arranged another meeting place?"

"No," said Carnowski wearily. "While Mrs. Lackland is ill Miss Hernshaw and Miss Quentin must never be from the house, not more than half an hour, perhaps, and never together. She ring for them. Always she ring for them. If it is to say nothing, still she ring for them. That is to keep them in the house, you understand."

Pardoe understood, and did not for one moment doubt the truth of Carnowski's words. Lacklands had been a pretty effective prison, and in such a place what more likely than murder conceived and executed?

"I understand Miss Bullen was out on Wednesday evening. Do you know whether she came back before you left?"

"No," said Carnowski. "She does not return before I go. Or I do not hear her come in."

Pardoe was amused at the caution of the last remark, a possible concession to official suspicion and demand for fact. None of this was leading anywhere in particular, he thought, when the actor suddenly spoke again.

"There is something which perhaps you like to know," he said, with a hint of graciousness that made Pardoe feel he was a small and not very intelligent boy whose persistent curiosity was being indulged. "I do not think of it till now. But now I think there is something funny there because it happen twice, both when I arrive and when I go."

"Yes?" Pardoe prompted.

"I see a man by the house who seem to be waiting for something. He is there both times."

"How near to the house? Tell me what happened."

"The first time it is when I open the gate and go up the path to the front door. Somebody pass me going away from the house. But later I do not think that. When I go away after ten o'clock I walk down the path, open the gate and turn along the square towards River Street, and there is again the man. This time he stand pressing himself to the street wall of the garden. At the moment he see me he walk away rather quick, head down again, in front of me. But not to River Street, no. He goes to the left, across the square."

He stopped a moment, and in the pause Pardoe inquired what there had been in the second encounter which had made Carnowski change his mind about something in the first.

"It is seeing him the twice," the actor said. "It make me remember the other time. And then I think that he could not be coming from the house when I see him first, because when I open the gate I would hear the door close. But there was nothing to hear. And it was as if he begin to walk only when he see me come through the gate." He made a slightly impatient sound at his own inability to explain as graphically as he would have liked. "You understand? It was as if he had been waiting the first time also, but I do not remember that until I see him at the last waiting by the wall."

"But," said Pardoe, "he might still have come from the house a minute sooner when you were entering St. Michael's Square, and then have been standing on the path."

"Ye-es," Carnowski admitted dubiously. "But still I do not think so. He seem to be facing the house, then turn and walk sharply as I open the gate, just as I see him quickly walk on when I come down the road that night."

"Are you sure it was the same man?" the inspector asked.

Carnowski looked surprised. "But yes. There is not a doubt."

"I ask because you imply you were not paying particular attention the first time. As it was then light can you describe this man to me?"

"Not so well," Carnowski said frankly. "I did not look carefully, of course. He was rather short, I think, dressed dark. He wears a soft hat pulled down, and walks quick and light with his head hanging, so." He depressed his own chin in dejected fashion. "There is the same hat and hanging look and the same walk from the man in the road. So I know it is the same."

"Was he obviously a tramping man?" Pardoe asked.

"No, he was not. I do not look close, but I think he is dressed with some show, a little bad taste, you understand. Besides, if he beg he have the chance twice to beg of me and he does nothing," he finished shrewdly.

Pardoe approved his deductions. But there was something in all this he wanted to think over. He stood up.

"Thank you, Mr. Carnowski," he said as the actor rose too. "What you have told me may be important. Your strange man's errand may have been innocent enough, but there's certainly something peculiar about his presence almost in the same spot after a lapse of three hours. I'll leave you now, but would like to know that we can easily get in touch with you if necessary."

Carnowski showed no surprise at the intimation, but gave Pardoe his phone number and mentioned the fact that he was at present resting between engagements. He did not ring for his servant, but himself accompanied the inspector into the little hall.

Taking his hat, Pardoe turned to the actor and said, with casual abruptness. "By the way, was it from Miss Hernshaw you learned of Mrs. Lackland's death?"

"Yes. She rang me up on Thursday afternoon."

Pardoe nodded. It was characteristic of him to appear heedless of the reply and to follow his first question with a quick second.

"Has anybody ever sent you an anonymous letter, Mr. Carnowski?" he asked lightly, but his eyes were keen.

He was interested in the actor's hesitation until he noticed he was merely pondering the term "anonymous."

"I mean a letter that isn't signed, and—"

"Oh, but I know," said Carnowski. "The letters which alone tell the truth of one. No, it has not come to me? Should it then?"

"We will hope not," said Pardoe, laughing shortly as he went away.

There were points about the interview he found intriguing. Apart from the personality of Carnowski, which would have lifted a fruitless errand above the commonplace, there were certain passages in the actor's account of Wednesday night with which the inspector was wholly occupied on his return journey to Minsterbridge.

Why, for instance, had Carnowski received as news the fact that Mrs. Lackland had been poisoned, while admitting that he had been told of her death as early as Thursday afternoon? It was improbable that Jenny, who had known otherwise since the doctor's last visit, would have led Carnowski to think that her grandmother's death was due to natural causes. Even if she had committed herself to little on the telephone she had most certainly had time in two days to amplify her information. Pardoe did not believe in the actor's assumed ignorance, nor did he find it easy to reconcile with complete innocence the readiness with which Carnowski had concluded murder had been done. He had not once suggested suicide, but had brought into the open with what Pardoe felt was theatrical skill rather than frankness, the suspicion in which the household at Lacklands was held by the police before there had been any official voicing of it.

Nor did the inspector put much faith in the story of the man lurking outside the house. Again it smacked of the theatrical. Carnowski had produced it late enough too to rob it of just that quality of spontaneity which would have best served his interest. It had the air of an artifice, like a trick suddenly pulled out of a hat so as to fill an uncomfortable gap in the performance. Had Carnowski provided this bit of melodrama as a mere decoy for police activities?

Anyway, Pardoe decided, as his train sped through the sun-soaked afternoon, the actor and his evidence, false or true, were worth keeping an eye on.

Chapter X

SHADOW OVER LACKLANDS

> Methinks I read distraction in your face!
> Something less gentle than the fate you tell me:
> You shake and tremble too! Your blood runs cold!
>
> Thomas Otway: *Venice Preserved*

E mily Bullen sat well forward on her chair in so uncomfortable an attitude that Sergeant Salt was almost provoked to remonstrate. It was a posture which made her appear more flabby and graceless than was necessary, but something rigid in the way this woman met his eye checked even the suggestion of familiarity from the sergeant.

The two detectives and Miss Bullen were in the small front sitting room where Dr. Faithful had talked with Jenny and Carol three days ago. Having lunched on his return from visiting Carnowski, Pardoe had gone round to Lacklands with the sergeant to see the family and particularly Emily Bullen, who had so far escaped police attention. A brief introduction to Miss Hernshaw had followed. Miss Quentin was out. She would be back for tea. He had made a cursory examination of the room in which Mrs. Lackland had died, and of the adjacent rooms, and on coming down had inquired after Miss Bullen.

He had the natural man's horror of hysteria, and it was with some misgiving that he had made his first tentative request for the companion. To the surprise of both detectives she was apparently as eager for an interview as they were themselves. She had come in with a kind of taut calm about her which, if it did not deceive

Pardoe, immediately persuaded Salt that her recent collapse must have been reported with gross exaggeration, and was now plainly engaged in critical examination of the two officers before committing herself.

Pardoe, watching her with unobtrusive keenness, wondered how much her shallow gaze took in. The cheap figured dress she was wearing so tastelessly made him think of the contrast struck between the beauty and discrimination discernible in the furnishings of the house and the shabby, almost straitened appearance of the women. Even Jenny, whose youth to a great extent camouflaged this air of neglect, had seemed to be wearing a frock unsuccessfully adapted to modern style. She was waiting for her mourning, he supposed.

Emily Bullen began to speak. She was fingering an object which provided the sergeant with some amusement. It was a "reticule, they called 'em," he decided, in corded velvet of an electric-blue tint, with a reeving string puckering the top of it and dark-blue cords to loop over the wrist. "And a regular bran-tub, most likely," he soliloquized, eyeing its protuberances suspiciously.

"I have been anxious to see you, Inspector," Emily Bullen remarked in precise tones. "We have all had a terrible shock—at least some of us have," she amended ominously, "and I say to myself, what are the police for if not to straighten out our troubles? So I intend to put mine before you immediately."

"Quite right, Miss Bullen," said Pardoe with cautious geniality, quick to recognize that he had no normal woman with whom to deal. "What is it we can straighten out for you?"

He was amused at the way in which she was taking the lead, but could hardly have said what it was he expected. It was certainly not what he got.

Emily Bullen drew open her reticule with maddening care. "She put in her thumb and pulled out a plum," Sergeant Salt felt like singing, when what came out was a folded piece of paper which at first glance held some familiarity for Pardoe.

He looked from the paper she held to her face. Her eyes, almost level with the sallow pudgy cheeks, were regarding him blankly. Despite their brown colour, they were like pebbles, he thought.

"I hear that inquiries have been made about anonymous letters. Carol and Jenny have never had one, but I have!" The triumphant note in the concluding words gave a shrillness to the flat tones. She smiled suddenly with repulsive childishness. "It came—let me see, it must be a week ago. One morning, with another letter. I think it was last Friday, a week yesterday." Her voice again lapsed to its former level.

"May I see it?" Pardoe asked patiently, extending a hand.

It was as he expected, the same rather ill-formed capitals on the same coarse paper as had served for the doctor's letters. He read the message:

Keep your eye on the old lady. You ought to know what is happening.

Pardoe passed the paper without comment to Salt.

"Have you the envelope this came in, Miss Bullen?"

"No, Inspector, I'm afraid I haven't," she replied with prim self-reproach. "I ought to have saved it, of course, but it was badly torn after being opened. I have a strong dislike for keeping untidy things, and did not think at the time that I would ever show it to anyone."

"You weren't alarmed then when you received it?"

"Not really. Of course I felt indignant that anybody should write to me in such a way, but I wasn't frightened. And I didn't think then that it referred at all to Mrs. Lackland's health."

"No," Pardoe agreed smoothly, "there is certainly nothing to show that that was what the writer meant. What meaning did you attach to it?"

His question was put abruptly, and two hot patches of colour appeared on Emily Bullen's cheeks.

"I hardly know. At least"—she plunged defiantly—"I thought it must be referring to her money. Mrs. Lackland was fond of revising

her will, you know. Not that I could have influenced her at all if she
had proposed making a fresh one."

To her evident surprise Pardoe accepted her judgement immediately. "That was probably the writer's meaning," he said. "Do you
know whether you are likely to benefit by Mrs. Lackland's will?"

She reddened uncomfortably and lowered her eyes, but not before
the inspector had caught sight of the naked greed in them.

"No, I don't. She never told me anything of the kind." She closed
her lips sullenly.

"Are you sure, Miss Bullen? If Mrs. Lackland never spoke to you
about her will, that is hardly consistent with what we know of her
habits. It seems she wasn't only fond of altering it, but of discussing
it a good deal too."

She gave him a careful, crafty look, and for a moment made no
reply. Both men got the impression that she was considering just how
far she ought to commit herself.

"Of course," she said at last in a smug voice, "Mrs. Lackland
sometimes spoke to me about her money. She mentioned the difficulty
of allotting it fairly, and so on. But it would be quite untrue to suggest
that she ever mentioned leaving any of it to me."

She bridled a little, as if to hint at such confidence was the greatest
impropriety. Pardoe noted that she had regained what he supposed
was her habitual self-control. Salt kept his eyes on his notebook most
of the time. It might be grubby but it did not give him the unwhole-
some feeling he got every time he chanced to look at Emily Bullen.

"How long have you been in Mrs. Lackland's service, Miss
Bullen?" the inspector asked.

"Twelve years. The poor soul was only reminding me of our long
association on the very afternoon before she passed away."

"Ah yes. In the afternoon. Was that the last time you saw Mrs.
Lackland in her usual health?"

"Yes, I left her just before she had tea. You see, I am free on
Wednesday evenings, so I go out usually. Not that I wouldn't have

stayed in any time the poor dear had wanted me, but she was always so particular about my free time, insisting that I shouldn't give it up on any account."

"Will you tell me, please, how you spent your free evening?" Pardoe asked, passing over the matter of Mrs. Lackland's altruism.

"Oh yes," said Emily Bullen, but a pause preceded her next words. "I went to a violin recital at the girls' school."

"At what time was that?"

"At eight o'clock. I was in the garden a short time after tea before changing to go out."

"And when did you return home?"

"I think it was a quarter-past ten."

"The recital was rather a long one then?"

"Oh, I wasn't there all the time. It must have been over by nine. So I called on a friend before coming home, to talk over her plans for a charity entertainment she's shortly giving."

"I think I had better have the name of your friend, Miss Bullen," said Pardoe. "As a check on times, you know," he added quietly.

"Certainly, Inspector," she replied readily and with an air of self-importance. "Mrs. Makin is the name, from Broombush, the large detached house in the Crescent, over there." She flapped a hand vaguely in the direction of the window. "She is giving a garden party the week after next, with dramatic and other entertainments, to help the League of Nations. And of course she needs helpers with some organizing ability."

"Of course," Pardoe murmured. "Now after you got home did you see Mrs. Lackland at all that night?"

Her eyes dilated at the question. It seemed for a moment as if she would unleash the hysteria she had had under control.

"No, no, I didn't," she cried, her voice ugly with shrill emphasis, "I didn't! I ate the supper cook left for me and I went up to bed well before eleven, and I didn't go near her room! It's a lie if anybody says I did!"

"Don't distress yourself, Miss Bullen," Pardoe admonished sharply. "It's quite unnecessary. Nobody has suggested that you went to Mrs. Lackland's room that night. I ask merely for the sake of finding out when she was last seen alive by anybody."

"And I've told you," she replied more quietly but still unmollified. "I never saw her after I left the room in the afternoon, not till—till the doctor came in the night."

"Very well. When you were there in the afternoon did you stay while Dr. Faithful made his visit?"

"Not all the time, Inspector." Her voice suddenly assumed an unctuous quality that made it even less agreeable than before. "The doctor was *very* conscientious with Mrs. Lackland. He always stayed a long time. She made a confidant of him, you know. So after he had given her her medicine, the dose she was always meant to take after lunch, and had asked me the questions about her health that he always asked, I went away. She didn't like me to stay the whole time. She appreciated the doctor's attentions very, very much."

You've got an idea, thought Salt grimly, of the way that proposed new will was going.

Pardoe regarded her thoughtfully. "Have you any idea who might have written you that anonymous letter?"

The sudden irrelevance of the question was too much for her precariously balanced calm. Fear showed in her eyes and in the way her fingers groped loosely at her throat.

"No, of course not," she whispered. She shot Pardoe a suspicious glance. "Didn't anybody else get them?" she asked under her breath.

He ignored the question. "I'll keep this one for the present," he said. "Please let me know directly if you receive another."

She nodded, still frightened. "There's something you ought to know," she hurried on breathlessly, as if she would escape from one fear into another. "I think it may be very important. It may be a terrible thing. On the afternoon she was last talking to me, poor dear Mrs. Lackland complained about the noises in the night. People walking about and whispering. I don't know what it was. But I feel it may have something to do with all the—the *horror* round us!"

Her voice rose again. Salt wished the chief would finish with her. She was getting on his nerves buzzing up and down like this.

"Do you mean the noises had disturbed Mrs. Lackland on the previous night, Tuesday?" the inspector asked.

"No. No, I don't know. Yes, I think she said last night when she talked of it. She was very angry. She thought it must be," she added with a kind of hurt indignation.

"I shouldn't worry about it, Miss Bullen," said Pardoe briskly, and not unkindly. "We'll look into it. But movements and chatter in a house at night are not so rare as to be necessarily sinister, you know. Movement without talk would be more to the point."

She did not look reassured, however. Her body was trembling, and she kept her eyes on Pardoe as if hypnotized. There was something else he had meant to ask her, but her own final piece of information had driven it entirely out of his head. In any case he felt it would be better to give her time to recover her calm before administering fresh fears. So he got up, and consulting his notes asked her if she would send Hetty Park, the housemaid to him.

Clutching her reticule to her, Emily Bullen rose in a flurry, and casting a look both penetrating and frightened at the two detectives, went away wordlessly.

Salt glanced significantly at his chief and emitted a long breath.

"Glad she's the other side the door," he confessed dryly. "Bad inferiority complex, I'd say," he went on, with barely concealed pride in his ability to use the new jargon. "See how pleased she was to have to announce that poison-pen letter? You'd think somebody was handing her the goods in the shape of a legacy or something, instead of a bit of malicious hot stuff like that."

Pardoe looked at him thoughtfully. "A legacy?" he repeated.

"'Mm. That's just about what she's getting. Bear in mind that the old lady was murdered before the doctor could net the lot."

Salt agreed grimly. "*And* she knew there was a pretty big chance of the doctor getting all there was to get. She rubbed it well in about the old woman appreciating him, eh?"

"It's a pretty problem how big she imagined the will to be," Pardoe said. "If, as they all say, the old lady wouldn't let on whether or not she had control of old Lackland's capital, Emily Bullen may easily—"

Before he could finish there was a timid knock on the door. Hetty Park came in, for all the world as if she expected immediate annihilation. She even closed her eyes a moment in readiness for the imagined blow to fall. When she closed the door it was with her back towards it, her hand gripping the knob as if for support. She was a little fair thing, meant to be plumply pretty, but the pitiable terror by which she was mastered was making havoc of her infantile features. Her eyes were swollen with crying, her mouth sagged, her normally fluffy hair was untidy with much futile adjustment. Pardoe, accustomed to fear in many disguises, had seldom encountered it in so glaring a form.

"Come on in, Hetty," he said in as offhand a voice as he could muster. "There's not really much I want to ask you, but in a case like this, you know, we've got to see everybody."

She was sitting now in the chair Emily Bullen had left, but not with the taut pose that suggested a pounce at any moment; she sat in a huddled, shrunken fashion that drew her into its depths as though she sought comfort and protection in its large proportions.

"I don't know anything at all," she said in a single breath, twisting her hands so fiercely that Salt, watching those betraying members, could see the ebb and flow of blood in the red and white patches.

"Well, that's quite likely," Pardoe replied soothingly. "But it's surprising how much one finds one knows after a bit of thought. I don't want to hurry you. You can take as long as you like," he shot a humorous look at the resigned Salt, "and when you've thought it over, tell me anything you can remember about last Wednesday which appears to you connected with Mrs. Lackland. You may have noticed something other people have missed."

The girl received what he said in the same huddled, finger-twisting silence, her eyes shifting from Pardoe's feet to Salt's and back again. It was hard to say whether she was listening at all. In a minute, however, she darted a terrified glance at the inspector and began to give an incoherent account of her whole day, cluttered with a mass of irrelevancies.

Pardoe let her run on. He had learned not to check a voluntary statement, however muddled, made under severe emotional stress. If he showed impatience or an attempt to direct the information into certain clear-cut channels, she would either be scared into complete silence or, more likely, would lose the tangled thread she was pursuing, with equally unproductive results.

So he did not interrupt, but himself extracted the salient facts, which were few.

She had not been in Mrs. Lackland's bedroom since the morning. Her duties later in the day were mainly in the kitchen. She had not noticed anything specially unusual about her mistress, who was always sharp and talkative with Miss Bullen in the mornings. Mrs. Lackland had spoken to her only once that morning to inquire about her young man and to say that he was up to no good. He was a labourer at Corbie Farm, near Bullham, and Mrs. Lackland didn't know him, no, she didn't, but she always liked to say things like that because it seemed as how she didn't ever want anybody to get married. She must even run him down to Dr. Faithful, for no reason at all, because the doctor, who was always nice to her, used to say sometimes: "And how's that bad young man of yours, Hetty?" He used to chuckle when he said it, but it must have been because of Mrs. Lackland's gossip that he ever mentioned George at all. Nothing happened all day that she could remember. She went to bed as usual about ten o'clock. That was before Miss Bullen came in. She knew there was company in the house, and guessed it was the foreign actor. But everybody kept very quiet about it, and cook was always saying to mind her own business if she so much as asked one question. She was roused by cook about two in the morning, because they had sent for the doctor to come to the mistress. She thought she was the last to wake up.

When she stopped it was with a gulp, as of rising tears.

"Now don't cry," Pardoe said promptly. "You've done very well indeed, and remembered a great deal. No, no," he went on firmly as she continued to cry unrestrainedly, "stop it, Hetty. What's the matter? Is it because you're very sorry at losing Mrs. Lackland?"

She shook her head with instant and touching sincerity.

"No. Well, is it because you've been dismissed? Tell me why that was."

She lifted her head and looked at Pardoe with streaming eyes.

"I didn't listen at doors, I didn't, I didn't!" she wailed. "It was just because I didn't like going in directly when there was company, and doctor was there with them that afternoon, so when I heard his voice I didn't knock for just a minute, but I couldn't hear anything they were saying, and Miss Carol she was sharp with me at the time but she didn't say no more then. And I couldn't believe it next morning when cook told me I was to go for listening at doors."

"Who told cook you were to go?" Pardoe asked.

"Miss Carol," she whispered, and buried her face in her hands.

"When?" Pardoe persisted.

"The—the night before." She lifted her face wearily. "She must have been thinking about it ever since the afternoon, but she didn't say anything to me till the morning when the mistress had passed away."

"Well, cheer up, Hetty," said the inspector. "You won't be going just yet, will you, so there's time perhaps for a change of mind after the first annoyance has passed. Anyway a smart girl like you will soon get another post."

"No, no!" she cried. "I'm not staying at all! I've got to go on Monday when the funeral's over. They're paying me my wages instead of proper notice, and I'm going home."

Pardoe raised his brows. He glanced at Salt, but the sergeant was making dots with his pencil down the margin of his notebook.

"I see. Well, the associations here can't be pleasant ones now, so it's just as well perhaps to leave early. Where do you live?"

"In Bullham." Her voice was muffled again.

"Where in Bullham?"

If it had been possible for anything but woebegone fear to show on her face, Hetty would have looked surprised.

"At 2, Bryony Cottages," she said in a reserved but less tearful voice. "My mother and brother live there."

"All right." Pardoe nodded reassuringly. "You go home on Monday and leave all your worries behind."

She looked at him quickly, half frightened, half appealing. Pardoe was puzzled. There was something here for which he could not account. At the risk of a fresh upset he tried to draw her out again.

"If there is anything on your mind, Hetty, anything you feel you ought to tell me, now's the time, you know. It will be all right. You may say what you like here to me, and nobody else will know."

He saw her dart uncontrolled glances at the door, at Salt's homely, taciturn countenance, at himself. Her breathing was uneasy.

"Is there anything?" he urged.

He felt, he could not explain why, on the brink of something exciting. He succeeded in holding her gaze, but the sick fright on her face was emphasized.

Salt watched her too, his pencil idle.

"There's nothing," she said at last below her breath, and relaxed so weakly that Pardoe thought for a second she had fainted. Before he could move, however, she was on her feet, steeled, it seemed, by a pathetic resolution to be questioned no further. The inspector did not try to delay her. Instead he got up and patted her shoulder.

"Don't worry," he said, recognizing as he used it the futility of the worn-out phrase. "You'll be home in a day or so, and forgetting all about this. And if you feel later on that you've got something on your chest you'd like to get off, let me know directly."

He saw that she deliberately avoided his eyes.

"Get along now, Hetty, and wash your face and try to brighten up. And just ask Miss Hernshaw if I may speak to her for a minute."

She went towards the door with a suddenness of movement suggesting release from a trap.

Meeting Salt's eye when the door had closed, Pardoe saw that the sergeant's customary calm was replaced by a look part irritability, part bewilderment.

"What the devil's wrong with the whole crew?" he grunted in worried expostulation. "That girl's got something up her sleeve, and she ought—"

"She ought to be let get out of this," snapped Pardoe, who, hands in pockets, stood looking out of the window on to the deserted square. "She won't talk in this place, but she will at home."

He looked worried, in the mood to fancy criticism and to resent unspoken comment. He felt he had done right in not pressing the frightened girl for information he was sure she could give. She was likely to talk more freely in the familiar atmosphere of her home in Bullham.

He turned at a sound. Jenny Hernshaw had entered noiselessly and was standing midway between himself and the door, a look of slightly haughty inquiry on her face.

"Ah, Miss Hernshaw, thank you. I won't keep you long. Has Miss Quentin returned yet?"

"No," said Jenny coldly, coming forward easily and sitting down on a chair with its back to the window. "She went to town about the mourning that's needed and rung me up just now to say she's having tea there."

Pardoe was not perturbed. Both Jenny and Carol were being too effectually shadowed for a London trip to cause him any uneasiness. Whatever discrepancies arose from this shopping expedition would be reported to him in good time.

"Will she call on Mr. Carnowski?" he asked bluntly. Observing how chilly Jenny was and sensing that she probably knew of his morning visit to Tite Square, he saw no reason to fence.

She flushed quickly, and it was only when her cheeks lighted with the sudden colour that Pardoe noticed how ghastly she was actually looking.

"Not that I know of," she said. "Why should she?"

He towered above her, for since Hetty's departure he had felt too restless to sit down again. She tilted back her head to look at him, and Pardoe, noticing the strained gaze and shadowed eyes, knew that this girl had passed sleepless nights. He ignored her question.

"Sit down," he said brusquely, then: "When did you last communicate with Carnowski?"

He saw her colour deepen and the faintly trembling lips compress.

"I wrote to him last night," she said.

"And before that?"

"On Thursday. What do you want to know for?"

"And when you wrote on Thursday did you explain what you had been unable to say on the telephone, that the police were investigating your grandmother's death?"

She shrank back a little from the menace she thought she detected in his voice.

"Yes, I did." Her own voice took on a note of defiance. "Nobody had forbidden it."

"Of course not. Another thing I would like to know, Miss Hernshaw. Have you known lately of any undesirable strangers calling at the house or hanging about?"

He saw her frown and clench firmly the hand lying in her lap.

"Not one," she replied, with such ready firmness that Salt was immediately sceptical of her good faith.

Pardoe, who had not removed his gaze from her face, nodded.

"All right. Let me know if there should be anything of the sort. Now, is it for eavesdropping alone that Hetty Park has been dismissed?"

For the first time she lowered her head a little and looked down into her lap. "I suppose you're entitled," she said wearily, "to ask these silly questions. No, not altogether for eavesdropping. I never caught her at that myself, but my cousin says that last Wednesday wasn't the first time. There was general inefficiency besides that. She's been here nearly seven months, but she's still not learned some of the most elementary things about the house, and what's more seems genuinely incapable of learning them. I like Hetty myself, but this has been the wrong place for her. She will be much happier in a different situation, and probably quite efficient." She looked up at Pardoe. "You've noticed how tearful she is, of course? But that—that's only natural in a house where there's been—murder."

The last word was spoken almost gently, but with such value accorded its syllables that Salt admitted afterwards it gave him the creeps more than anything that had been said that afternoon.

"Yes," said Pardoe gravely, "it's unhealthy for everybody, and Hetty is normally a healthy girl, I'd say."

His irritability had dropped from him now, but his manner remained distant.

"I wonder, Miss Hernshaw," he said, "if your memory is good enough to recall a visitor who called here on the afternoon of June 7th? You accompanied him, or her, to the gate, at the same time that Dr. Faithful was leaving the house."

Jenny stared at him in frank surprise. Then she sighed and pressed both hands to her forehead in a hard, stroking movement.

"No, I'm afraid my memory isn't good enough," she said. "There have been many visitors since Grandma was ill. And I don't keep a diary."

"The doctor's car was waiting outside that afternoon," Pardoe said softly, ignoring her tone and keeping his eyes on her face.

She gave him back look for look.

"It nearly always was," she said composedly. "Perhaps the doctor might remember my visitor."

"Perhaps he might," was the noncommittal reply. "Have you anything, Miss Hernshaw, you'd like to add to the information you gave Superintendent Littlejohn?"

In the short, acutely felt silence that followed Salt had the idea that Jenny was remembering something to some purpose. But she shook her head. Her eyes looked bright with controlled tears.

"Nothing but this," she said, with the artificial lightness of one resolved to keep calm. "I didn't kill my grandmother."

The sergeant pulled down his mouth at the unorthodox disclaimer. Pardoe turned away coldly.

"Nobody's made the accusation, Miss Hernshaw," he said coldly, checking with raised hand whatever retort she was about to make. "I've nothing more to ask you now, but hope that as soon as you've any information you think will help me you'll voluntarily give it. I'd like to see Miss Bullen again for a few minutes, please."

Jenny got up at the offhand dismissal in his voice and levelled a disconcertingly candid gaze at him. But Pardoe was not to be put out of countenance.

"I am willing to tell you what I know," she said crisply, "although you don't seem to think I am. But I don't propose to invent or decorate facts to give the police an excuse for showing off their activity about nothing. If my facts happen to be bald you must have them bald. If you concentrated more on how my grandmother came by her death and less on such old-fashioned melodrama as strange men lurking outside the house, we should be free of this horrible business more quickly."

"One of Mr. Carnowski's old-fashioned ideas, that," Pardoe murmured deprecatingly, "which perhaps explains the melodrama."

He saw the sudden fright on her face. She was speechless.

"All right, Miss Hernshaw," Pardoe nodded. As she went silently from the room he watched her with the first smile Salt had observed from him that afternoon.

When Emily Bullen rejoined them she was apparently a different being from the distraught creature who had talked to them earlier. Not that the air of bright servility she now wore made her any less unattractive to Sergeant Salt, who was finding it very hard to overcome his initial repulsion. The inspector, who seemed unaccountably cheered by his passage-at-arms with Jenny, wanted to laugh at the almost comical distaste with which Salt was surveying the woman as she tripped coyly into the room with an assumption of grace and eagerness to serve that sat ill upon her.

Pardoe was looking at her with an absent-minded thoughtfulness that made his stare impolite.

"Oh yes, Miss Bullen," he said suavely as she approached him, "I'm sorry to bother you so soon again, but there was something important which I forgot to ask you."

He saw her bridle a little, immediately conscious of her own value at being considered able to supply an answer.

"Yes, Inspector?"

"When you were returning home from your visit to Mrs. Makin on Wednesday night—" He broke off with: "By the way, I presume you walked back?"

"Oh yes." She giggled at the suggestion she would do anything else. "It's such a short way, you know."

"Yes. Well, when you came along the square and drew near the house do you remember seeing a stranger, a man, loitering near, or standing by the gate or wall?"

Her eyes opened wider with the old glassy look, but she simpered as she replied.

"A *man*? And near the house?" As if it was a Bengal tiger, thought Salt. "Dear me, Inspector, do you think then there was a burglary contemplated? No, I can't say I saw anybody. I should have told you already if I had," she concluded smugly.

"Did you meet anyone on the way back?"

She affected to think, but Pardoe was sure her mind was actually busy with his own reasons for wanting to know.

"No, I didn't, I'm afraid," she said regretfully, conveying the impression that she would have liked to concoct an encounter of some sort but hadn't time to make up a convincing one.

"That's all right, Miss Bullen," Pardoe said cheerfully. "It's almost as much help to me, you know, to hear you didn't come across him as to hear you did."

He glanced at Salt, and the sergeant got up. As Pardoe prepared to leave he fixed Emily Bullen with a slow stare.

"You will have seen enough of us for one day, Miss Bullen," he remarked jocularly. "Remember two things, please. Let me know directly you receive another anonymous letter. Bear in mind that the stranger I've just inquired about may have something to do with the disturbing noises Mrs. Lackland complained of, so I shall want to hear all about any strangers you may have calling at the house from now on."

With apparent unconcern for the quaking fears he had succeeded in restoring, he strode to the door and opened it for her.

Muttering: "Oh yes, I'll let you know. Oh yes. Good afternoon," Emily Bullen went out. The inspector and Salt followed, to see her quickly mounting the stairs.

A maid coming down passed her near the bottom of the flight. Pardoe, who had not seen the girl before, glanced at the slender, composed figure in her fresh cap as she drew aside to allow Emily Bullen passage, and advanced with assurance.

"Miss Dawes, isn't it?" he said politely.

The girl nodded, her sallow face expressionless.

"I'm Inspector Pardoe from Scotland Yard, and this is Sergeant Salt," he said quickly. "You were very clear in the evidence you gave Superintendent Littlejohn the other day. You can keep your head. Now I'm wondering if you have remembered yet what other thing it was you noticed on Mrs. Lackland's night table when you took in the tea, something extra to the articles you mentioned?"

The girl had heard him at first with a rather supercilious indifference that seemed impervious to any flattery, but when he had finished Pardoe saw her flush angrily.

"Some other thing?" she echoed, her voice unnaturally heightened. "You're on the wrong track, Inspector."

"How?" asked Pardoe quietly.

"Because I never saw anything else at all! Because I never told the super I had! Because he—you, you're all trying to fix something on me with your lies!"

The sudden fear that swept her drove a note of vulgarity into her trembling voice. She turned on her heel and leaving the detectives looking after her went down the passage towards the domestic quarters.

Chapter XI

THE CASE AGAINST X

Which of you have done this?

Macbeth

On Saturday night Inspector Pardoe made a second call at Lacklands to see if Carol had returned. His luck was in. She received him coolly but with an engaging candour in marked contrast to her cousin's hostility, and was perfectly ready at his request to go over the evidence she had given Littlejohn. She looked tired, Pardoe thought, and something of the strained fear which belonged to everybody he had so far seen in the house showed in the too-direct gaze with which she scanned his face.

Short interviews with Hennessy and Mrs. Beadle completed his knowledge of the staff. He was favourably impressed by the butler, who told a plain tale convincingly, neither stressing nor attempting to conceal his dislike of his late mistress, and whose apprehensions were not, as Pardoe felt sure, on his own account. Mrs. Beadle, torn between her lamentations over calamity and her resentment at the interference of Scotland Yard, seemed to the inspector the one normal occupant of Lacklands.

Sunday provided a respite for everybody except the police. Inquiry about the morphia sulphate among the chemists had so far drawn a blank, as Pardoe had expected. They were engaged now in threshing the evidence they had so far secured and in trying to identify the man whom Carnowski alleged he had seen outside Lacklands on two occasions. In the absence of corroborative evidence Salt was disposed to share the chief's earlier view, that the unknown stranger was, likely enough, a figment of the actor's imagination. But since the lunch hour yesterday something had inclined Pardoe to the belief that the lurking man was a reality, though for the present the sergeant's desire for enlightenment remained ungratified.

By Sunday night no report relating to the stranger had come in, and Salt was beginning to display a little triumph. Pardoe spent the day quietly going through his own and Littlejohn's notes, and making the sort of rough tabulation he was accustomed to when there were numerous points for consideration. He wanted the stimulation a thorough discussion of these with Salt would give him; but the sergeant was too busy today, "nosing a bad herring," as he himself termed it. Besides, Pardoe was impatient to get the inquest opened and adjourned. With that and the funeral over, he anticipated what he had sometimes got before, a certain degree of relaxation on the part of the household which had been strung up ever since the death to a pitch of nervous tension. The arena cleared, his own work, he had often found, became simplified, whatever difficulties might still lie ahead. He had learned by experience not to disparage what was called "a cold trail." Cold trails were not infrequently productive of the most valuable clues. Everybody was bound to be a little off guard when a trail was cooling, and everybody included the murderer.

When Salt turned up that evening, tired and grumpy, after running to earth an innocuous salesman of Magico Cleansing Powder whom a Minsterbridge police constable had seen twice in the vicinity of Lacklands, and whose most unfortunate habit seemed that of sloping his hat brim over his eyes, he found Pardoe in a genial mood.

For all that the inspector was not communicative. He made it plain that further business was banned till after the inquest, and when they had eaten supper of an excellency common to the Swan and Ferry, left the sergeant to his own devices, which he knew might turn to possibly useful tittle-tattle with the landlord, while he himself went for a walk in the river meadows to refresh his mind with gazing on an angler's paradise.

The inquest opened at ten o'clock on a sullen, clouded morning. The glittering sunlight of the past week was absent, so that in the dusty rooms of the town hall and its environs the oppressive quality of the heat seemed less tolerable. The public, purposeful and aimless alike, that contended for entry or hung about gossiping, was provided with more disappointment than thrill.

The proceedings occupied less than half an hour and entirely lacked spectacular verve of any description. The coroner, a retired solicitor of an impeccability if not charm equal to Mr. Rennie's own, was an exception to those gentlemen who figure so prominently in the columns of the indignant press. He knew both the privileges and limitations of his job, and cut no acrobatics in the execution of it. Minsterbridge thought him dry and dull, and said so. The police thanked heaven for him, and kept quiet about it. He was at his best in the short time at his disposal this morning, which might, according to your taste, be equally judged his worst. Bullying, lost tempers, misplaced wit, amazing disclosures and swooning witnesses were what the well-bred citizens of Minsterbridge hankered for, and never got. Instead their portion was the exemplary medical evidence of Dr. Faithful, who delivered it in an objective manner with the flat restraint of which he was capable on occasions, and a couple of minutes of low-voiced responses from Carol who testified to finding her grandmother dying and to sending for the doctor. Notice of adjournment to that day fortnight followed. The dispersing crowd felt cheated enough even to believe that Dr. Tom had let them down.

To one person, however, the hasty formality he had just witnessed did not lack drama. Running his eye over the protagonists present, Pardoe knew that at least the secret of Mrs. Lackland's death, if not her murderer, was present in that court. He was pretty sure the murderer was there, for the only absentees were Beadle and the two maids. He watched the girls, Jenny rigid in her pose, her glance travelling from face to face yet carrying a faraway expression, Carol pale and small in her mourning, sparing a look for nobody but the coroner. Twice the inspector had caught Jenny directing a quick conscious look at the doctor in the course of his evidence, and each time look hastily away. But Carol watched nobody. Emily Bullen sat very still, red of face and apparently hypnotized by the fact that she was part of this indecorous proceeding. At the back of the room was Carnowski who, in spite of his inconspicuous position, attracted more interest than anybody with a speaking part. Pardoe observed that Hennessy, the butler, seemed only to remove his gaze from the actor's face to force it back there the next minute. Carnowski himself did nothing but make a few vain attempts to intercept Jenny's wandering eyes. He looked like a rather benign being planted in the midst of representatives of an alien race whom he was regarding with a kind of puzzled indulgence.

Directly the court rose Pardoe hurried Salt back with him to the Swan and Ferry. Now that the thing was over and nothing that mattered had been given away, he was full of that sense of optimism which a free hand and an uninterrupted period of time ahead always gave him.

"I want to run over the case with the facts we've got up to date and just see what our suspects look like," he said as soon as they were indoors, seating himself at the table with a briskness Salt knew of old.

"Suspects? That'll be all of 'em," the sergeant remarked with lugubrious resignation. The heat of the court room had not contributed to his zest for work after last night, but he sat down opposite the inspector and prepared for what he termed a bit of brain-fag.

"Not exactly," Pardoe replied. "Well, I suppose we can't eliminate anybody offhand, but I prefer the common sense view that shuts out one or two of 'em after a very short look-over."

"The servants?"

"Not the lot. Mrs. Beadle certainly. It doesn't need much knowledge of human nature to know that she's pretty well incapable of murder by poisoning. Besides which, in her position as cook she was queen in her own domain, you might say, and had less perhaps than anybody to endure of the old lady's tantrums. The legacy she stands to gain is sixty pounds, and I can't imagine Beadle murdering for that amount even supposing she knew the old will was going to be scrapped."

"The butler's a different pair of shoes, though," said Salt.

"At first glance. But his share of the standing will is only sixty too, not enough temptation to make money the motive, for Littlejohn tells me he's fairly well-to-do, has got a banking account and needn't bother from the financial standpoint if he is turned off. No, nothing but temper at getting the sack after a quarter of a century's service would account for it if he's our man. And he doesn't strike me as the type that lets resentment get hold of him to that extent."

"No," the sergeant agreed, "if he was going to feel that mad about it he'd have kept the film chap locked out safe enough."

"He'd less opportunity, too, than any of the women," Pardoe went on, "for whoever murdered Mrs. Lackland had either to poison the medicine, give her the dose, and polish the bottle at one visit to her room, or make more than one visit, which increases the risk of discovery. If you think it over you'll see that whoever did it is somebody whose presence in the old lady's bedroom wasn't at all unusual. Hennessy's was."

"But suppose he had somebody in with him?" Salt suggested.

"Not very likely. Who'd share Hennessy's motive, which common sense says could only have been revenge? Where'd you find anybody that would help in a murder because somebody else was offended at getting the sack?"

Salt did not reply and the inspector continued.

"I think myself Hennessy's told what he knows. But the two maids are a different proposition. What do you think of 'em?"

The sergeant was prompt. "Neither of those girls killed her," he said, "but both of 'em know something about it."

"I agree with you. Take the parlourmaid, Dawes. She stands to lose a job and to gain nothing by the death, and if she'd killed her herself she wouldn't first have tried to remember something about that table by the bed, and then repented of it a couple of days later and flamed out at us for reminding her of it. Something happened after Thursday to make her reconsider telling the police what she knows, or what she thinks she knows. And I'd like to hear about it."

Pardoe was silent for a minute and Salt remarked: "Maybe she thought it over and worked out some puzzle for herself that told her who the killer was, and she spotted the danger of talking any more."

The inspector nodded. "Maybe. It's the other, Hetty Park, that's worrying me. There's something pretty bad there."

"Well, the kid's going home today."

"Yes. The best thing that can happen. And there's the chance she'll say in Bullham what she didn't dare say in that house. There's something behind that listening at doors."

"Something behind the doors, you mean," said the sergeant with heavy humour. "I wouldn't mind betting though there's nothing to it but some sharp words when she was sent packing, and she was hysterical about it because of the murder and all."

He was inclined to think the inspector too much occupied with the housemaid's tribulations, but he did not succeed in dispelling his gravity.

"I hope you're right," was Pardoe's curt rejoinder.

"Well, she had no motive we know of to kill the old lady," said Salt. "And 'tisn't likely that a girl in that state could have done it and not given the show away."

Pardoe looked thoughtful. "That leaves us the two girls, the doctor, and the companion," he said. "So let's dispose of Dr. Faithful first."

"Right," the sergeant said. "We can do that without much palaver. Where's his motive?"

"There isn't one. He had every incentive to keep alive a good patient who seems to have had implicit trust in him as well as being financially profitable, and to see that she lived to change her will in his favour. We know what she told him on Wednesday was true.

We've Rennie to confirm it. So with her death Faithful's seen a fifteen thousand legacy go west.

"Besides, supposing there was motive, how did he have the chance to give her the stuff? He administered a dose we know to have been harmless in the afternoon and he didn't come again till he was sent for about twelve hours later."

"He could have put the morphia in the stuff," said Salt in a totally unconvinced tone, "and have left it to the old lady to pour out the last dose herself."

"Then who wiped the bottle so carefully?"

"An accomplice," said the sergeant flippantly.

"Bright, aren't you? Well, there's something here that won't wash. If Faithful put the tabloids into the bottle when did he do it? His only chance was between the time he gave her the medicine and the time he left on Wednesday afternoon, a matter of about a quarter of an hour, with the old lady lively and talkative all the time and the Bullen woman in the room."

"But she said she went out after he'd given her the tonic."

"So she did. But it doesn't make much difference. Think of it, Salt. Those morphia sulphate tabloids each contain a quarter of a grain of the stuff, and there were nearly three grains in the body. So that means twelve tabloids had to be put in her medicine and dissolved with the old lady only a foot or so away, watching, talking, claiming his attention! It's sheer rubbish. And if he brought the stuff in solution he had just as much difficulty, if not more, in getting it into that small bottle."

"That's what's worrying me," said Salt.

"What?"

"Why the stuff was in the bottle."

"Me too. Why not the glass? Somebody had got hold of morphia, that's certain, and managed to put it in the medicine. But why did the murderer's choice fall on the bottle instead of on the glass when it would have been easier to pour out a genuine dose, turn one's back on some pretext, and slip in an already prepared solution of the poison into the medicine glass? If somebody in the house stole those tabloids in June there was plenty of time to make such a preparation, without the risk that must actually have been run at the last. Why, that bottle was on the table all the time! It was harmless at two-thirty Wednesday afternoon and poisoned at we don't know what hour afterwards. And I can't see how. Mrs. Lackland didn't go to sleep, so far as we know, before her supper came, and we're told she was a light sleeper at best, so anybody who may have found her asleep was running the worst risk imaginable by going in then to tamper with the bottle. Could have been done, of course, especially if the stuff was in solution, but there's something senseless in it which doesn't tally with the rest of the diabolical scheme."

Salt's comfortable face wore a heavy frown.

"Seems as if she *had* to be killed just then," he decided. "Wonder why the poison was kept for the last dose."

Pardoe did not answer for a moment, then he said slowly: "I suppose it was known the doctor would call that afternoon, and there was the chance he'd detect something."

"Then it wasn't the murderer wrote those letters to him? Else it would've been just right, getting him to give her the poisoned dose."

"No," said the inspector firmly, "it wasn't the murderer. It's easy to see that things have not turned out as poison-pen expected, with the doctor nicely out of the murder in the nick of time and the loser of a fortune. The murderer, if he'd been poison-pen trying to fasten it on the doctor, would have managed better than that. I've got an idea myself of the origin of those letters, which we'll come to later, but I'm puzzled about it, for I believe the writer sent 'em quite independently of the murderer's plans, and what the devil for I can't fathom."

Salt was thinking hard. "D'you suppose the murderer got to know about the letters and didn't want Faithful suspected, so fixed the murder so as to clear him?"

Pardoe laughed. "A tender-hearted killer! No, old man, I don't think so. Assuming such benevolence, though, who wiped the bottle afterwards but left the doctor's prints sticking out like a prize exhibit?"

"Poison-pen," retorted the sergeant, undaunted.

"This is turning into a duel between poison-bottle and poison-pen," said Pardoe, "and we're not getting anywhere. Let's stick to the point and talk about the people we're left with, the girls, Carnowski, Miss Bullen. And first Jenny Hernshaw."

"Things are pretty black for her," said Salt.

"Yes. Well, we've got Rennie's story, and neither of the girls can be considered without remembering John Lackland and the background to their lives. Now, what motive had Jenny? Plenty. To begin with, money. It's no good putting complete faith in the story that they were ignorant whether they stood to gain anything by Mrs. Lackland's death. They admit she was always talking about her money, and for all we know she may have spoken with a certainty they won't allow. Anyway, Jenny could have known that she was an heiress, and I want better proof than I've had yet that she knew nothing of the sort. There's your motive. Added to which her grandmother's death means for Jenny an escape from a hateful tyranny and the freedom to marry Carnowski if that's the mutual desire, a marriage for which she would never have got permission while the old lady lived.

"This triple motive is overwhelmingly in favour of Jenny Hernshaw as the killer. Besides that we've got to bear in mind that the situation centring round Carnowski was precipitated to a crisis by the row last Friday week, a row with a curious sequel next day when Mrs. Lackland was taken suddenly ill with a mysterious malady."

Salt nodded. "It looks as if she tried to do it then and it didn't come off, and then she had to do it before the old woman saw her lawyer on Thursday."

Pardoe leaned across the table, his mouth grim. "Yes. Before she could draw up a new will. And if it was true that the girls were ignorant of the terms of their grandfather's will, then Jenny may very well have thought that the whole amount was to be left elsewhere and killed her in panic at the thought that she was going to lose every penny."

"You're thinking it's too good to be true, aren't you?" the sergeant asked. He knew the chief's suggestion was not that of a man who sees the end of a chase in view.

"I do. It falls into place too patly, Salt. At the same time I'm afraid of that very feeling too. It could be Jenny, it ought to be Jenny, and it isn't safe to say that for the reason that everything points neatly to her it can't be her. It's a pretty silly argument that because circumstantial evidence against X is about as bad as it can be therefore X is innocent. Things are sometimes what they seem, you know. So let's get on.

"Opportunity? Quite enough. She could have given her the dose when she gave her supper if she lied to us about Mrs. Lackland's refusal of the medicine at seven o'clock, and in that case her nine o'clock visit to the bedroom would actually have been to see if the poison was acting properly. If, on the other hand, the girl was telling the truth in saying that her grandmother wouldn't drink the medicine at seven, then if she murdered her she gave her the morphia at nine o'clock. See any weak point in that?"

Salt thought. "Can't say I do," he said finally.

"Well, it seems to me unlikely that last visit to her grandmother's room was for the purpose of killing her. It was done too ostentatiously, under the noses of Carnowski and the other girl. If Jenny killed the old lady I think she did at the latter's supper time. Now, we'll suppose she's done it, and waive for the minute all speculations how, and why she poisoned the bottle and not the glass. Does Carnowski know she's done it? And is Carol Quentin trying to shield her?"

"Why d'you think that?" the sergeant asked.

"I didn't say I thought it. But you've got to remember it was Carol who tried to minimize to us Mrs. Lackland's dislike of Carnowski. She pretended it was simply because he was a film actor. It was Carol too who said nothing about her grandmother's coming interview with Rennie—"

"Perhaps that was to shield herself."

"May have been. Equally it may have been to cover up Jenny's additional motive for murder, for remember it was Jenny who'd had the big row a few days earlier and who might be cut out of the new will in consequence."

"That flare-up with the old lady don't make things too bright for her," the sergeant conceded.

"No. And remember it was she who asked Rennie about their future position, and she who insisted on the fact of Hennessy's dismissal to Littlejohn while not mentioning Carnowski's presence that night, as well as looking odd when the super brought up the subject of the anonymous letters."

"Perhaps she sent 'em herself," Salt said grudgingly.

"Perhaps she did. If she did, though, I'm no judge of character. But there's one thing I feel sure Jenny Hernshaw knows."

"Who killed the old lady?" Salt suggested.

Pardoe gave him a steady look. "That's pretty sound, Salt. She may, and that of course doesn't eliminate her as the murderer herself. But that wasn't in my mind at the moment. You wondered yesterday why I believed Carnowski's story of the fellow you've been chasing, didn't you?"

"Fellow?" Salt grunted. "Giddy phantom."

"No, flesh and blood, I'll be bound. I was sceptical myself till I mentioned him to Jenny Hernshaw. Didn't you notice how she first denied knowing anything, and then afterwards when I'd dropped the subject brought it up herself as an example of wasted activity on the part of the police?"

"Yes, but how—"

Pardoe brought his hand down quickly on the table.

"Like this. When I told her it was one of Carnowski's ideas, why did she look scared to death all at once and never say another word? If the man didn't exist, there was no need for her to take fright because Carnowski had had a notion. I think she knows him. I think she went back to the subject herself without any pressure from me because it had been in her mind ever since I spoke of it, and she wanted to put me off the scent by ridiculing it."

"Sounds likely enough," said the sergeant. "But see here. Suppose she suspects Carnowski killed the old woman, and suppose she thought he put up that tale so as to invent another suspect? That 'ud make her sure he did it."

"You're working double-quick this morning, Salt," said Pardoe. "Well, it might be. It still leaves her with knowledge of something pretty vital to the case. Now what about the cousin, Carol Quentin?"

"She's in the same boat, isn't she?" said Salt. "I mean there isn't much to choose between 'em."

"Equal opportunity, certainly," Pardoe replied. "But I don't think you'll find a motive so urgent as in Jenny's case. The money motive, of course, remains, and freedom from the kind of slavery the old woman practised. Motives enough, but it was Jenny who was in disgrace and who is in love with a man who presumably loves her. We've no evidence to show that Mrs. Lackland's death was of such immediate importance to Carol Quentin as it was to the other girl."

Pardoe frowned, and then went on more slowly.

"I'm puzzled why she was killed on Wednesday night and not earlier when she was so downright ill it's possible Faithful wouldn't have questioned her death."

"Because of the will she was going to alter," said the sergeant.

"Yes, I know. That's a reason for killing her now, but it isn't a reason for not killing her weeks ago. That morphia was missing early in June, yet the murderer waits till her convalescence is so well established that there's no question of passing off the murder as natural death!"

"Whoever did it must have hoped to fool the doctor, I suppose."

Pardoe shook his head. "Not with a poison she wasn't taking then even in the smallest quantities. But to return to Carol. She had the chance to administer the dose when she went upstairs for a handkerchief, as she says, at about eight-twenty. Our difficulty with that visit is in assessing the time she was absent from the sitting room. If Carol's been trying to shield Jenny, Jenny may just as well be trying to make things look good for Carol by pretending not to know at what time she returned and by getting Carnowski to back her up. The cook's no good there, either. Says Carol left her at ten to nine, but can't remember whether they talked for 'ten minutes or twenty.' Whichever it was though she had time to kill her grandmother before going to the kitchen."

"Must be a cool one," said Salt, "to go straight from a killing to gossip about sacking the maid. And we're no nearer knowing how the bally stuff got into the bottle."

"No. I'll not believe that anybody who killed Mrs. Lackland took the trouble on their last visit to her room to put the morphia into the bottle only to pour it out again. It's senseless. That stuff must have been put in some time before, and if I didn't know she'd had a harmless dose in the afternoon I'd have said it was put in some days before too. The poison being in the bottle and not in the glass is the worst puzzle of the lot, and I believe if we could solve that the other pieces would fall into place."

"There's something else to remember about the Quentin girl," said Salt irrelevantly. "She scouted the idea of suicide from the first, Littlejohn said."

"Well, how does that strike you?"

"I'd say it's pretty good for her. If she'd done it herself or if she knew Jenny'd done it, wouldn't she want to push the suicide theory for all she was worth?"

Pardoe smiled. "That might be just what she wanted you to think, old man."

"Oh lor'," said Salt.

"Now we're left with Emily Bullen——"

"And Carnowski," the sergeant finished.

"Let's do the household first. And tell me," said Pardoe, a glint of mischief in his eye, "just what you think of the late Mrs. Lackland's companion?"

But Salt was not to be drawn. "We've got a character study there," was the only response he made.

The inspector, however, did not seem to find it unilluminating.

"You've said it," he replied; "a crafty, hysterical, harmful, but ultimately stupid type. She has all the traits of the disappointed spinster that has to face a future of starved affections and economic insecurity."

Salt heaved a sigh in mock appreciation of his eloquence, and Pardoe went on: "If we assume that Emily Bullen murdered her mistress, what motive are we going to supply? A mixed one, I think, including desire for money and desire for revenge after twelve years of a dog's life."

"But she said she didn't know any money was coming to her."

"We'll suppose she did know, or guessed. It's likely enough she's lying. There's nothing fanciful in the idea that Mrs. Lackland told her about her legacy and let her know afterwards that she proposed to deprive her of it by leaving the doctor the whole amount. There's motive for you—a case as desperate in its way as that of either of the girls, for if she'd known there was money coming to her, God knows how anybody in Emily Bullen's position must have counted on the prospect of it. She'd be frantic at the sight of it slipping away from her grasp."

"And she'd have as much opportunity as the girls to murder her," said Salt eagerly.

"She could have given her the dose when she came in shortly after ten o'clock, yes," Pardoe replied. "But in that case she never planned to give it her herself. Ten o'clock and after wasn't Mrs. Lackland's medicine time, so if Emily Bullen was the murderer and introduced the stuff into the bottle she meant one of the girls to administer it while she was out. But coming back and finding the dose still there she had to give it herself, so wiped the bottle afterwards. That could be it."

"And that 'ud explain why the morphia was in the bottle," said Salt. "The murderer didn't mean to be the one to pour out the dose. Somebody else was to do that and get the blame."

"Then whoever wiped the bottle did it because the plan went amiss," Pardoe answered. "That would mean the murderer counted on the prints hanging somebody. But when you think of it on those lines, Salt, it's rubbish. That bottle is interesting only when it's cleaned up. So long as it was left alone the confusion of fingermarks couldn't have convicted anybody, especially as so many people at one time or another were likely to pour out her medicine." He sighed. "There's a dead-end somehow whichever way we turn."

"I'm thinking," said Salt, "she made up that bit about noises in the night."

"Well, I don't know," said Pardoe. "Remember that touch about the old woman accusing her of it? Bullen isn't a clever woman, you know, and that remark seemed to me perfectly genuine. Only a subtle mind would have invented it. That's why I don't fancy her as the murderer. She hasn't got a cool head, nor a good brain. She couldn't sustain the role successfully. But is there something else you can imagine her doing, Salt?"

The sergeant considered a minute, then tentatively remarked: "Anonymous letters?"

"That's it. She fills that bill admirably. She's got all the characteristics, even to the trick of writing one to herself to throw us Nosey Parkers off the scent. Did you notice something old about that letter?"

"It wasn't as nasty as those the doctor had."

"No, it wasn't. It didn't accuse her of the remotest connection with the murder, but only perhaps of some laxity in observing what was going on under her nose. There was something else too. That letter, unlike the doctor's, was very lately written, freshly blotted, with no time allowed for the ink to darken. Yet she said she got it a week ago. And she couldn't produce the envelope."

"But say she did write it to herself, why couldn't she put it in an envelope and post it?"

"What, with the postmark showing the date? She didn't hear about the questions Jenny and Carol had had on the subject till it was too late to do any posting. That'll be it. Why she should have written 'em remains a mystery for the present, but the longer we are finding the murderer the nastier it's going to be for Emily Bullen if she didn't do the murder. She knows that, and that in itself would cause hysteria."

"The doctor's last letter came from Bullham," said Salt thoughtfully.

"Yes, and Hetty Park lives at Bullham. If the woman's as stupid as I think, she's quite capable of giving Hetty that letter to post so as to make it appear to have been written elsewhere than in Minsterbridge. Find out which was the maid's afternoon off. I'll be bound it was Tuesday. Or Bullen herself could have taken the bus there."

"Her time was Wednesday evenings," the sergeant objected.

"She may have had an afternoon too. She got more liberty than the girls. Anyway, check up on that, and see that Mrs. Makin she's supposed to have called on after the concert. The school, too—pretend you want to establish the time exactly, and ask when she left the concert. You can do that this afternoon. And while they're at the funeral I'm going to rummage their rooms. Bullen's in particular."

"What d'you expect to find?"

Pardoe shrugged. "Some familiar writing paper, maybe."

Salt grinned. "She'd be daft to leave it about. But you never know. Anyway, we're left with the film star now. What about him?"

"He has the motive," said Pardoe, and frowned. "Marriage with Jenny, and a possible fortune. Even if he shared their alleged ignorance about it he's man-of-the-world enough to guess there's likely to be a lot of money coming his way. I'm going to find his banker and look into his affairs. He seems sound enough, but he does himself very well and it's probable he's blessed with the artist's usual disregard of commercial values."

"Morals too, I bet," Salt growled. "Being divorced and all." The way he said it made it sound like a disreputable disease. "He didn't mind sneaking in where he wasn't wanted, so maybe he wouldn't stick at poison."

"Hold on," Pardoe smiled. "There's still a long stride, old man, from gate-crashing to murder. We've got to consider him though. He had the opportunity when on his own admission he went up to the bathroom. It may easily be all my eye about not knowing where Mrs. Lackland slept. On the other hand, there's a strong argument in Carnowski's favour—with a bellrope within easy reach of her hand would an old lady of the type of Mrs. Lackland not only admit a strange man to her room but let him administer a dose of medicine to her?"

"I'd say not," said the sergeant decisively.

"Another thing," Pardoe continued. "Carnowski was seemingly a rare visitor to the house, so it would have been a dam' fool thing to arrange for the old lady's murder a night he was there."

"For the Hernshaw girl too," said Salt. "She wouldn't want to do it at a time her young man was there."

"No. Only we've got to remember it probably had to be that night because of the old dame's intention to see Rennie next day. What we want to know is, who's got their knife in the doctor? Somebody's been trying to suggest he's a murderer for a good time now, and somebody has dished him of fifteen thousand pounds. A nasty blow for any fellow."

"He's taken it pretty well," said Salt.

"And," the inspector said in conclusion, "if Emily Bullen wrote the letters did she do the murder too? It's consistent. But I don't think so. She *could* have put the morphia in the bottle, she *could* have planned for somebody else to pour it out and then found she had to do it herself, and being stupid she *could* have wiped the bottle afterwards, thinking she was doing something clever. But it's out of character, and like the old woman confronted with a giraffe, 'I don't believe it'!"

"Something'll break soon," said Salt. "You'll see."

Chapter XII

UPSTAIRS AND DOWN

They don't keep this room so tidy as the other.

Alice Through the Looking-Glass

As a prelude to the sergeant's prophecy, Pardoe found his luck in when he called at Lacklands in the afternoon. He had guessed correctly that the attendant publicity as well as convention would keep any of the women away from the funeral, at which Rennie and the doctor were to be present with the police to ensure order. He was prepared therefore for some hampering of his movements in the house and need for a ruse to obtain the necessary freedom for his actions.

But when Edith answered his ring he was agreeably surprised to find on inquiry that both girls were sitting in the garden, "because of all the blinds being down," while Miss Bullen had gone out to stay with a friend for the afternoon. Hetty Park was packing to leave by the evening bus. Hennessy had gone to the funeral.

"Don't disturb Miss Quentin or Miss Hernshaw," he told the girl. "I only want another look at Mrs. Lackland's bedroom. I'll go straight up."

Edith seemed glad of the brusque leave he took of her. "Probably expected some more questions about that table," he thought, noting her sullen, brooding face and slightly reddened eyes.

He had memorized on Saturday the position of the rooms in relation to one another. As he turned at the head of the stairs there was Carol's on his left, with windows on the front, next to it a vacant guest-chamber, then Jenny's. Almost opposite Jenny's door a short

corridor ran down to a window overlooking the garden. On the right
of this passage was the murdered woman's bedroom, with a smaller
room next to it that had been unoccupied since the nurse's departure.
On the left was a bathroom and another spare bedroom, and a linen
cupboard at the end with the door facing Jenny's room. Opposite
Carol's a door led into the room occupied by Emily Bullen. A service
stairs behind that led to the servants' rooms above.

Pardoe wasted no time on Mrs. Lackland's room. It had been
stripped of character by now. He spent a few seconds going in and out
of the bathroom, looking up the passage as he did so and noticing how
much of the main corridor remained visible. Then he went straight to
Jenny's bedroom. This was large and though sparely furnished not
uncomfortable. At this hour it should have been filled with sunlight,
but the blinds were down and outside the sky hung like a warm grey
blanket patterned here and there with copper-rimmed clouds. The
airless quality of the room was apparent in spite of open windows.
A certain untidiness gave it a more homely appearance than its large
spaces suggested. There were books in a heavy case, a frock or two
not put away, a pair of shoes kicked over. Holding the door shut
behind him Pardoe stood just inside it and let his eyes travel slowly
and keenly round. Then he advanced into the room, ignoring the long
drawers of the bureau and the wardrobe with its door slightly aswing,
and examined without touching them objects on the dressing table.
An oval mirror swung between two very little drawers on top of the
table. He pulled out the one on his right. It ran smoothly and revealed
nothing but an unopened packet of hair shampoo. Pardoe turned to
the other. He pulled but nothing happened. He pulled again, there
was a sudden creak, then the drawer shot out into his hand. At first
glance it seemed as unproductive as the other. A bit of dry seaweed
and two pennies mocked his inquisitive gaze. Then something white
in one of the corners caught his eye, and on taking it out he saw it
was a tightly screwed up piece of paper. He unfolded it carefully, and
five little white tabloids slid into his hand.

The inspector stared at them for a few seconds with no change of expression except a tightening of the lips. Then he carefully replaced them in the paper and put the tiny package into a breast pocket. For a minute he stood still, motionless in the motionless room where only the half-hearted booming of an imprisoned bee disturbed the silence. He would show his find to the doctor, though he did not need telling what it was. He raised his eyes, to catch his own reflection in the mirror. His glance was bright and hard. The drawer went back with difficulty and many jerks. The other slid out again at the merest touch. With no attention for anything else Pardoe went out and along the passage to Carol's room.

In size and shape this bedroom was twin to the one he had just seen, but of a contrasting neatness that made it almost feature-less. Everything had the pretty self-possession of its owner. Pardoe approached the dressing table, ran an eye over it, drew out its two drawers which contained innocuous undies, and moved to the ward-robe which was locked with the key in it. A glance inside showed everything in apple-pie order and he left it for the rest of the furniture which, like that in Jenny's room, was good and fairly modern though of a quality inferior to the period stuff downstairs.

There was nothing in the bureau to hold his attention, but he stood for some minutes in front of a small light chest of drawers in a corner by the window. This had a long drawer, which opened easily and contained nothing but a little linen, beneath two shorter ones that were locked. It was these which engaged Pardoe's attention. When he finally closed the door behind him and crossed to Emily Bullen's room his face wore a thoughtful expression.

He did not emerge again for some time, and when he finally came downstairs had been in the house half an hour. As far as he could see or hear he might be its only inhabitant. He made his way quietly in the direction of the kitchen in search of Mrs. Beadle and must have somehow betrayed himself in the act, for a green baize door was opened quietly and the cook appeared, encased—Pardoe could think of no better term—in a harsh black dress of apparently unyielding material. She eyed him suspiciously.

"The very person I was looking for," said the inspector pleasantly. "Can you tell me, Mrs. Beadle, when a locksmith visited the house last?"

The cook's severity changed to surprise. "This is no time to be asking questions," she censured him. "There's such a thing as respec' for the dead, though it seems of small account nowadays. A locksmith, did you say?" she went on, curiosity mastering propriety. "That would be the one Miss Carol had in April, after her grandma was took bad. Mrs. Lackland would never have any workmen in but what she'd sent for 'em, but there was no 'by your leave' of that sort, you'll understand, when the old lady was ill, and Miss Carol she said she didn't fancy having all her drawers without keys to 'em and some even without locks, for you never knew who might be about the house as was light-fingered. No more you do," she added defiantly, as if in anticipation of contradiction from Pardoe.

But the inspector was regarding her mildly.

"Thanks," he said, and forestalling questions added quickly: "One other thing. Your mention of Mrs. Lackland being the one to call in workmen reminded me. I suppose nobody except your late mistress could engage a new servant?"

"Oh no, certainly not. Why, if anybody in the house had brought in one of these 'ere pareegons as maid, if such creatures exist which I don't believe, she'd have sacked 'em the next minute only because she hadn't engaged 'em herself."

She stopped abruptly, fearful lest Pardoe should suppose she was maligning one who at that very moment was being consigned to her last resting place. But Pardoe was looking unbecomingly cheerful.

"Just as I thought," he said happily. "Now can I get to the garden this way?"

Mrs. Beadle pointed to a short flagged passage just behind him. "The door at the bottom," she said coldly, with the feeling that as far as she was concerned this police game was all give and no take.

The inspector had not been in the garden before and regretted that he had now no time in which to explore and appreciate its beauty. Old John Lackland had known what to covet and how to get it. Past trellis and pergola and between the grave magnificence of Dutch yews Pardoe walked, in front of him the terraces descending to the river, and over all the thick menacing sky, so vaporous that the outline of the cathedral tower was lost in a dull yellow haze. He was beginning to think he had somehow missed the girls, who might have gone indoors after all, when he suddenly caught sight of them sitting in deck chairs at the entrance to a tiny summerhouse that had been built in the shade of a fine mulberry tree.

Carol had a book to which she was giving desultory attention but Jenny was apparently unoccupied. As he drew near Pardoe saw that she was smoking fast and nervously. They were not talking, and at his conspicuous approach both looked up.

"Miserably hot, isn't it?" he said easily. "And I hate disturbing you. But I wonder, Miss Quentin, if you'd mind showing me how I can get to the other side of the river from here. I believe there's a bridge a bit higher up."

"You've only to go through the gate at the bottom and follow the path to the right," said Jenny hurriedly.

"I'm a duffer without guidance," he answered placidly, turning his smile on her. He looked back at Carol. "D'you mind?"

She gave him a keen glance suddenly, then got up unsmilingly, dropping her book in the chair. "Come with me."

They moved away together towards a narrow path skirting the left of the terraces. There were shallow steps at intervals permitting room for only one at a time, so that conversation was difficult until they had reached the foot. Here a small heavy gate bolted at the bottom gave on to a public footpath bordered with grass and parallel to the river bank. They were hidden from view of anyone in the house or on the other side of the terraces.

Pardoe stopped at the gate and coming up with Carol as she

unbolted it looked down at her gravely. She returned the look, her face pale, her eyes troubled.

"A ruse, Miss Quentin," he said with quiet frankness, "as you saw. It isn't always advisable in my job to talk in threes, and"—he hesitated—"there are reasons why I wish only you at the moment to hear what I have to say."

Her face cleared and she made a charmingly expressive gesture with her hands.

"Oh, but you can say to Jenny just what you'd say to me!" she cried.

"Well, let's pretend this time I want to say it to you by yourself. So, will you please tell me whether to your knowledge there is anybody in the house at present, or has been recently, whom you'd suspect of being a thief?"

She kept her eyes on his face until he had finished, then slowly gazed across to the motionless alders on the other side of the river.

"At one time we rather thought Edith took things," she said at length without removing her gaze from the opposite bank. "In the way, you know, of not being able to help it. Grandma was quite certain she did."

"But in that case why keep her?" the inspector asked, remembering Mrs. Lackland's merciless reputation.

Carol half wheeled to look at him sharply.

"I don't know." She was quite unaccountable. "No. It wasn't philanthropy, of course." She added softly: "She enjoyed power over people, and if they had made any mistakes, well—" Her shrug was eloquent.

Pardoe nodded.

"Did you ever miss anything yourself, or did Miss Hernshaw?"

Carol was watching him with a vaguely puzzled expression. She did not answer for a few moments, then she said: "I don't know about Jenny. She may have. I didn't. But I didn't think we ought to keep Edith."

"Then nobody but Mrs. Lackland could dismiss the servants?" he asked quickly.

"Gracious, no!" Carol almost laughed. "We couldn't even suggest it. Not at least without ensuring that that particular servant would be kept on, more firmly rooted than ever. But why all this, Inspector?"

Pardoe smiled and turned to go. With his hand on the half-opened gate he halted and looked at her again.

"Part of my job, Miss Quentin, getting to know as fully as possible the people with whom we've got to deal. Looked at like that, nothing's irrelevant." He lowered his voice. "Don't, in the next day or two, confide too readily in anybody in the house. I don't want you to be alarmed, but it's just as well to feel that until your grandmother's murderer is discovered nobody—nobody is free from danger."

He slipped through the gate and without waiting for a reply lifted his hand in leave-taking, walking quickly away along the path towards the bridge which was about two hundred yards upstream. He did not look back, so failed to see the little watching figure that still lingered by the gate.

When Salt came back to the Swan and Ferry after tea, inspector and sergeant pooled their information. Pardoe gave an impartial account of his examination of the rooms, but in spite of the widening of Salt's eyes at news of the find in Jenny Hernshaw's did not invite comment then. Instead he went straight on to describe Emily Bullen's room and the complete lack of evidence in the form of notepaper or envelopes.

"As many family faces as in a photographer's studio," he finished, "but of our poison letters nary a sign beyond a bottle of ink and a pen on a tin tray. The nib's the kind that could make those capitals, but that's all."

"And quite enough for the likes of her," Salt grunted. He seemed excited about something, and before Pardoe could question him burst out with: "Look here, there's nothing on the square about that dame. I went to the girls' school like you said, and what d'you think I found?"

"That she'd not been there after all," said Pardoe with a smile.

Salt stared. "Right. She had not. I passed it off as well as I could, but I wasn't feeling that good towards her. Then I went straight to this Mrs. Makin, thinking I'd get to know from her without letting on that we'd ever been told where it was she went. But lor', what I had to cut through to get down to bedrock—" He broke off, and pulled the kind of face that gave Pardoe more than an inkling of that interview.

"Talked, did she?" he said. "All round and back again?"

"Talk?" Salt repeated. "It's the best dam' squitter I ever listened to, an' I've heard some. Nonstop an' all. I can't remember opening me mouth except to gasp, but I must have done so, I suppose, for I've got her answers here—or a bit of 'em."

He pulled out his fat untidy notebook that somehow bore a vague resemblance to himself, and began to thumb its pages carefully.

"Now if only you'd had a dictaphone," Pardoe remarked cheerfully, "we might have had some fun."

"I've had mine," the sergeant rejoined grimly, and reached the place he was looking for.

Reduced to precis but without translation into official language, Mrs. Makin's evidence was to the effect that Miss Bullen, "poor thing," had called on her at about a quarter-past nine last Wednesday night to discuss arrangements for the forthcoming garden party. She was always so conscientious and so willing to help with a good cause. Not that her help was really of very much account, but it wasn't for any of them, was it, to despise the goodwill efforts of the humblest among them? Now there was the doctor—Dr. Faithful, of course—who everybody knew was the best conjurer anywhere round, but was very selfish in keeping his talents to himself simply because he thought he'd be more run after that way. But people soon got to know of that sort of thing, didn't they?

"'A great man with the ladies, you know, officer,' the old hag simpered at me," said Salt with the savage mimicry he reserved for the Makins of his career, "'and I don't think it's quite nice in a doctor. People will talk.'"

It seemed indeed that they had talked of the doctor in the usual vein, saddling him with a number of prospective wives and, as Salt had read the innuendos, with an equal number of competing mistresses. Well, Miss Bullen, "poor thing," said that at one time he had seemed to want to make a match with Miss Hernshaw, the dark cold girl, you know, officer. Now if it had been her cousin one might have understood it better, but the other is so offhand and secretive, don't you think?

The sergeant had wearied all the more of this interminable skulking round the fringe of scandal because he knew that to stop it might check a useful piece of information for which all the spiteful superfluities might eventually be worthwhile. So he had let her run on.

"But she's surely got her knife deep in the doc. I got to think at last that she was the poison-pen, with the Bullen woman keeping her primed with what was going on at Lacklands, an' perhaps doing the murder."

"What *was* going on at Lacklands, though, when those letters were being written?" Pardoe asked.

Salt looked doubtful. "No. Well, anyways, I got her back to earth, so to speak, by asking casual-like if she knew where Miss Bullen had been that evening before she called."

Mrs. Makin, it appeared, did know. Emily Bullen had been to the pictures at the Imperial Cinema in Cuffe Street. The poor thing was badly in need of relaxation always, and she got just what she wanted there, you know, something not *too* intellectual. She hadn't thought it was very good that time, though. A picture with that foreign actor, it was—she was afraid she couldn't remember his name—that everyone was praising *so* extravagantly and who was supposed to be fortune-hunting at Lacklands. But you could *never* believe what people said, could you, and if you ask me, girls nowadays don't need to be run after. It's they who do *all* the running.

"So there you are," Salt finished, a mingled triumph and excitement in his manner. "Bullen's told a bald lie and a wobbly one at that, for she must have known we'd check up on it. Why d'you think she made out she'd been to the school? There don't seem any point in it to me."

Pardoe chuckled. "Perhaps it's an easy one after all. I'd say she'd got the habit of lying to the old lady about her amusements because Mrs. Lackland was rabid on the subject of the flicks. So starting off with the violin recital she went on with it, without bothering so far ahead as our checkup." He paused before adding: "I said before that she was really a stupid woman."

"Maybe," said the sergeant firmly, "but being stupid needn't have stopped her murdering the old woman. All poisoners aren't clever."

"True. And this one has got his blind spot, you can be sure. But it wasn't an ultimately stupid brain that planned this murder, whatever tip-up may come afterwards."

Salt did not contradict this, though he continued to look dogged. "Well, don't put the Bullen out of your calculations. If you think she wrote the letters, why not see her as the murderer too, seeing that it don't make sense even when we let killer and poison-pen be separate johnnies?" He broke off abruptly. "I asked Hetty which was her afternoon off."

"When did you see her?"

"Just now. On my way back. She was waiting for her bus, suit-case and all. She said her day was Monday, not Tuesday, so that's off—thinking she had a hand in the posting. But I asked her about Bullen and she said she didn't really know, but she thought she got afternoons free, no fixed day. That would be besides the Wednesday evening, of course."

Pardoe looked a little preoccupied. "How did the girl seem?" he asked.

"So-so," said Salt. "Quiet like, not in the tear she was in when you talked to her."

"Well, she'll be home by now," the inspector rejoined, a satisfaction in his tone for which Salt could hardly account. He did not pursue the subject, however, but returned to the discovery of the tabloids in Jenny's room.

"Clear enough, isn't it?" he said. "There's nothing innocent she'd be keeping those for. And she was the one in the road the day the doctor missed 'em."

"But I thought you'd picked Emily Bullen for the murderer just now?" Pardoe's voice held mock surprise.

"And I'm not saying she didn't do it," was the retort. "Why shouldn't they both be in it?"

"Because it would be a remarkably far-fetched and pointless alliance," Pardoe replied. "If Jenny Hernshaw stole the morphia with the intention of killing the old lady and had every opportunity of administering it, as we know she did, why should it be necessary for her to run the risk of letting a second party into her plot? Especially one who must have been notoriously unable to keep her head."

"All right," said Salt. "Then either the Hernshaw girl did it or somebody's planted the stuff on her to make us think so."

"Well, think it over," was the inspector's answer.

At half-past seven that evening the storm which had shadowed the city and surrounding countryside all day broke with appalling violence. The sky had slowly deepened from the colour of soiled wool to a sulphurous grey and thence to ugly purple with fire-tipped clouds trailing the horizon, one full-bellied monster hanging above the centre of the town with what seemed conscious malice. From the first sly breeze preceding the first impact of thunder and crazy leap of lightning, through the surge and riot of contending wind and flogging rain that washed gardens into paths and paths into a mess of pebbles and sandy slush, to the last reluctant grumble of the clouds and rush of astonished gutters, less than an hour elapsed. But in that fifty minutes or so two elms, rooted on the river bank for sixty years, crashed in splintered wood, a man in drenched clothes urging his horses and hay under cover died a few seconds after being struck, a bullock was killed, St. Michael's vane was struck, and eight houses in River Street received a wash of water six inches deep on their ground floors.

More than this, Murder, his work achieved, drove back with the blue light flickering in ceaseless play round the radiator of his car, the solid sweep of the rain trying, it seemed, to build a wall between him and his security; while wind and weather obliterating his retreat raged unheeded round the body of his victim.

Chapter XIII

APPEARANCE AND DISAPPEARANCE

They have their exits and their entrances.

As You Like It

The air that night had an unaccustomed sweetness. To the jaded lungs of Minsterbridge it was like a miracle. An extraordinary stillness too, that was unlike the earlier menace, had succeeded the storm's artillery, so that the voices of sheep from distant pastures bleated timid relief and there was rare music in the splash from leaf to leaf of slowly gathered raindrops and the low chime of trickling water.

In the morning the freshness was fortified by the sun's brave glitter on wet earth and foliage of a greenness unexpected at the close of July. Pardoe's spirits rose with the general sparkle around him. At breakfast with Salt he felt as if tangles were being loosened, contradictions dissolved, and success waiting at the next turn. News of it seemed to ring in the clop of a pony's hoof in the courtyard outside, in the tuneless wholehearted whistling of one of the hands engaged in washing down a car, and not least in the honest smell of the fried rasher he was just finishing and the sergeant's familiar sturdiness sitting opposite.

He was just about to pour himself a third cup of tea and make a remark to Salt about the thoughts that had been ripening in his mind since waking, when a tap at the door interrupted him. It was the landlord with the message that the superintendent was on the phone asking for Inspector Pardoe. Pardoe got up and went out into the little hall, leaving Salt to munch his toast and speculate on what the local police could have got.

He was back in little more than a minute. Before he spoke the sergeant knew that something had happened to please him.

"Come on," he said crisply. "We're going to the station. Littlejohn's got a fellow there says he's the chap Carnowski met coming from Lacklands that night. Won't say anything except to 'Scotland Yard.' So Scotland Yard it is."

At the police station Littlejohn greeted them, mildly inclined to credit himself with the responsibility of bringing the unknown to book. He took them into his office where, standing by the window but closely watching the door, was the man who claimed to be the lurking stranger.

He was a middle-aged individual rather above the average height but looking shorter because of the slightness of his build. His face was clearly defined as to jaw and cheekbones, the eyes bright and hard under short, bushy brows, the hair growing close to his head in harsh grey curls. There was about him a decayed handsomeness that seemed never to have reached its prime, and the shabby breeches he wore with a yellow pullover gave him a horsey air that was somehow spurious. A Homburg hat lay in the chair beside him.

Pardoe came forward and met his gaze.

"I'm Inspector Pardoe of New Scotland Yard," he said. "I understand you've something to tell me. What's your name?"

The man was regarding him with a jaunty inquisitiveness.

"Well," he began in a husky voice that must once have been of singular power, "I knew the Yard was in charge of this inquiry and when I found out there'd been talk about me I came along here. But I wasn't giving anything away to the police in this city. I'd rather deal direct if you get my meaning."

He spoke with a cultured accent which belied the flashiness of his appearance.

"What is your name?"

"I'm Will Hernshaw," said the stranger, with the conscious air of having given his listeners something to think about. "Jenny's father, y'know. I was at my Peckham digs over the weekend, and only heard this morning you were looking for me. So having nothing to hide I came along."

"Who told you we wanted to see you?" Pardoe asked a trifle sharply. He had not expected this development, and judging by Salt's grunt behind him and Littlejohn's expression neither had his companions.

Hernshaw gave him a dubious glance, a hint of craft in it.

"Is that likely to get my informant into trouble?" he asked.

Littlejohn shot an amused glance at the inspector.

"Well," Pardoe countered, "since it's brought you to us we needn't look for trouble in that direction, I think. I suppose it was Miss Hernshaw?"

"Right," said Hernshaw easily. In spite of a certain wariness in his pose he did not show any real discomposure. "Get this clear. I've been seeing my daughter off and on this summer without the old woman's knowledge. She wouldn't have had me set foot in the house, and I swear I've not clapped an eye on her any of the times I saw Jenny. When I left last Wednesday night as far as I knew everything was the same in the house as it had been all along, and the first I heard of the old woman's death was Friday when I got a letter from Jenny advising me not to come again till she let me know."

"Why did you think she did that?" Pardoe asked.

"Well, I suppose with the inquest and all the rest of it, and police making free with the place, she thought I'd be one too many. Anyway you could have knocked me down with a feather when I heard there was to be an inquest on the old dame. Barking up the wrong tree, aren't you, seeing how long she's been laid up?"

For answer Pardoe jerked his head in the direction of the chair near Hernshaw.

"Better sit down," he said. "There's a lot you can tell me."

As Hernshaw complied he himself took one of the small office chairs, while the superintendent sat down at his desk and Salt with ponderous caution perched on the table edge.

"You can tell me," Pardoe continued, "why you've lately made yourself known to your daughter after years of absence, and what you've been doing between now and the time her grandfather adopted her."

Hernshaw did not attempt to hide his surprise at this intimacy with family affairs. Pardoe judged that there was a simple streak in the man which enabled him to live composedly enough in the present while disregarding past and future alike and never troubling to probe beneath the surface of things. It obviously had not occurred to him that Jenny's affairs were public matter by now. His astonishment, however, did something to mitigate a slight aggressive quality in his manner roused by the inspector's questions. After one or two false starts he seemed to accept the fact that the police were in possession of too much to make prevarication worthwhile, and launched out on the usual wastrel's story of repudiated responsibilities—repudiated, that is, until renewed contact with his family appeared likely to be profitable.

He admitted that until about two months ago he had not seen Jenny since 1916 when her mother had died and her grandfather adopted her. In reply to Pardoe's question as to the legality of the adoption Hernshaw said that John Lackland had insisted upon "a lot of red tape," ensuring complete surrender of parental rights and control, and implied that as far as he was concerned such insistence was superfluous. He had plainly not wanted his regained bachelor freedom burdened with the responsibility of a child. To do him justice he did not try to whitewash his abandonment of Jenny by pretending that the material blessings offered her by adoption justified his giving her up. On the contrary, he said old Lackland was a devil, only surpassed in devilry by the old woman who fortunately for everybody concerned had just come to her end.

Hernshaw himself for the past twenty years had had a knockabout existence entirely in harmony with a temperament which coveted the solidity a settled job would give only to relinquish it as soon as got. A sort of meretricious pride, it seemed, had got in the way of his hanging on to his theatrical work, even if he had been able to, in face of the continual drift to the army of men of his own age. Less than a month after giving Jenny up he was wearing khaki, and for the rest of the war was in action at one or other of the fronts, escaping both illness and battle scars with the proverbial luck of the carefree. The first years after demobilization had found him in Australia, beginning a series of jobs, finishing none. He returned home, working his passage back, only when it became clear that his welcome in a land to which he did not propose to contribute anything of value was wearing a little thin.

In England the increasing menace of unemployment had held few terrors for him. He never wooed work, and in the perverse nature of things work of sorts pursued him. He managed without much difficulty to renew acquaintance with his old calling, and played for some years with third-class repertory and provincial companies.

All this time he made no attempt to concern himself with Lackland affairs. It was only in the last year or so when he had found himself in London in receipt of a depressing wage from a more than usually unstable venture that he thought of his rich relations. The thought nagged at him—Jenny, a young woman now, perhaps an heiress, and his own child. The upshot was he made tentative inquiries which not only located the family but brought him news of old Lackland's death some years previously. After an unannounced visit to Minsterbridge in the spring, where he picked up some idea of the character of Mrs. Lackland and the impregnability of her fortress, he wrote carefully to Jenny, a course he regretted immediately afterwards for fear the old lady censored all letters. By then, however, though he did not know it, she was ill, and within a week Jenny had replied, a brief noncommittal letter explaining the impossibility of his coming to Lackland and the difficulties which lay in the way of her going to him. He was prepared to lie low for a while in the hope that it was the old lady's last illness, and was therefore agreeably surprised a few weeks later to receive a note from his daughter suggesting a meeting at his lodgings in a day or two.

"But after the first visit she wasn't able to come again for a long time. The old woman got worse and had to have all the attention. So I didn't bother 'em," he added virtuously, "except to get Jenny to keep me posted with news of her grandma."

There was something, Pardoe thought, vulturish in the implication that he had waited on the death so patiently. The inspector had a sudden uncomfortable picture of a household racked with anxieties they could not get rid of, with hopes they dared not encourage, and hovering in the background Hernshaw avid for whatever personal gain might result at the end. The thought made his voice sharp when he addressed the actor.

"What made you come to Minsterbridge in these circumstances? You knew it was against your daughter's wish."

"I had to find out how things were," Hernshaw said. "Once or twice lately, this month, I mean, Jenny's been able to slip over to Peckham again for an hour or two. Both times she told me the old woman was pretty nearly well again, and insisted on me staying where I was. But I felt I ought to be on the spot to see for myself."

"In other words," said Pardoe coldly, "you were not going to take your daughter's word for it."

"Oh, it wasn't that," the other replied airily, and added in a manner which swept away in one moment the twenty years he had not allowed the image of Jenny to invade his mind, "After all, she is my child, and it was up to me to see that she got a square deal."

There was clearly no answer to this.

"What was the last occasion Miss Hernshaw came to London to see you?" Pardoe asked.

Hernshaw's eyes grew rounder. "Don't mean to say you don't know? Gosh, I thought you had everything at your fingertips by now. Well, it was last Tuesday, the day before I followed her to Minsterbridge. I saw her in the evening and she went back on a late train. The other girl knew about it and was to let her in."

"I see. What time did you get to Lacklands on Wednesday?"

Hernshaw looked quickly from one to another with the first sign of perturbation he had shown.

"Here, what're you getting at? Think it was me bumped the old dame off? Well, I never set foot in the house then or any other time. I got to town just before seven. Evening was the safest time, because even if she was well enough to be up she'd have gone back to bed by then. I walked up from the station, hung about the town a bit, and was at the house soon after the hour struck. But would they let me in? A butler fellow answered the door and when I said I wanted to see Miss Hernshaw, said Miss Hernshaw could see nobody. I wasn't going to hand over my name, so I told him to say the man from Peckham had called, but the flunky shut the door in my face."

"Hardly surprising," said Pardoe, and Salt chuckled. "When you left the house d'you remember seeing anybody coming up to it?"

"Yes," Hernshaw said promptly. "A tall chap was coming up the path. He went on round to the back of the house."

He looked questioningly at the inspector, but receiving no enlightenment went on: "Funny thing, but I nearly ran into him again hours later. I went to the flicks most of the evening, then back to the house at ten o'clock. I thought there might be a chance of seeing Jenny then. But no sooner was I back by the gate than this same fellow came out and looked hard at me. So I cleared off in case he was going to watch."

"That's all right," Pardoe said briefly. "We know about him. So you didn't go back to Lacklands that night?"

"No. I couldn't. There wasn't time after that. What are you going to do about it now? Because I'd like to see my daughter if there's no objection."

"None, of course. But I'd prefer her to see you here before you leave," Pardoe answered.

He felt there was the chance Hernshaw was bluffing, though he did not really think so. But suppose Jenny had never seen him since his first communication with her, had always contrived to keep him at arm's length, and that last week's visit was merely another attempt on his part to achieve his purpose of talking to her? If so Pardoe determined to call his bluff by confronting him with the girl. He turned to Littlejohn.

"Will you put a call through, Superintendent? Ask Miss Hernshaw to be good enough to call here, as we have some news for her."

Though Hernshaw did not look pleased about it, he made no direct protest, but was careful nevertheless to watch while the superintendent lifted the receiver as if he feared some trap was being prepared for him. He fell silent, nor did Pardoe or Salt speak.

"Hello," Littlejohn was saying, "this is the superintendent speaking from the police station. Is Miss Hernshaw in? Please say I would like to speak to her immediately... Hello... Miss Hernshaw, I'd be glad if you'd come round here as soon as you can. I have some news for you... What?... Hold on a minute, please... The housemaid? Well, come as quickly as you can. The inspector is here."

Littlejohn replaced the receiver and getting up turned to Pardoe and Salt, who had been listening eagerly.

"Miss Hernshaw says they had a call from Bullham police station this morning to say that Hetty Park didn't arrive home last night."

Salt gave a low whistle and shot a look at the chief. The effect on Pardoe was startling. A mask seemed suddenly to have dropped over his face, his eyes were bright and grim and he struck his palm sharply with his fist.

"Damn," he said softly.

Littlejohn looked bewildered.

"What's this?" he asked. "Was the girl to go home then?"

Pardoe made no reply. He looked plunged in unpleasant thought. Hernshaw was for the moment forgotten. It was Salt who answered the superintendent.

"She got the sack," he said briefly. "She left on the evening bus yesterday. I saw her go."

Pardoe interrupted: "Miss Hernshaw on her way, Superintendent?"

"She said she was coming directly," was Littlejohn's reply.

Chapter XIV

POSTSCRIPT

Best open the writing and see what it doth speak.

Nicholas Udall: *Ralph Roister Doister*

Jenny Hernshaw arrived little more than ten minutes after-wards. When she came in Pardoe thought that he would hardly have recognized her as the girl of a couple of days earlier. Smart semi-mourning admirably setting off the grace and decision of her carriage had replaced the shabby frocks of a short time ago, and makeup applied with discretion had given a new confidence to her features. That this was merely superficial, however, was apparent at first glance. Jenny was plainly wrought up to a tension requiring all the control she possessed to keep from snapping.

As soon as she was in the room her glance fell on Hernshaw. Her breath caught audibly. She flushed brightly, then as suddenly whitened.

"What are you doing here, Father?" Her voice was sharp. "You know I said—"

She checked, aware of her listeners. Before Hernshaw, who was grinning sheepishly, could make a remark, Pardoe interposed quickly, at the same time putting forward a chair.

"Please sit down, Miss Hernshaw. Your father came here to give voluntary evidence of his identity and of his movements on the night of Mrs. Lackland's death."

He looked at her keenly. "You will remember Mr. Carnowski met him that night."

Jenny gave him a steady look as she sat down, and said with a defiance bred of uneasiness: "You told me Mr. Carnowski had said he met someone. Mr. Carnowski didn't mention it to me, so how was I to know who it might be?"

"Of course you couldn't," Pardoe agreed. "That is why you thought Mr. Carnowski had made up the story to supply us with a murderer, wasn't it?"

Jenny's colour rose. She moved her hands slightly in a resigned gesture.

"Yes—I thought—no," she murmured incoherently. "I don't really know now what I thought."

Hernshaw was looking both puzzled and resentful. He had not quite grasped the inspector's reference to a murderer just now, but it seemed to be connected with himself and he didn't like it. Jenny's discomfort, with which he was too selfish to feel any sympathy, communicated itself to him.

"Look here—" he began, but Pardoe interrupted him.

"You will be able to talk with Miss Hernshaw afterwards," he said in a tone of finality. "For the present your own affairs are not under discussion. I want to go into an entirely different matter. So there's nothing more to keep you now."

Pardoe was sure he detected a look of relief on Jenny's face. Hernshaw still appeared doubtful, but evidently concluding that no particular treachery could be perpetrated behind his back prepared to go.

"You might leave us the address of your lodgings," Pardoe observed pleasantly, "and it would oblige me if I knew we could easily get into touch with you until we've cleared things up."

Hernshaw voiced no demur, but scribbled his address on a slip of paper with a mute acquiescence that had about it little of the jauntiness with which he had opened his passage with the police. He had found things of a sterner significance than he had supposed. As Salt took the paper from him, Jenny addressed Pardoe.

"Would there be any objection to my father having lunch with us?" she asked composedly.

"None," Pardoe answered. "Mr. Hernshaw is perfectly free to go where he likes. It's merely a question of finding him quickly if we need to, just as we might need to get into touch with anyone concerned in the case."

"I'm not concerned," said Hernshaw sulkily.

"By relationship with Miss Hernshaw at least," was Pardoe's equable reply before Jenny cut in.

"It's all right, Father. If you want to grumble about your luck now you should have done as I said, stayed away from Minsterbridge. Be round to lunch at one. I'll talk to you then." She nodded a curt dismissal.

Hernshaw departed, waving a hand to Jenny and to the inspector, tossing a "None of that third-degree business, mind!" in Parthian valediction. As he went Salt seated himself quietly at the table and pulled out his notes. Littlejohn was sitting at his desk, slewed round to where Pardoe stood looking down at Jenny.

"Now about Hetty Park," the inspector said directly in a quiet voice. "Please tell me exactly what the Bullham police had to say this morning."

Jenny told him. The call had come through while they were at breakfast, about eight-forty, she thought. Carol had taken it. The village police sergeant had said that Mrs. Park had come to the station that morning with the complaint that her daughter, whom she'd expected on the seven o'clock bus the night before, had not been home. She had had no message from her to say that she was not coming. The police station therefore wanted to know if the girl had left Lacklands and at what time.

"I couldn't have told them," Jenny said, "because I was out yesterday evening, and had left the house before Hetty. But both Carol and Mrs. Beadle knew when she went."

"Where did you go?" Pardoe asked.

"For a spin in the car. Nowhere in particular. I felt I couldn't breathe yesterday, and after tea I decided to try to drive out of the heat somewhere into the country. I went Cosset way and through Little Minster. Surely it was cooler somewhere, I thought. It was— for I ran slap into the storm on my way back. That was terrifying."

"So I should think," Pardoe answered. "Well, it will be easy to find out whether Hetty actually took the bus. You saw her waiting for it, didn't you, Salt, but not on it?"

The sergeant was tapping his pencil against his teeth, a rueful expression on his face.

"That's right. I left her before it came."

"Bullham station's probably sounding the bus people about it," Pardoe said. "I'll want to see Miss Quentin as soon as possible, so will be at Lacklands soon after you, Miss Hernshaw, if you'd like to return now. And, Superintendent," he added, as Jenny rose, "you might put a call through to Bullham and explain I'm in charge of affairs at Lacklands and can handle the business that end if it's O.K."

It was certainly O.K. with Bullham, disposed to account the whereabouts of Hetty Park of minor importance until it received the Minsterbridge call. A laconic exchange of civilities with the office of the Minsterbridge and District Omnibus Company had elicited the information that the driver and conductor of the evening bus the girl was alleged to have taken were at present out, but due back at the head office at ten minutes past twelve. The sergeant at Bullham, sole representative of the law in that village, had intended, he said, notifying the city station of the matter so that inquiry might be made at the bus office without delay. The superintendent suspected that the good sergeant had minimized Mrs. Park's anxiety and the necessity for finding Hetty speedily, and that it was taking him some little time to realize Scotland Yard's interest in the case.

Pardoe consulted his watch. "No good going to the office for another hour and more. We'll get hold of something first round at the house."

At Lacklands Hennessy admitted them into the morning room where Littlejohn and Vale had waited the day of the death. As they passed across the hall the sound of voices raised above their normal pitch reached them from the sitting room, then abruptly stopped; but not before Pardoe had recognized the doctor's as one of them.

A few moments after the butler had left them, Carol, very soignée in a black frock the cut of which seemed to mock its own gravity, came in. Pink patches glowed in her cheeks and a certain hurry of movement and glance was contrary to her usual poise.

"Please sit down," she began quickly, herself taking a chair by the open window. "My cousin says you want to ask me about Hetty. I'm afraid there's very little I can say to help you. Nothing, in fact, except that she left the house with her case at half-past five."

"She was alone when she left?" Pardoe asked quickly.

"Quite. I had offered for Francis, the chauffeur, who hadn't gone home then, to carry her case to the bus corner. But she refused, and I admit I was feeling rather too sore with Hetty to urge it. So she went, and I can't tell you anything of her later movements."

She sounded a trifle snappy, but Pardoe affected not to notice.

"That was after Miss Hernshaw had gone out?" he said.

Salt caught a meditative glance from Carol to the inspector.

"Why, yes," she said after a momentary hesitation, "it was. I remember now. Jenny felt nervy, had a headache. The heat was awful. She took the car out about five."

She seemed as if she would have said more, but remained silent, her gaze fixed upon Pardoe with almost fascinated expectancy.

"Yes," he said mildly, without any indication that he attached importance to what she had said. "Well, we will presume Hetty left St. Michael's Square on the bus. Do you know, Miss Quentin, whether or not it goes right into Bullham village?"

Carol shook her head. "I've no idea. I've never been to Bullham on the bus. But surely it would go as far, else Hetty would have had to walk and she'd hardly do that with a heavy case to carry."

"I wasn't meaning she'd have to walk," the inspector explained. "One sometimes has to change country buses before reaching a destination. But we'll soon know that. What I'd like you to tell me, Miss Quentin, is whether the girl left here as depressed as she's been these past days, and if you know the cause of that depression."

Carol met his eyes steadily. "About the first question," she said, "no, I don't think she was nearly so miserable yesterday as she had been. She wasn't exactly cheerful, perhaps, but by what Beadle said and from the few occasions I actually saw her she was impatiently looking forward to going in the evening."

She paused, but as Pardoe made no reply, went on quickly: "As for why she was so depressed I can give you my own opinion, which satisfies me, but as it's only conjecture—" She shrugged indifferently. "Well, it's obviously ridiculous to suppose that Hetty could be at all upset by Grandma's death. She had less to do with her than anybody else, and was always timid and uneasy in her presence. No, I'm sure all the fuss she made was entirely on account of her young man, a quarrel or something of that sort. He's a farm labourer near her home. Hetty told me once that he was very run after, though she laughed about it then."

"Rather a coincidence, wasn't it," Pardoe asked dryly, "for a quarrel with her young man to upset her so badly just at the time Mrs. Lackland died?"

"No, not really. There were often tiffs. Besides, it would be only natural if the strain we'd all been through had its effect on her when she was bothered with her own affairs. But frankly," Carol added, the irritation she had shown all through suddenly mastering her, "I'm too tired of Hetty and her woes to find any discussion of them interesting. I was very glad to see her go, but even now it seems that she must leave trouble behind. But I expect in the end you'll find that she's eloped with George—or with somebody else." She laughed with a carelessness that did not ring true.

"We will hope for so simple a solution," said Pardoe gravely as he rose to go. Salt stood up too, when Carol checked them with a hasty gesture as she got to her feet.

"I'd almost forgotten. Don't go for a minute, please. Dr. Faithful is here and wants particularly to see you, Inspector. He had another anonymous letter this morning. I'll bring him to you now."

Pardoe who had been wearing a preoccupied expression looked suddenly alert.

"*Another?*" he echoed with an emphasis that struck Salt as peculiar. "Yes, I'll see him now."

Carol favoured them with a smile as she went out. Directly the door had closed Salt turned eagerly to the inspector.

"Seems like this might get us somewhere. That George may be the goods."

The inspector shot him a bright glance but said nothing, and Salt knew that his mind was engaged with an entirely different train of thought.

The door opened and Dr. Faithful came in. He looked a little more tired than when Pardoe had last seen him, and was wearing a faintly disgusted expression though he bore himself with the same easy domination. Pardoe lifted his brows inquiringly and waited for the doctor to speak.

As Faithful came up to the two men he took from his pocket an envelope which he handed to Pardoe with an impassive countenance though a distasteful gesture.

"There's life still in my unknown correspondent, Inspector," he remarked lightly. "This came to enliven breakfast."

Pardoe turned the envelope over in his hands, then glanced sharply from contemplation of the vulgar capitals to the doctor's face.

"You've not opened it then?" he said.

Faithful shook his head. "No. I was inquisitive, I'll admit, but I thought you should do it yourself this time."

Without answering the inspector took a penknife from his pocket and neatly slit the envelope, which was white and of the same manufacture as the last the doctor had received. The paper when he pulled it out was a page torn roughly from a cheap exercise book.

Across the middle, regardless of the lines, the scribe had written in his unattractive block lettering:

> *How are you going to get out of it?*
> *P.S. Why not look for the thief who stole the morphine tablets?*

The three men bent over the message together. Salt muttered the words half audibly, while the doctor, apparently the first to digest them, watched Pardoe to note his reactions. The inspector appeared to be staring at the words rather than reading them. For a few seconds before he raised his head his eyelids were motionless. Then he looked squarely at Faithful and smiled.

"We may be getting somewhere at last, Doctor," he said quietly.

The doctor's grim expression changed to something almost eager.

"This gives you a clue?" he queried with the first touch of boyish excitement Pardoe had seen in him.

"We won't commit ourselves at the moment," was the inspector's half-jocular reply, "but yes, I'm bound to say this tells me something. It may be that the writer has gone a little too far at last. I can't say more at the moment but I'll take this letter and attend to it as soon as ever we've cleared up the matter of the girl's disappearance."

"You mean Hetty?" said the doctor, as Pardoe deftly returned the letter to its envelope and slipped it into an inner pocket. "Carol was telling me about it just now. Is it really a matter for the police? The girl is a giddy little thing, you know, and with her young fellow so handy in the locality—"

"Yes, of course," Pardoe interrupted him with rare brusquerie, "and we'll hope this is the usual mare's nest. But investigations are being made, so, if you'll excuse me, Doctor, I'll be off." A slight smile came to his lips. "And somewhat cheered too by our correspondent's latest evidence of thoughtfulness."

Dr. Faithful laughed shortly, but it struck Salt that he was not too pleased at the summary curtailment of his suggestions about

Hetty. They left the room together, and in the passage encountered Carol who appeared to Pardoe to be hanging about in the hope of intercepting somebody.

As the doctor passed her he asked casually: "Is Jenny in?"

"Yes, she's upstairs, I think. Do you want her?" was the reply.

Faithful shook his head and, lifting a hand in general farewell, left the house.

Carol glanced inquiringly at the inspector. She looked very pale and uneasy, he thought.

"We're just going, Miss Quentin," he assured her, "and when next I see you I hope some definite advance will have been made. The most pressing job at the moment is to follow up this business of Hetty Park. And about that, there's one point on which you could materially assist me. Was Mrs. Lackland aware of Hetty's misbehaviour in listening at doors?"

Carol shook her head. "Oh no. We didn't bother her with that. The row likely to have been made wasn't worth it. Besides, the girl's worst eavesdropping—" She broke off abruptly and stared at the inspector. "But *why* all this silly fuss about a girl like that when there is so much else to attend to? I want to know, I tell you I want to know, who killed my grandmother, yet you find it necessary to sidetrack all the things that matter while you go hunting after a girl who's probably sitting at home this very minute laughing at you all!"

She sounded on the verge of hysteria. It's getting her down, thought Salt with a touch of compassion, for until now he had judged her the coolest member of this edgy household.

Pardoe's voice and look were steady.

"Believe me, Miss Quentin, I'm losing sight of nothing that matters. Hetty is part of the puzzle. And if, as you suggest, she's safe at home at the present moment, then we may congratulate ourselves that very little time's been lost in looking for her." He motioned Salt on and, with a nod to the silent girl, made his way out with the sergeant.

Chapter XV

HETTY

There was only one road through the wood.

Alice Through the Looking-Glass

The driver of the Bullham bus was an alert youth who took police interrogation in his stride without hesitation or confusion. His statement was to the effect that he clearly remembered Hetty as a passenger the previous evening. He was well acquainted with her and in the habit of conveying her regularly to Bullham on her half days. Yesterday she had caught the five-fifty bus from St. Michael's Square and was taken as far as the Three Herons, a public house near the crossroads three-quarters of a mile distant from Bullham village. That was the terminus of the evening bus serving Minsterbridge and District.

"What time do you reach the Three Herons?" Pardoe asked.

"At six thirty-eight," the driver replied. "And we were on time last night."

"Would any passenger alighting there and wanting to get to Bullham be obliged to walk the rest of the way then?"

"No, sir. In the ordinary way Hetty Park—Miss Park—would have walked, but she had a heavy suitcase yesterday and she said she should wait for the country bus that comes from Flaxby and stops at the Herons at five to seven before going on to Bullham." He pronounced it Blum.

Pardoe was plainly interested. "Then you left her standing there at the roadside?"

"Yes. We only wait a couple of minutes. We were gone by six-forty, and she was waiting on the grass verge then."

"Who else got down at the terminus?"

"Nobody, sir. She was the last in the bus. There was only a few passengers, and nobody else was going to Bullham."

This was corroborated by the conductor of the bus.

With the loan of Littlejohn's car and Sergeant Vale for his local knowledge, the Yard men were soon hurrying along the road the girl had taken the day before. It ran across undulating country flanked by open pasture most of the way, but as they approached the Three Herons, Pardoe noticed that the road dipped to the crossways, rising again on the Bullham side to a sharp height crowned with a thatch of dark trees.

They stopped the car at the crossroads and Pardoe, leaving his companions, slipped out to question the proprietor of the inn. He saw that this did not stand directly at the meeting of the roads but about fifty yards along the right-hand fork and opposite the road to Flaxby which, Vale had told him, was a small market town about nine miles away. It was apparent at a glance that Hetty would not have had to wait by the inn or even on that side of the road for the bus which would take her into Bullham, and if he was disappointed he was hardly surprised when the innkeeper was unable to give him any information. He was aware, of course, that the Minsterbridge bus had got in just before twenty to seven, he said, but he hadn't taken any notice of it yesterday evening nor seen anyone get down.

"If they was going on to Bullham, sir, and didn't want a drink, they wouldn't come over here at all, and you couldn't see 'em from the front, not unless you was trying. Anybody in the garden, now, they might see folk waiting. Depend where they was standing, for the field 'edges back there," he waved a hand behind him, "are pretty 'igh."

Pardoe nodded. "And I take it there wasn't anybody in the garden between half-past six and seven last night?"

The innkeeper shook his head despondently. He was feeling his importance dwindle at his inability to furnish an eyewitness.

There was nothing for it but go straight on to Bullham. Up the hill they drove, and some yards past the dark coppice turned sharp right and bowled along a high level stretch for half a mile and more, the road curving slightly all the way in the direction they had come.

The village was a narrow one, consisting of a single long street cresting the hill. A bleak spot in winter, Pardoe thought, eyeing the tops of the dark trees that crept up the right hand slope.

They called first at the police station, a modest brick house near the top of the street, where Sergeant Cowles received them with a mixture of awe and suppressed excitement. Bullham was looking up these days.

No, nothing had come out that would throw any light on the girl's disappearance. He had made inquiries among the villagers but not a soul had seen her that evening. His manner was stolid and unimpressive, but when Pardoe spoke of a phone call to Flaxby bus office he found that Cowles had already put it through.

"I reckoned she'd never have walked in from the Herons," he explained, "since she had some luggage, her mother said. So being at that time it would be the Flaxby bus. They put me on to the driver, but no luck. He didn't pick anybody up at the pub for Bullham, and there wasn't anybody standing there either when he came through."

"All right," said Pardoe. "I didn't expect it. And in a way it's luck, for this narrows the question by definitely limiting the time in which she disappeared. She was last seen at twenty to seven standing at the roadside, but when the second bus came in at five minutes to seven she was gone. What happened in that quarter of an hour?"

He looked thoughtfully from one man to another without actually seeing them. For a moment he was back in the sitting room at Lacklands with Hetty huddled in a chair in front of him. Then his voice and manner grew brisk.

"We must search for her," he said promptly. "Or for traces, at any rate. Salt, you go back to the Herons and make that a starting point. If Sergeant Vale cares to go with you take him along. But wait a minute."

He turned to Cowles.

"By the way, is there another cut to the village besides the road?"

"Oh yes." The sergeant waved a hand vaguely in the direction of the door. "Through the wood, you know. Corbies, they call it hereabouts. There's a path that comes out at a stile down the bottom end of the street, but—" He hesitated and looked doubtful.

"But you don't think it likely she came that way?" the inspector asked.

Sergeant Cowles shook his head. "Not if she was carrying a case. It's a thick part, plenty of growth there, and after the first bit uphill all the way."

Vale turned to Pardoe suddenly, his pale face flushing. "What about the storm? Mightn't—"

"Gosh," Cowles broke in, "and I never thought of it. She may've been struck among all them trees."

Pardoe and Salt exchanged a swift glance.

"What time did the storm break here?" Pardoe asked Cowles.

The sergeant thought. "It 'ud be about a quarter-past seven it was worst. Not later than that. But the first drops was falling some time before that."

"A bit sooner than we got it," Salt murmured.

"Work your way through the wood back to the village, Salt," the inspector said, "but start where she was last seen. When I've called on Mrs. Park I'll go through the wood from this end and join you unless I've heard from you first."

As Salt and Vale went out Pardoe turned to Sergeant Cowles.

"How far are Cosset and Little Minster from here?" he asked abruptly.

The sergeant looked surprised. "A goodish way. At least Little Minster's handy, I suppose, but the roads are bad. And Cosset's a tiny place about ten miles further on."

"So coming from Cosset to Minsterbridge by car you wouldn't be likely to run through Bullham?"

"Not you," said Cowles. "Secondary roads and a stiff pull, as well as a longer way round. No, you wouldn't touch on Bullham. Not unless you had business there," he added.

Pardoe made no reply. He was wondering if Jenny Hernshaw had had business there.

Cowles accompanied the inspector to Bryony Cottages where Mrs. Park lived. He explained that Hetty's mother was a widow. Park had been a thatcher at Corbies Farm and had died of some gastric trouble a year or so ago.

Mrs. Park opened the door to them so promptly that Pardoe had the idea she must have been watching for their arrival. She was a slender little woman, youngish though grey-haired, with features strongly reminiscent of her daughter's.

She took them into the living room, which was neat but dark and overstuffed. Thick clusters of a small yellowish rose at the window shut out some of the light. A little boy sitting at the table sucking a pencil, with a thumbed copybook in front of him, clambered off the chair when he caught sight of the sergeant's uniform.

"You go on with your job, Norman," Cowles reassured him, and turning to Mrs. Park introduced Pardoe to her.

"Please sit down," she said, indicating a little sofa under the window. She seated herself in a chair and patiently waited for something to be said.

Pardoe, struck with her steady bearing and relieved at it, explained the situation as it stood and told her briefly what inquiries had been made. He made no mention of the wood or the storm, but Mrs. Park herself touched on the one.

"Of course," she said, "when that awful tempest came last night I thought Hetty silly-like hadn't waited for the bus and must have been walking home, and then when the rain started went back to the Herons, perhaps to shelter. It was only when I found she hadn't done that I began to worry, and then I thought she might have been kept unexpectedly at Mrs. Lackland's."

"Naturally," said Pardoe. "But if she'd walked home wouldn't you have expected her to be nearer her own home than to the inn when the storm broke?"

"Well, she had her case to carry," Mrs. Park replied, "and she might have——" Her voice faltered, then she went on: "She might have stopped talking at first."

"Yes," Pardoe agreed. "And that brings me to the question of Hetty's friends. Isn't there a young man in the village she has been very friendly with?"

Mrs. Park flushed. "You mean George Coster, I suppose. Well, they were friendly, but it didn't go very deep. They went to the same dances. You know what boys and girls are like."

"I know," said Pardoe. "And George Coster—he works on a farm nearby?"

"Oh yes," she answered. "At Corbie, where my husband used to be. But George wouldn't know nothing about Hetty last night. He'd be at work at that time, and the farm's in the hollow right the other side the wood. He didn't know she was to have come home last night."

"All right, Mrs. Park," Pardoe said. Watching her closely he thought her more agitated than a few minutes ago. He changed the subject. "When did you last see Hetty?"

"More than a week ago. On her last Monday half day. That was before Mrs. Lackland died."

"And what about letters? Has she written since?"

"Only once. That wasn't like Hetty either. She's always the one to send a card or two in the week. But I didn't bother about that, because I put it down to all the dreadful things as was happening at the house, and them being so busy."

"And when did the letter come?" Pardoe asked patiently.

"Last Saturday," she said, adding quickly: "I've got it now if you'd like to see it."

She went to a little sideboard, and from behind a pink and white jar holding some sprays of plush leaves took an envelope which she handed to the inspector.

Before Pardoe's fingers touched it he knew it was identical with those in which the anonymous letters had been posted. Nothing very significant in that, he reflected, since the manufacture and quality were of a type widely obtainable. He drew out the letter, which was undated, and read:

> *Lacklands,*
> *Minsterbridge.*

Dear Mum,

> *Thanks for the letter. We are in an awful fix here. I expect you heard the old lady has died. But it's worse than that, we have got the police here today. I can't write about it. I will tell you everything after. I have got the sack, so I shall be home soon I suppose then I will tell you. I can't write it. She would be sure to find out. I hope I shall be home soon. Sorry the Lockes have measles. Mind Norman don't get it. Look out for me soon and I will tell you everything. No more now.*

> *Love,*

> *Hetty.*

Pardoe rose, his face grave, and handed the letter to Sergeant Cowles, who had been casting a longing eye in its direction.

"I'll keep this for the time being, Mrs. Park," the inspector said. "It may help us. Have you any idea to whom Hetty was referring when she wrote, 'she would be sure to find out'?"

"No," Mrs. Park replied. "It couldn't be Mrs. Lackland, of course, because she was dead then. So I don't know which of the others, unless she means cook."

Before Pardoe could reply she went on agitatedly: "Oh, sir, you don't really think anything has happened to her, do you?"

Pardoe tried to infuse his tone with a confidence he did not feel. "Let's look forward to good news. Our men are making inquiries now, and directly anything is found out you shall be told."

They took leave of her and of Norman who, in defiance of established rule, mounted the sofa and flattened his nose on the window pane to watch their departure.

Pardoe asked Cowles to point out to him the stile which gave the village entry to the wood. He said he would go down that way and join Salt and Vale, and suggested that Cowles should return to the station to be on the spot should a telephone message from Littlejohn come through. The sergeant's inward reluctance to comply was somewhat modified by the thought that he would be the first to receive such a message.

Pardoe noticed that the wood was no thinner at the point where it met the road. The trees stopped abruptly near the stile, dark and silent, in sharp contrast to the open sunny road. Beyond the entrance to the wood the road bore to the right, climbing downhill and, Pardoe guessed, in the direction of Corbie Farm. He got over the stile and found himself on a narrow path that cut between ranks of motionless larches rising from a dank earth devoid of undergrowth. For some distance the path was fairly level and worn, but pretty soon it grew more precipitous with little outcroppings of stone ready to catch the toes of unheeding travellers and pitch them headlong. Firs began to give place to oak, beech and hazel, all densely grown and heavy with their summer foliage. Pardoe noticed evidence of the storm in the washed surface of the path in places and in the quantity of freshly fallen twigs, but there was little sign of moisture now, so thickly grown were the trees. The sky seemed completely excluded from this twilit world, and in this part of the wood at any rate no tracks between the trees were visible. There was only the path on which he walked, climbing downward all the way. He noticed how with the absence of light all air too seemed to have been sucked from the wood. There was no freshness, no motion. The undergrowth was rank and undisturbed, but the wood spurge and hart's tongue looked yellowed by the struggle towards the light they could never reach and the few foxgloves that still lingered near the path were frail and sickly.

The breathless, obscure nature of the place lent its dismal hue to the inspector's thoughts. He went over the bald phrases of Hetty's letter again. Was it his own foreboding merely that made him interpret them as he did? But Hetty had been afraid of something, of somebody. That was certain. She had presumably written this on Friday, and it was on Saturday he had talked to her for the first time and observed the state of collapse she was in. Who was "she," and what was it "she would—"?

Pardoe suddenly blinked as he came out into a clearing dotted only with scrub and saplings. To the left where the ground sloped steeply he could hear the tinkle of invisible water. The sun was shining from a placid sky. He had been walking at a good pace for more than five minutes and decided he ought now to be within hailing distance of Salt. He stopped and gave a short halloo.

Almost instantly a faint shout came up to him. They were still in the lower part of the wood then. He went on down the path, his senses suddenly quickened. The trees began to grow thicker again but not so closely as to prevent the sunlight filtering through, and here and there were little pathless glades massed with the foliage of last spring's bluebells.

A twig snapped. Then another. There was a gruff and rather breathless "Hallo!" and the sound of heavy footsteps. Before Pardoe could utter an answering shout Salt came in sight, negotiating with town-bred caution the stony gradients of the path. As soon as he caught sight of the inspector he pressed on, coming up with him in a few seconds.

"We've found her," he said, breathing heavily. "A minute ago. I was coming for you."

Pardoe knew there was no need for the look of interrogation he shot at Salt, nor for the headshake that answered him. Silently they turned right where the wood grew level and easier, and crossed a little open ride between young beeches. At the end of it and about a dozen yards from the path they had left, Vale was stooping over an indistinct shape on the grass. He stood up as they approached and stepped aside.

Hetty lay on her face, one arm outflung, the other doubled beneath her. Both fists were clenched tightly. Her legs were a little bent and her clothing appeared tidy, but the cotton frock she wore was saturated with the previous night's rain. A foot or so away lay her sodden hat and near it a crumpled raincoat, the lining uppermost. Next to these lay a suitcase on its side, the cheap fabric blackened by the rain. Her face was pressed to the earth and the soaked strands of her hair had been beaten around her cheeks.

"I haven't disturbed her," said Salt. "Vale found her. She's been strangled, I reckon."

He and Vale stood a little apart while Pardoe knelt carefully beside the dead girl and taking her by the shoulders turned her gently on her back. The front of her dress was quite dry. The cause of death was patent. Great livid marks showed dully on the sides of her throat, bruises that stood for the pressure of human fingers. Pardoe, with a shuddering memory of Hetty's blonde prettiness, spread a handkerchief over the pitiful staring features. Then he stood up and met Salt's gaze. His face had hardened into lines that made it almost expressionless, his voice was flat and unemotional when he spoke:

"You came down in the car, didn't you? Take it back to Bullham police station and put a call through to Littlejohn. Ambulance and police surgeon. Then join me here. Stay if you like, Vale."

Vale acquiesced readily. He was looking rather white and mutely excited. This was his first murder, and it was he who had stumbled upon the body while Salt was searching the far side of the path. He had never seen a Yard man at work and was eager to miss nothing.

"We didn't touch her case nor the clothes," he said, pointing to the hat and raincoat.

Pardoe nodded absently. He waved his hand towards the trees below them. "How far are we from the field behind the Three Herons?" he asked.

"Close to it," said Vale. "If you go back to the path you're not two minutes from the gate Sergeant Salt and I came in at."

Pardoe was rapidly scanning the ground that stretched between the dead girl and the path.

"You came along here by chance, didn't you?" he questioned Vale.

"We divided the wood between us. One to the left of the path, one to the right. So I came down the opening here because I thought it would be more likely if she'd been enticed away that it would be here instead of in a denser part."

"Yes. With grass as short and dry as this was before the storm even a struggle would leave few traces. But she may have been killed further off and brought here for concealment. The path is out of sight from this point."

"Yes," said Vale. Then he added tentatively: "But you'd think in that case whoever killed her would have hidden the body more securely. It's pretty open here and easy to find really, once you've started a search."

Pardoe looked at him thoughtfully. "That's a suggestive remark," he said, and stooped again over the body.

Vale saw him pick something from the frock close to the armpit. He drew near, and when Pardoe straightened himself saw that the inspector was holding what looked like a bit of dirty rag. It was a soiled thumbstall, bloodstained and very dirty but quite dry.

"I didn't see that," Vale said in an interested voice.

"No, it must have been underneath her," Pardoe replied, "and clung to the front of the dress when I moved the body. A filthy scrap. But it may hang a man all the same."

Chapter XVI

THREE VISITS

Here's company enough for me to prate to.

Ford: *The Lover's Melancholy*

"There's a short cut to the farm through the wood," Vale said more than two hours later when the Minsterbridge ambulance had come and gone and Pardoe, Salt and himself had finished a hasty meal at the Three Herons.

It was close on four o'clock. The Divisional Surgeon had made a cursory examination of the dead girl before her removal to Minsterbridge, and had given it as his definite opinion that death was due to strangulation, though a post-mortem would reveal whether drug or poison had been administered beforehand. He added cautiously that Hetty had probably died not more than twenty and not less than seventeen hours before the discovery of the body.

Inexactitude in this respect did not worry Pardoe. In this particular case there happened to be a helpful precision about times. While the doctor's ruling placed her death possibly as early as five-forty the previous evening, the inspector knew that, excluding the murderer, the last known persons to have seen her alive were the driver and conductor of the Minsterbridge bus, who had left her standing in the road at six-forty. The driver from Flaxby who had got in at five to seven had seen nobody on the road from the Three Herons as far as Bullham village. It was safe to assume, therefore, that Hetty was in the wood before seven o'clock, and that judging by the part in which her body was found must have been murdered very soon after she got there. Seventeen hours as a minimum gave eight-thirty as the latest possible time at which she could have been killed. But the storm's intervention had effectively disposed of that as the hour of the murder, even if there had been any other circumstance in its favour. Whether Hetty had been in the glade at the time or carried there dead, the deed had been done before it rained. The ground beneath her body had been quite dry, and only the exposed parts of her clothes wet. Even the knees of her stockings and where they covered the shins were as dry as if it had never rained. Cowles had said that the storm had broken over Bullham at seven-fifteen. The landlord of the Herons, when questioned again, agreed. These factors together, therefore, practically fixed the exact time of the murder, which must have been committed about seven o'clock, a few minutes before or a few minutes after.

The next thing to do was to find George Coster. Cowles had the unenviable job of breaking the news of Hetty's death to her mother, while Vale, who knew the farm though he was unacquainted with Coster, showed them the quickest route there.

Leaving the car at the Three Herons they retraced their steps by the field path, the same road as Hetty must have taken on her fatal walk. What inducements, Pardoe wondered, had persuaded her to leave the highway for the darkness of the wood and death? Inside the trees still bore their secretive, withdrawn air. Only the shadows had changed direction a little.

This time they bore to the right, across a scrubby clearing and down to a brook whose music Pardoe had heard in his descent of the wood a few hours ago. Before yesterday's rains it had been a discouraged trickle; now it chuckled past, swollen and brown. On the other side was a stile and beyond it a barley field lately mown. Before stepping across the stream, a mere gutter in width, the inspector noticed that the low bank between it and the stile had slipped, leaving a raw cavern where the earth had slid into the water. Effects of the storm perhaps; but equally well traces of a human being's passage after the murder was done.

Climbing the stile they walked down between the damp stooks of barley, and in a minute or so the farm came in sight, a pleasant huddle of white buildings flanked by ricks and byre with the road to Bullham twisting past. Nobody was in sight, but when they had gone through a gate into a grain-strewn yard where young turkeys and guinea fowl gobbled, a woman came out of a back door with a pail of scraps which she flung to the scrambling birds. She was of middle age, finely built and hard-featured, and Vale just had time to mutter to Pardoe that this was Mrs. Selby, the widow who farmed Corbie, when she advanced towards the three men and asked them their business.

When Pardoe had explained that they would like a word with George Coster: "What's he been doing now?" she flung at him sharply, more of resentment than curiosity in her voice.

"Nothing that we know of," Pardoe replied immediately in as casual a tone as he could muster, "but we think he can help us in an investigation we're making."

She looked at him with a touch of contempt. "I hope he may help you. It's more than he does me. He's not pulling his weight these days."

She turned her back on them squarely and flounced towards the house, tossing over her shoulder as she went: "You'll maybe find him in the stables round the corner."

Salt gave Pardoe a whimsical look as they moved towards some buildings on the right. Not over-inquisitive, he thought. A cheerful whistling was brought to an abrupt close as they came in sight of a red-faced boy vigorously washing down an elderly-looking Ford. At sight of them all power of speech seemed to desert him, for when Pardoe inquired for Coster he only jerked a thumb at the stables and went on staring.

No sound came from the yard, but as they crossed the straw-littered kidney stones out of sight of the gaping lad, and came round the corner of a stable, a man got up slowly from an upturned bucket and faced them.

The sun shining full upon him in the otherwise empty yard gave almost heroic proportions to his height and bearing. Pardoe judged him about twenty-five or twenty-six, noting the sulky handsome face and deeply bronzed skin. It was an uncommon type of good looks to find in a farmyard, a combined grace and virility that distinguished him from every other country labourer the inspector had met.

"Mr. Coster?" Pardoe inquired, and when the other had nodded warily: "I'd like a word with you about Miss Hetty Park. We are making inquiries into her failure to come home last night."

"Well, she's been murdered," was the bitter reply. "I thought you was the first to know it."

Sergeant Salt shot a glance at Vale. Direct action this, he was thinking, but Vale, judging it not to be his pigeon, had strolled a few yards off and was apparently deep in admiration of the stables.

"How did you know?" Pardoe asked.

Coster jerked his head in the direction from which they had come. "The kid came back from the village with it an hour ago. It's all over the place. You found her, didn't you?" he finished aggressively.

"Yes, we found her. Perhaps you also know how it was done?" There was a hard note in the inspector's voice.

Coster hesitated. "She was strangled, wasn't she? Gosh, who'd do it? Who'd want to do it?"

His voice had fallen a little quieter as if he were questioning himself.

"Who indeed?" Pardoe echoed sharply. "When did you last see her?" Then he added in a less insistent voice: "You're not obliged to answer my questions, of course, and I must warn you that anything you say may be used later in evidence. But if you've nothing to hide you will help yourself as much as help me by stating anything you know."

George Coster appeared to hear nothing but what he felt was the implication of the inspector's remarks.

"So you think I did it, I suppose?" he said savagely. "So you think it was me saw her last yesterday and killed her in Corbies? Well,

I didn't. Not that that would make you think any different. But p'raps this will. How d'you think I'd choke anybody with a hand this way?"

With a quick, defiant gesture he held out his left hand which had been hanging partially concealed at his side. The thumb was heavily dressed in clean bandages tied professionally at the wrist. Salt's face brightened, and Vale drew closer, but Pardoe though he looked at it with interest betrayed no surprise.

"How did you come by that, and when?" he asked.

"Last Thursday in the chaff-cutter," was the laconic reply. Presumably he thought he had established his innocence. There was a lazy triumph in his manner which Pardoe resented while touched by something naïf in the sudden cooling of Coster's indignation.

"Pretty bad, was it?" he asked.

Coster shrugged. "A nasty slice. I doctored it meself till Saturday. Then Mrs. Selby, she says I'm to go to the doctor. So I went in on Saturday night, and he dressed it up for me. But you can see I can't use it?"

"Where d'you mean you went? Isn't there a doctor in the village?" Pardoe asked.

"No. The nearest is at Flaxby. But it isn't so easy to get there and back latish, so I went to Minsterbridge, where there's a late bus Saturdays, and saw Dr. Faithful. I been to him other times."

Pardoe glanced down at the comparative cleanliness of the dressing. "Who bandaged it for you afterwards?"

"The doctor." He sounded sullen again.

"He saw it again then?"

Coster looked at him suspiciously. "What you getting at? Yes, he did, if it's anything to you. He was in Monday for the measles the kids in the village 've got, and he came and put it right again."

"What time of day was that?" the inspector, ignoring the man's belligerent air, wanted to know.

At that Coster flared up again. "Hell, you're some Nosey Parker, aren't you? Think you're checking me up all right?"

"Don't be a fool, Coster," the inspector said bluntly. "If I wanted to check up on you, as you put it, I could do it in a much less round-about way than getting at you through a doctor's visit. In any case Dr. Faithful will tell me."

"All right, all right," Coster said sulkily. "It was after tea."

Pardoe appeared to be paying little attention. His hand went suddenly to his pocket. He drew something out and held it for Coster to see. It was the soiled thumbstall.

"Know anything about this?" he asked casually.

Coster put his hand out curiously to touch the bit of rag, then drew it back quickly. He shifted a little with the uneasy movement of an animal that suspects a trap he cannot see.

"I don't know what it is," he answered slowly.

"I think you do," Pardoe returned stolidly. "You wore this at some time or another after you had injured your hand." He held up his own to check a fiery protest and added calmly: "Perhaps you will remember better when I tell you that this was found beneath Hetty Park's body where she lay murdered."

There was a momentary silence in which not a muscle of the group moved. Then both Salt and Vale made an involuntary step forward. They had thought Coster was going to strike the inspector. It was only a matter of seconds. The fury died out of the man's face, and with it the violence of the fear that had possessed him. He was frightened, but it was a fear inspired by bewilderment rather than indignation. He made as if to speak but no sound came.

"Come on," Pardoe urged patiently. "If you've nothing to hide you'll find the best thing you can do is to give me a straightforward account of when you wore this and when you left it off."

Though incoherences and interlarded protests marred Coster's explanation, the gist of it was plain. He had worn the original band-age applied on Saturday night by the doctor until Sunday evening, when finding that it impeded his work and was already much soiled he replaced it by an improvised stall that fitted closely and let him get on with his jobs more quickly. It was clear that he had in full measure the contempt for medical advice that is the associate of ignorance, and thought a lot of fuss had been made over a cut which because it had stopped bleeding had ceased to be important in his eyes.

"So you were wearing this when the doctor came Monday evening?" the inspector asked.

Coster cast a miserable glance at the rag and hesitated. "I don't know—I don't think so. It came off once or twice."

"You should remember if you were wearing it when Dr. Faithful called. He didn't approve of what you'd done, I suppose?"

Coster nodded. "That's right. Said I was a fool to play about with it. But it seemed pretty fair by then. And doctors 'ud say that anyway," he added tolerantly.

His natural optimism seemed to be reviving. But Salt observed how sickly his colour was and how constantly his eyes returned to the rag Pardoe was holding.

"Pretty fair, eh?" the inspector took him up. "But not good enough, in your own words, to choke anybody with?"

"I never done it, I tell you!" Coster clenched his right hand savagely. "I wasn't nowhere near the wood. I never went in the village last night. I—"

"Suppose you say exactly what you were doing between half-past six and seven last night?" Pardoe broke in.

Coster had no answer ready. After a minute he said he had been tedding in the lower hayfield. No, nobody had been with him.

Pardoe noticed that the field in question, though a good distance from Corbies, lay out of sight of the farmhouse and adjacent to the road which led into Bullham and on to the bus stop. Coster could have left the field for the road, met Hetty before the Flaxby bus got in, and returned to his work the longer way through wood and meadows after committing the murder. It was plain that he had no alibi for the hour at which the murderer had been active. Mrs.

Park's statement that he hadn't known Hetty was coming home yesterday evening might very well not agree with the facts. How was she to know whether or not they corresponded while the girl was in Minsterbridge?

"You knew, of course, that Hetty Park had left her situation and was returning home yesterday?" Pardoe watched Coster closely.

"That I didn't then," he returned promptly.

"Weren't you in the habit of seeing her the days she came home?"

"Yes. Sometimes," Coster added after an appreciable pause.

"Then as yesterday would have been her normal half day off didn't you wonder where she was in the afternoon?"

Coster flushed slightly. The sullen look came back to his face. "I didn't care. We'd had a tiff. I mean—" He caught himself up, but it was too late. "I mean I didn't see her every week. There was Saturday night dances we both went to, and Monday was a bit close. And I knew there was trouble about the old woman she worked for, so I didn't expect as 'ow she'd get time off this Monday."

The fixity of Coster's stare at the inspector suggested to Salt that he was trying desperately to cover up his first admission. Pardoe let him run down.

"So you quarrelled, eh?" he said smoothly. "When was this?"

Coster tried unsuccessfully to hedge. "Oh, it was nothing. A fair time ago," he said with assumed carelessness. "She was jealous about—about things. And 'twasn't as though we was engaged."

"Jealous of other girls?"

"That's about it." There was an over-eagerness of assent noticeable in the reply, but Pardoe did not pursue the matter.

"Well, that's all for now," he said quietly. "Just hang on here in case I shall want to see you again. By the way," he added more briskly, "aren't you rather short of men here?"

Coster looked so nonplussed that for the moment the inspector thought he had not understood the question.

"Understaffed on the farm, aren't you?" he repeated.

"Oh. Ah, I suppose we are." Coster flushed heavily. Feeling some explanation was due he added: "Some of 'em don't care for working for 'er. Drives 'em a bit. But they come and go."

There was a defiant edge to his voice that did not escape Pardoe, who thought that here at least was one who had not gone but had stayed on in a place that seemed an unlikely setting for his personality.

They left the farm by the road this time without seeing Mrs. Selby. At Bullham police station, Cowles, his face still wearing the shocked expression it had carried since he learned of the tragedy, said that a call had come through for Inspector Pardoe from Superintendent Littlejohn about a quarter of an hour ago to say that someone was waiting at the station with information possibly bearing on the girl's murder.

"Did he mention a name?" Pardoe asked quickly, a sudden anticipatory light in his eyes. This was quick work, but otherwise not more than he had expected.

Not at first. But, the sergeant added apologetically, on being asked who it was the superintendent had given a name that he, Cowles, had been quite unable to catch. Though Littlejohn had repeated it he still could not get hold of it, so the super had rung off and said it didn't matter.

Pardoe's own confidence that he knew who it was prompted him to supply the name himself, but he took up the receiver and asked for the Minsterbridge police. After a brief exchange of conversation he hung up and turned to the others, a crestfallen smile on his lips. Salt knew that whoever was waiting for the inspector in Minsterbridge it was not the person he had expected.

"Carnowski," he said noncommittally, and catching Cowles's eye added: "From Poland, Sergeant, so that's why it didn't come across well."

By the time they reached the Herons and got the car out it was close on five. With a clear road ahead they were in Minsterbridge inside a few minutes. In the superintendent's office Carnowski rose to greet the inspector. His mobile features were less controlled than the first time Pardoe had seen him and he began to speak at once, as if their entry was his cue.

"Inspector, I am glad to see you," he said. "Here is something I do not understand. It is funny when it happen, but it is more funny now that I know the girl is killed."

"Who told you a girl was killed?" Pardoe asked.

Littlejohn interposed. "Mr. Carnowski has already given me his story, Inspector, and I told him of the discovery at Corbies this afternoon." He gave Pardoe a shrewd look. "I think you'll find he has some evidence to offer that may be valuable."

Pardoe nodded. "Good. Please let me have it."

They sat down, and Carnowski, who was visibly excited, began his story again.

It appeared that until today he had not seen any of the inhabitants of Lacklands, except at the inquest, since the death of Mrs. Lackland. But each day he had exchanged brief and cautiously worded conversations with Jenny, until on Monday morning when he had seen her for a few moments after the inquest she had asked him not to ring her any more while the police were still in and out of the house. She gave no explanation of the request and seemed anxious to get away, so that he was very surprised when at teatime that day his telephone bell rang and a voice asked him urgently to drive to Bullham in the evening and meet Miss Hernshaw at the stile leading to Corbie Wood at seven o'clock. She had something very important to tell him. If she was not there he was to wait a quarter of an hour before returning home, as her absence would mean that she had found it impossible to leave Lacklands just then; but more harm than good would be done by his continuing his journey into Minsterbridge to see her, and on no account must he telephone to the house.

"Your caller refused to give a name?" the inspector asked.

"Yes. I mean he ring off when I ask."

"You say 'he.' It was a man then?"

Carnowski spread his hands in an eloquent gesture. "But I do not know. It was impossible to know. So far away it was, like an echo. Yet it seem anxious, in a hurry—how shall I say? But I was sure then it was not Miss Hernshaw."

"Why were you sure?"

"Because if it is she she would not keep her name hid. She would say, ''Ello, this is Jenny,' as always. And if she do not want others to hear her she would not have talked so long and said so much where to go and the time to wait. Besides," he added simply, "I know now that she know nothing about it."

"How do you know that?" Pardoe inquired.

"I see her just now. Before coming here. I tell her all that happen. She does not know any of it. There was nothing she want to tell me, no meeting she want to arrange. So I come to the police, because I wonder why somebody want me in Bullham just then. And now I learn a girl is killed."

Pardoe felt annoyed that Carnowski had taken what he knew really was the inevitable step of seeing Jenny before coming to the station. A sudden thought made him ask: "As it was from Superintendent Littlejohn you heard of Hetty Park's death, I presume Miss Hernshaw didn't speak of it to you?"

Carnowski looked surprised. "But no," he said coldly. "Neither of us know it, so naturally we do not speak of it."

Pardoe dismissed the matter, and began to question the actor about his vain journey to Bullham and back, labouring to arrive at some definite knowledge of precise times. Carnowski could help here. The call had come through, he noticed, at four-twenty. Though doubtful from the start of the bona fide nature of the message, he was much too anxious not to fail Jenny to take the risk of its being a hoax. So allowing for a margin each side the appointed hour he had arrived at the stile shortly before seven and had stayed till half-past. He would have stayed longer, in the hope that she might turn up after all, but by the time he started back to London the storm was raging, and he had no mind to sit through it by the side of the road. He had got back to his flat by a quarter to nine and had written a hasty note to Jenny in which, without going into any details, he had told her how long he had waited at Corbies and asked her to let him know whether she was all right. He was sure in his own mind, he said, that the whole thing was a hoax, but he had posted the letter to her in case it should have been genuine, and anyway he intended calling next day. He had at first thought that perhaps there was a plan to burgle his flat in his absence, as on Monday evenings his man was out, but he had found nothing wrong. Questioned further Carnowski admitted that though he had met and overtaken several cars on the London road quite close to the village, in Bullham itself he had seen nobody. It was already raining and a bad storm imminent when he reached the stile, so it was probable everybody was in shelter by then.

Pardoe, who did not draw his attention to it, thought that by the actor's tone he did not attach any importance to this lack of corroboration of his story. This indifference might mean innocence; on the other hand it could be the bluff of a guilt that was both subtle and bold. But if Carnowski had killed Hetty why had he been so prompt to announce his presence practically on the scene and at the hour of the murder? Part of the same bluff, perhaps. And it had to be remembered that the man was a consummate actor.

"Well, Mr. Carnowski," the inspector said, becoming conscious of the other's intent gaze, "you gave me your telephone number some days ago, and we'll see if we can trace yesterday afternoon's call. There's not much chance of doing so, though, as if it was a trap it's unlikely you were rung up from a traceable source. But I'd advise you to carry on as usual, and if anything turns up I'll let you know immediately."

Then, as the actor prepared to take his leave Pardoe checked him with a sudden question.

"When you were talking to Miss Hernshaw just now did she tell you why she had asked you not to telephone?"

Carnowski hesitated. Pardoe had the idea he was going to reply in the negative when he said slowly: "Miss Hernshaw have the thought her calls are known to the police. So she make no more."

He gave each of the men a cold, steady stare as he took courteous leave of them.

When he had gone Pardoe had a short talk with Littlejohn on the events of the afternoon. He asked the superintendent what he knew about George Coster.

Littlejohn pursed his lips, weighing his words carefully before speaking. A look of contempt came into his face.

"What with picture palaces and dances so handy, the country places aren't half what they used to be, and young fellers like that can soon get a bit above themselves. The girls would see to it that they did, anyhow. But we haven't got anything against him up to now. They do say that he and that Mrs. Selby he works for—" He paused and looked significantly at the inspector.

Pardoe grinned. "So Bullham's faithful, is it, to the traditions of village scandal? Well, who are we to say Bullham's wrong?"

The lightness of his tone only accentuated the look of strain on his face. The unconscious dread he had cherished for Hetty Park's welfare had solidified into hideous fact for which no remedy existed. That he believed it had brought in sight the goal of his work did nothing to arouse elation.

Before leaving the station he rang up Exchange to inquire about the call through to Carnowski at four-twenty the previous day. As he had surmised, he drew a blank. The unknown had evidently used a call-box. As he and Salt made their way back to the Swan and Ferry, Pardoe was occupied with thoughts of the work that lay ahead. He must see Dr. Faithful, who could help him in the final stages of it. Then in the morning too he would have to go to Lacklands. Now all that he wanted was a bath.

Even that was to be deferred, however. For when they got in, mine host met Pardoe with the news that a young lady, who had declined to give her name, was waiting in the sitting room to see him.

"And fair agitated she is too, sir. I told her you might not be in for a long time, but she wouldn't go away. Said it wouldn't be safe for her to go back. She's been there over the half-hour now."

Pardoe thought instantly of Jenny. Salt's first picture was of Carol; then he wondered if any man could be so polite as to describe Emily Bullen as a young lady.

It was none of these. When the inspector, followed by Salt, entered the quiet little room at the back, the tall figure that rose nervously from a chair by the table was at first sight unfamiliar to both in the comparatively dull light. But when she moved and spoke Pardoe saw that it was Edith Dawes.

The parlourmaid's usually neat appearance was marred by the alarm which evidently beset her. Composure had fled, and the natural sallow of her skin was faded to a sickly white. She was clutching a small leather shopping bag between her hands, supporting it on the table in front of her, and at sight of Pardoe the relief she obviously felt found vent in a rush of words.

"Oh, Inspector," she cried, while Salt closed the door carefully and stood near it, "it is true then? Hetty's been found dead! They told me in a shop this afternoon. None of us are safe—none of us! Oh, what shall I do? What can I do? I can't ever go back to the house!"

Pardoe, observing her dry lips and the whiteness of her knuckles, put a hand on her arm and spoke firmly.

"Now, Miss Dawes, sit down and pull yourself together. Going on like this will only make you feel worse about everything."

He sat lightly on the edge of the table when he had got her into the chair, and went on: "Yes, Hetty has been found. Dead, as you say. It's bad business, but there's no need for you to frighten yourself as you're doing. Tell me why you came to me."

The girl was breathing as if she had been running. Without raising her eyes she said hoarsely: "I'm frightened. They could kill me as they've killed her. And there's something I must tell you. I had it to tell you, only I was afraid to. But now I'm afraid not to."

"Then tell me," Pardoe said. "By the way, have you come straight here from Lacklands?"

Edith shook her head. "It was my afternoon off. I'd been home. I live here in Minsterbridge, you see."

Pardoe considered her for a minute, noticing how fear had skinned off the veneer of superiority she had worn. She caught his eye and a look of resolution tinged with pathetic dignity came into her face.

"I shall never go back to Lacklands," she said quietly, but with a tremor in her voice. "I don't know why Hetty was—was killed. But if Hetty, why not me? There were things I did that they could hold against me." Her voice sank to a whisper.

"What things?" Pardoe asked kindly.

"I didn't want to tell the police. Mrs. Lackland always said I could go to prison for it. I was afraid."

She lifted her chin and looked fiercely at Pardoe.

"But I don't care," she continued more rapidly. "It's worse now keeping quiet about it than telling." A dull red flush covered her face. "I took some things belonging to Mrs. Lackland. Last spring. Before she was ill. Miss Bullen found out and told Mrs. Lackland, and Mrs. Lackland said I was a thief and could be sent to prison and never have a job again, but she would look over it that once and keep me on. And so I stayed. But all the time, whenever there was anything that didn't please her, she kept hinting at jail and handing me over to the police. Then the old devil got ill, but there was still Miss Carol. Mrs. Lackland had told her all about it, and worse than what it was, I know, because she often said little things to let me know they had a hold over me."

Her voice was trembling, more, Pardoe felt, with hatred of her employers than distress at her own confession.

"What sort of things did you take?" the inspector asked gently.

"Money. A brooch, and a little trinket box. She never looked at them anyway. But she made me give them back. But there was something else she never knew I had." She gave a wintry smile as she recalled this empty victory over the dead woman.

"It wasn't any good to me, but I felt worse about handing it back than I had about returning the note and the jewellery. I waited and waited for her to say something, but she never did. She never missed it, I suppose. Then when she got ill I knew I was safe, so I didn't think any more about giving it back."

She plunged her hand with sudden feverish resolution into the bag she had been holding so closely, and took out a packet of letters loosely tied with tape. She held them out to Pardoe.

"They're no use to anybody," she said contemptuously, "but I was afraid to go on keeping them now. I'm afraid to have anything of theirs. Some man wrote them to Mrs. Lackland years ago. They're just love letters."

Salt who had drawn near and was eyeing the packet in the inspector's hand snorted audibly. Love letters. And they had just come from a murder. What did the girl think she was talking about?

Pardoe, however, was looking down unsmilingly at what he held.

"All right, Edith. I'll look after them—until I give them to the lawyer who has charge of Mrs. Lackland's estate."

Alarm sprang into the girl's eyes again. "You won't say anything about me?" she breathed.

"Not a word. And get it out of your head that any harm is coming to you. Because you lived a long time under a threat doesn't mean there was anything to it. You gave the things back, didn't you? Well, then. And now you've finished with it by handing these over to me."

Relief that was close to tears flooded Edith's face.

"Finished with it," Pardoe repeated firmly. "I'd advise you to go back to Lacklands, Edith, as though nothing had happened. Nothing will happen—to you. Go on with your ordinary work—"

He broke off as the girl got hastily to her feet. She caught his arm tightly in both her hands.

"I'm not going back!" she cried. "I'm never going back! I can't! I'm afraid even to go home this evening. What happened to Hetty will happen—"

"Be quiet," Pardoe said roughly. He took her by the arms and forced her back into the chair. She was sobbing tearlessly.

"Nothing's going to happen to you, I tell you. The sergeant here shall take you home. Will that do?"

She nodded, calmer, but still trembling.

"There's something else I had to tell you," she said more quietly. She shot a sudden look past Salt's substantial presence to the door, as if she expected to see somebody come in. "I remembered it afterwards."

"What?" the inspector asked.

"What I told the superintendent. There was something different about Mrs. Lackland's table when I took her tea up that last day. It all came back to me. But Miss Bullen asked me what the super had said and what I'd said, and when I told her she said it was silly to bother the police with such unimportant things, and anyway the more I kept out of their way the better for me considering my past. They would try to fasten something on me, she said. So when you asked me if I'd remembered, I was scared and pretended I didn't know what you were talking about."

"Yes?" Pardoe said, as she paused. "What was it you noticed was different?"

Her voice when she spoke was little more than a whisper. Pardoe had to bend to catch her words.

"The bottle. The bottle of medicine Mrs. Lackland was using that last day or two. It had a stained label. A long yellow stain down the side. I couldn't help noticing it every time. But when I took her tea up that day the bottle on the table had a clean label. There wasn't any stain at all."

Chapter XVII

A MURDERER STRIKES AGAIN

The right-valiant Banquo walk'd too late.

Macbeth

P ardoe went to bed that night tired enough to sleep, but sleep
did not come for a variety of reasons. After supper Salt and
he had gone through the letters Edith, in terror of sharing Hetty's
fate, had handed over to him. They were flaccid and slightly yellowed at the edges, and the dates they bore were all late in the
first decade of the century. As the girl had said, they were just
love letters, though in more than a few instances much warmer
than the common variety of their own or any other day. It was
probable that Edith had not looked further than the top ones. But
they interested Pardoe, for here and there the writer showed an
altogether unloverlike intimacy with Mrs. Lackland's worldly affairs.
Her financial condition had apparently been at times as near to
his heart as her betrayal of her husband. And that she had been
playing fast and loose with John Lackland's affections as late as
ten years after marriage these letters made clear. They were all
signed "Philip" and bore varying addresses, sometimes a London
club, sometimes a Hampstead address, occasionally a foreign hotel.
There were eighteen of them. The inspector did not imagine that
sentiment alone had preserved them. That must always have been
an ephemeral quality with Mrs. Lackland. Self-interest, most likely,
had been at the bottom of it. They might have constituted a pretty
effective weapon for the power she had undoubtedly wielded over
the unfortunate Philip. Pardoe resolved to show them to Rennie in

the morning. The solicitor was more likely than anyone else to be able to identify Mrs. Lackland's lover.

Meantime there was the important evidence Edith, after withholding it for days, had proffered about the medicine bottle. Important? It was revolutionary. It changed the whole face of the problem and disentangled apparent contradictions. Pardoe scarcely touched on it with Salt that night. He wanted to think about it in all its implications, and in the small hours when sleep eluded him the unrelated pieces of his puzzle revolved before his eyes and meekly fell into place.

Towards four he switched on the reading lamp beside his bed and took up the last of the anonymous letters received by Dr. Faithful. He read it carefully again. It had its part in the problem, greater than the writer had intended. When he turned the light out and lay back again on his pillow he had his case. There were still one or two pieces missing before a part that was conjecture became fact, but he would get those tomorrow. He had his case. He had his murderer. And a vile business it was.

Pardoe dressed early after sleeping a bare couple of hours. Nevertheless, he felt as refreshed as if he had slept the night through. The weariness of body and spirit that had assailed him yesterday with knowledge of Hetty Park's murder had given place to a new vigour. While he was not so foolish as to blame himself for the girl's death, he could not quell the memory of his own premonition the day he had questioned her. It stung him now to a ruthlessness of purpose that would have surprised anyone who had never probed beneath the inspector's comparatively mild exterior.

Today was Wednesday, the fifth day he had been on the case, and this would see the end of it. But there was much to be done first. He wanted to see Dr. Faithful, to show Rennie the letters, to put into execution a subsidiary plan he had thought of in the night and which he meant to outline to the doctor first. At breakfast he gave Salt a sketch of the day's earlier programme, though he forbore as yet to mention his ideas for later on, and before nine o'clock was putting a call through to Lacklands. Carol answered him and received his brief instructions. Then there was Carnowski to be rung up. Pardoe was not sure he would find the actor at home at that hour. He was there, however, his lazy voice with the faintest intonation of surprise in it suggesting that he was still in bed.

That settled, the next move was to see Faithful. But he was spared that call for just as he was preparing to leave, while Salt remained at the Swan and Ferry to take any message that might come in connection with the post-mortem on Hetty, the doctor himself turned up and was shown into the sitting room.

"I was coming to see you," Pardoe said, pushing forward a chair.

"I thought you would be," was the doctor's reply, "and as I start on my rounds at ten it occurred to me I may as well go a bit earlier and see you first. As you must know by now, I haven't the ghost of an alibi for yesterday evening."

His final remark was made with an abruptness that invited quick response. But instead of answering immediately Pardoe looked at him contemplatively, observing how harsh the lines of his face had become these last few days, how haggard the eyes. Sleeping badly, he thought, like everybody else in this damnable business.

Aloud he said: "Why do you think I must know?"

The doctor shrugged. "I don't imagine I went through Bullham yesterday in an invisible cloak. Besides, you'll have seen Coster."

There was none of the inflection of a query in his voice, and Pardoe accepted the statement without hedging.

"Yes, I saw Coster, naturally. And he told me you had doctored his hand for him."

"The fool, he doesn't deserve a hand to be doctored," Faithful burst out with sudden savagery. "And it wouldn't surprise me if he lost it, either. Can't let bad alone but he must make it worse. I put it all right for him on Saturday, and when I saw it yesterday he was wearing a wretched rag of his own, dirty to begin with, I'll be bound.

I gave him a piece of my mind and he was as sulky as the devil. Didn't want me to bandage it again and as much as said he'd have it off so as to get on with his work. Work, the lazy hulk. And I haven't a doubt he'd whipped mine off and had another bit of crawling rag on it the minute my back was turned."

Pardoe listened with interest, and as Faithful paused said quickly: "What time did you see Coster yesterday, Doctor?"

"As near to five-thirty as makes no difference. I saw him first because I had a good many calls to make and you can't be sure of catching these fly-by-nights later." He smiled grimly.

"And when did you leave Bullham?" the inspector asked.

"Haven't I told you I've got no alibi?" the doctor returned testily. "Not a feather of one. Well, here you are. Half the kids in Bullham have got measles, five at the Lockes' all down with it, and I didn't get away finally till after seven. I barged into the storm on the way back. The last house I called at in the village was Mrs. Alder's, so you can check up my departure there, and then I had a spot of trouble with my engine else I'd have been in before that infernal rain."

"Thanks, Doctor. I don't think I'm as keen as you fancy to check up on your time in Bullham. I knew you were there yesterday, but I wasn't so much interested in your alibi—"

"Well, you ought to be then," the doctor broke in, but with a more good-humoured note in his voice. "Haven't I been accused of one murder even before it was done? And now some maniac's chosen to kill this poor, wretched girl at the very hour I'm practically on the spot. Not an accidental choice, you can be sure."

"Perhaps not," said Pardoe. "But I think you know as well as I how much importance we are attaching to those letters. I'm coming to them in a minute. Now I'm going to be frank with you, and I know you understand that what I say is in strict confidence."

Faithful stared at Pardoe with an intentness from which all irritability had vanished. Even Salt, silent in the background, kept his eyes on the inspector, a faint surprise on his face.

"Everything that's ever told me is in strict confidence, I suppose," the doctor replied, "so a bit more shouldn't matter. But don't," he thrust out a protesting hand, "whatever you do, burden me with the responsibility of sharing your murderer's name, for that's more than I can bear at this stage!"

"You're sure it's one murderer then, Doctor?"

Dr. Faithful's eyebrows shot up. "Aren't you?" he countered.

"I'm afraid if I told you that I'd be foisting on you a responsibility you couldn't bear," the inspector said good-humouredly. "So we won't say. No, what I wanted to tell you is this. Underneath the girl's body we found a thumbstall that had evidently been worn."

He motioned to Salt who unlocked a case on a little side-table and handed the stall to Pardoe. The inspector passed it to Faithful.

"What I'm hoping you can tell me is whether this is what Coster was wearing when you saw him on Monday?"

The doctor, looking down at the rag as he twirled it between his fingers, shook his head slowly.

"It isn't. What he had twisted round his hand then was a strip of rag. That," he tossed it contemptuously on the table, "as you can see, has been cut from an old cotton glove."

"I can see that. But this makes it a funnier business still. For if Coster killed the girl, a thumbstall he wasn't wearing found on the body doesn't make sense."

"But it does," the doctor exclaimed, "if you look at it this way! Coster didn't want me to bandage his hand on Monday, and I felt sure he was going to rip it off as soon as I was gone. Suppose he put that stall on afterwards?"

"But he was wearing your dressing when we saw him," the inspector reminded him.

"Of course. He lost the stall, discovered the loss too late, and didn't dare return to look for it. So he restored the bandage."

"It was put on with a professional touch," said Pardoe thoughtfully.

"Mrs. Selby has done first-aid work," Faithful replied curtly. "And here's something else. If Coster meant to kill the girl with his hands he'd have to get rid of my dressing and use a stall."

"That's true," said the inspector. "Which brings me to another point. As a medical man would you say it was possible for Coster to have choked the girl with the force that was used with a hand in that condition?"

The doctor thought for a few moments.

"Yes," he said finally, "he could certainly have done it at the cost of some pain and a risk of reopening the wound. The thumb being in the nature of a lever, and strangulation by the hands being largely dependent on the thumb——" He broke off, took a deep breath, and said more slowly: "However, I wish I'd had the chance to look at his hand that evening when the girl was dead. There might have been indications. But what I said just now about his purpose in using a stall means this was a premeditated murder. And that seems to me out of character for Coster, I must say. I can imagine him killing on impulse but not to a preconceived plan."

"There I'm in entire agreement with you," said Pardoe so heartily that the doctor looked startled.

There was a short silence, and then the inspector, abruptly leaving the subject of George Coster, gave Faithful a concise account of the plan he proposed to put into execution that morning.

The doctor wore a doubtful expression as he listened, so that Pardoe felt impelled to vindicate his scheme.

"It's unorthodox, I know," he said bluntly, "and the morality's questionable. But when they've stopped posting, except," he amended, "for that last effusion yesterday, anonymous letter-writers are notoriously hard to catch by orthodox means. So that's when we resort to the more dubious to do the trick."

The doctor looked up heavily, his black eyes sombre. "You had Brassey's report?" he asked.

"A completely negative one. An expert in graphology, like a sound one in everything else, is well aware of his limitations, and all he could positively say was that the group of letters you handed over to me last week—he's not seen the latest, of course—were written by the same hand. Even sex baffled him, though he thought female."

"All of which we knew," the doctor finished for him. "Well, I'll be there. And let's hope it works."

He went away on a more cheerful note. Pardoe, before leaving to see the lawyer, instructed Salt to return to Bullham either by bus if there was one soon or in Littlejohn's car, outlining what he was to do there.

"Be back at Lacklands at eleven," he told him. "I'll want you."

Mr. Rennie was not in his lodgings close to the cathedral, but at his office ten minutes' walk away. A chubby boy with something of his master's cherubic appearance led Pardoe into a room behind, the cosiness of which seemed enhanced rather than disturbed by the presence of numerous well-dusted law books. The old solicitor accepted so early a visit without surprise. He courteously drew forward a chair and, after expressing his shock at Hetty Park's murder, sat down himself to examine the package his visitor handed to him.

"I am hoping, Mr. Rennie," said Pardoe, "that you can tell me who is the writer of these letters. Perhaps you recognize the hand?"

Minutes elapsed in silence while the old man examined meticulously one faded letter after another. Presently he sat with his head bent over them, eyes and hands still. He seemed oblivious alike of the inspector and his surroundings. Pardoe coughed, and at the sound Mr. Rennie lifted his head and met the eyes of his visitor. His own held disapproval.

"These are the property of my late client," he said gravely, "and as such should be in my possession, particularly as they can have no bearing on her death."

"That is for me to judge," Pardoe said politely. "When I have no further use for them, sir, they will be handed over to you. Meantime, I shall be much obliged if you will tell me whether you can identify the writer."

"Yes, I can," the old man replied reluctantly. "These letters were written by the late Dr. Philip Faithful, Dr. Tom's father."

Pardoe could not conceal his astonishment.

"Dr. Faithful?" he echoed. "Then he was——?"

"Mrs. Lackland's lover," said Mr. Rennie firmly. "Yes. And before any of them came to Minsterbridge."

"But if you knew this when you told me the family history——" Pardoe began reproachfully.

"Hearsay is not fact, Inspector," Mr. Rennie reproved him. "I did not know. But I am very well acquainted with Dr. Philip's handwriting, and these letters confirm the truth of what has been rumoured for many years. But neither of the only two people who were in a position to do so ever honoured me with such confidence, so I did not pretend to knowledge of the story."

"But others here in Minsterbridge knew of it?" Pardoe said a little impatiently.

"Others talked of it," the lawyer corrected him. "Not freely, else Dr. Philip would not have remained the respected practitioner he always was. Long before he died there was no mention of it. It had turned into a worn-out legend about two old people, and there was nobody who thought it worth reviving."

Pardoe thought rapidly. "Were there any additions to the story, I wonder?" he asked. "Did rumour suggest any other favours Mrs. Lackland may have bestowed on the doctor?"

Mr. Rennie looked at him shrewdly, hesitating. "Yes," he admitted quietly, apparently deciding that concealment was no longer expedient. "It was suggested that Mrs. Lackland had helped Dr. Faithful to set up in practice. She had known him in London, you see, when he was not the flourishing practitioner Minsterbridge knew."

Pardoe had one more question. "And do you suppose, Mr. Rennie, that Dr. Tom knows all this?"

The old man smiled a little sadly. "That is not for me to say. Dr. Faithful must have been a mere infant, perhaps not born, when this—this association began. We don't know what his father may eventually have told him, nor what he may have guessed for himself."

He paused, then added surprisingly: "I think, Inspector, if it is at all important, I would ask him if I were in your place."

"I think perhaps I will," said Pardoe.

He was still thinking it over when he left the office for Lacklands. Here at any rate was ample explanation of Mrs. Lackland's proposed legacy for Dr. Faithful. He had not only restored her to health, he was the son of her old lover. But by the time he reached the house he had decided that it was quite unnecessary to put the matter before the doctor.

In the morning room all the members of the household were assembled, as he had asked them to be. Hennessy opened the door to him and then joined the group shepherded by Salt, who had arrived about ten minutes before Pardoe.

They had a curiously artificial air, the inspector thought, waiting in uneasy silence, for they did not know what, in the bright quiet room where sunlight and breeze entered from the garden. Carol, pale and collected enough, sat moodily in an easy chair, her back to the window, but Jenny Hernshaw was standing, talking in undertones to Mrs. Beadle, on whose heavy face disapproval struggled with curiosity and both with a determination to tolerate as best she might these absurd official antics. Emily Bullen sat in another chair, facing Carol. Her prominent eyes were fixed stupidly on the window, at a point much above their level, which gave her the petrified look of a cataleptic. Salt was at a little round table near the bookcase, trying to appear as unobtrusive as was consistent with the wary eye he kept on his collection. He looked up relieved when Pardoe came in and Hennessy placed himself respectfully near the door, a lively interest on his face.

"The doc and Carnowski haven't come yet," he muttered. "Think he'll turn up?"

Pardoe knew he meant the actor.

"Yes," he said shortly. "We'll wait."

He had no objection to waiting. The suspense created by even a short delay might easily prove of value in a tension such as he felt here. The sergeant gave his chair to Pardoe and took up his position by the door after a quiet word to Hennessy, who slipped out.

But not a minute or two had gone by before there were sounds in the hall, the butler's voice and Dr. Faithful's, followed quickly by a third. The doctor's laugh was heard, then the door opened and he and Carnowski came in together, the butler behind them. The actor included them all in a little bow, caught Pardoe's eye without speaking, then moved over to Jenny immediately. They sat down on a small couch near the window, while Mrs. Beadle walked ponderously across to where Hennessy was, and taking a frail chair (by the scruff of the neck, thought Salt, watching her approach with some dismay) lowered herself on to it almost at the sergeant's elbow.

Dr. Faithful lifted a hand in general greeting, smiled at Carol, who did not respond, said: "On time, I hope, Inspector," and took up his position, hands in pockets, close to Pardoe's chair.

Pardoe looked up from the notes he was pretending to consult. But it was Carol whom he addressed.

"There is only one person I miss," he said, "and that is Edith Dawes. Where is she?"

"At home," said Carol briefly. "We had a rude note this morning in which she said she wasn't coming back."

Beyond simulating a faint surprise Pardoe did not acknowledge her remark. He looked from her to Jenny who, under lowered lashes, was steadily regarding the back of her cousin's head. Carnowski was watching Jenny. The servants were both waiting on his own next move. He could not see where Dr. Faithful's attention was drawn, but Emily Bullen still fixed her hungry stare on the window. "A human chain of cat-and-mouse," he thought, and wondered who would pounce first.

"You will be asking yourselves," he said in a detached voice, "why I have wanted you all to meet here at this time. Well, there is something I want each one of you to hear, and it's more economical of time and labour to say it once than to say it many times."

He looked away from the little French clock on which his eyes had been absently fixed, and let his gaze travel coolly from face to face.

"You know from questions that have been put to you in the last few days that somebody has been writing anonymous letters in connection with the death of Mrs. Lackland."

No one spoke in the pause. The room was so quiet it was odd to think it contained so many people.

"For several weeks these letters have been arriving at intervals, insinuating serious charges against one of you. The recipient has handed them all over to the police. Now anonymous letter-writing of a malicious nature is a grave matter at any time. When it happens to treat of murder it is still more grave. I don't think the writer of these letters realizes the dangerous position in which he or she stands."

Again he deliberately stopped speaking. Without moving he scanned every face but the doctor's. Carol was looking down at the toes of her shoes. The expression of the bent still features was hard to read. Jenny, with queer, frightened stare, seemed fascinated at the sight of Emily Bullen, who had abandoned her frozen attitude for a fidgety one, her head turning restlessly from side to side as if she had lost something. Pardoe heard a chair slightly drawn along behind him, and a heavy sigh as the doctor sat down.

"These letters," Pardoe continued with calculated solemnity, "have naturally directed suspicion to their author as the person responsible for Mrs. Lackland's death."

Jenny Hernshaw started forward slightly. Then she sank back again, and Pardoe saw Carnowski's restraining hand on her arm.

"I say this now because the matter has become much more serious since yesterday. For a week or so it appeared that the writer did not intend sending any more letters. But yesterday morning another was received, again by the same person, and today—" he repeated with emphasis, "today the police themselves—"

He broke off again, fumbling in his breast pocket.

"I have a letter which came this morning——"

He got no further.

There was a hoarse cry, half shout, half scream. Emily Bullen was on her feet, rage and terror convulsing her face. She raised clenched hands to the level of her breast and shook them impotently.

"It's a lie!" she shouted thickly. "I never wrote to the police—I never wrote a letter yesterday—I haven't written any of my letters since last week! And if the——" she spat a filthy epithet at Dr. Faithful, "says I did, he's a liar too!"

The quiet of the room seemed all at once to have cracked into pandemonium. The doctor was so quickly on his feet he almost kicked over his chair. Both girls had sprung up, Carnowski too. Mrs. Beadle had moved towards Emily Bullen with astonishing agility for one of her bulk, but she hung back now, daunted by the look of demoniacal fury on the companion's face. Only Pardoe remained seated.

"So it was you who wrote the letters?" Pardoe said in a gently conversational tone, his eyes steady on those of the possessed woman confronting him. But for all the glare in them he had the idea she did not really see him.

Suddenly she began to pour out in a low voice a torrent of foul language directed at nobody in particular. At that Pardoe got up, and as he did so Salt went over to her and caught her arm tightly.

"Enough of that," he said roughly. "You come out of here."

At the grasp on her arm she crumpled at once, changing from a red-faced fury to a cringing, pitiful creature that shook from head to foot and would have fallen but for the sergeant's grip. She began to moan in tearless fashion, and at the sound the cook started to cry weakly.

"Now, Beadle," Jenny Hernshaw said, and taking her arm in a strong clasp began to lead her towards the door. Her own voice trembled a little, though she was keeping her self-possession better than her cousin. Carol looked white, sick and repelled by the hideous little scene. She made no attempt to move until Pardoe addressed her peremptorily.

"Miss Quentin, will you be good enough to go with the sergeant and see that Miss Bullen is taken to her room?"

She went, though there was no readiness in her compliance, and the little procession moved slowly out, Bullen supported almost entirely by Salt, her feet scuffing against the floor. The inspector intercepted a questioning glance from the doctor who had stood his ground quietly, an uneasy, embarrassed figure.

"It will be all right, I think," Pardoe replied to his unspoken question. "She must have a doctor, and in her present state she isn't likely to pay any more attention to you than to the rest of us."

He looked round the room, so queerly hushed all at once. Only the men remained in it: Dr. Faithful at his elbow, Carnowski an immobile figure at the window, his back and a little of an enigmatic profile alone visible; Hennessy still by the door, the play of expression on his face oddly at contrast with his silence and unmoving pose. Like the Roman soldier at Pompeii, thought Pardoe with almost light-headed irrelevance. He felt a sudden incongruous gaiety. Things were working out exactly as he had hoped.

"I'd be glad if she could be got to bed and quieted, Doctor," he said. "There's very little I shall say to her now, but I must see her for a few minutes. She's not to be left alone. Miss Hernshaw or Miss Quentin had better stop in the room. Well, it worked, didn't it?"

The doctor suddenly smiled at him with a touch of derision.

"It certainly did. Poor devil." He sighed shortly. "And now nothing remains for you but to arrest the murderer, Inspector." He did not trouble to conceal the contempt in his voice.

Pardoe looked straight at him. But though his attention was wholly on the doctor he was aware from the corner of his eye of movement elsewhere. Carnowski, he was sure, had turned from the window and was surveying them both.

"Nothing. But not immediately," Pardoe replied without rancour.

"Isn't the best part of a week long enough for Scotland Yard then?" Faithful baited him.

"Rarely. In any case I'm going fishing this evening, and an arrest for murder would be a bad prelude, wouldn't it?"

The doctor laughed. "Dammit, man, don't remind me of the Highland trout I've missed this wretched week!"

Pardoe felt Carnowski's eyes on him but he would not look at the actor. It seemed to him suddenly that he and Doctor Faithful were repeating lines learned for an essential bit of play-acting.

"My apologies, Doctor," he said. "It's true I'd forgotten about that holiday of yours. I suppose you're thinking I've been the one to have it instead. Well, I've been walking by your river a few evenings, and that quiet bit of water on the bend by Barr's Meadow—isn't that what they call it?—takes my eye."

The doctor was regarding him with more amusement than scorn.

"It's pretty fair. At twilight, when the lovers have all gone. Well, I must take a look at my patient. Good luck to your fishing."

Hennessy opened the door for him. The butler, however, had eyes for nobody but Pardoe.

"Shall you be needing me any more, sir?" he asked formally.

Pardoe shook his head. "There's nothing else now, Hennessy. You can go."

When Hennessy had gone, Pardoe for the first time met Carnowski's eyes. The actor was looking at him unwinkingly, his gaze brilliant and burning.

"Are you a fisherman too, Mr. Carnowski?" the inspector inquired.

Carnowski did not smile. "I? No, I do not fish," was all he said softly.

When Pardoe had left him he still stood by the window, looking out on the garden once more with a kind of sombre excitement on his face.

Upstairs Emily Bullen lay still dressed on her bed. She was whimpering softly. There was nothing formidable about her now, nothing malign. Her mind, as she stirred restlessly and shuddered from time to time, was totally incapable of grasping the situation in which she lay trapped or even of realizing the fears that endangered her sanity. They drifted about her, formless but all the more menacing.

Dr. Faithful behaved admirably. This was a patient, not a woman who for weeks had been doing her best to get him hanged. He found Salt near the door of her bedroom, and inside, to his surprise, not Carol but Jenny. He stayed only a minute or two.

"She's suffering from severe shock, a bad nervous breakdown," he told Jenny briskly. "You must get her undressed. Keep her quiet. Don't let her be worried. I'll send something round directly."

Jenny was standing at the other side of the bed. "She's been very upset since the storm," she said in a low voice.

He noticed that she did not meet his eyes but kept her gaze on Bullen. He gave her a penetrating look before turning away. At the door he met Pardoe.

"She's not to be bothered," he said sharply. "I'll send something along that will make her sleep."

One glance at the shivering wreck on the bed showed Pardoe the impossibility of questioning her. He suggested that Jenny should get Mrs. Beadle's help in putting her to bed, and was about to go away again when the girl came quickly over to the door.

"I want to tell you something—outside, Inspector." Her tone was urgent.

He drew her out without speaking, and closed the door. Salt stared at the flush on her brown cheeks.

"It's this," she said hurriedly before Pardoe could speak. "She's only said one thing since she came up here. Carol heard her, and then I did. She said: 'He asked Jenny to marry him.' It seems to be on her mind."

"And what does she mean?" the inspector asked quietly.

Jenny met his gaze candidly. "She's talking of the time Dr. Faithful proposed marriage to me. A year ago. It must have been on her mind ever since. That's why she was so odd. I think—she was—I think she must have been in love with him."

Salt looked the incredulity he felt, but Pardoe showed no surprise.

"Did your grandmother know the doctor had asked you to marry him?" he questioned her irrelevantly.

"No. It's odd that Bullen didn't tell her when she found out. She kept nothing from her as a rule. But she couldn't have done so, else I know Grandma would have spoken to me about it."

Across Barr's Meadow the cathedral bells chimed the quarter after nine. Their unhurried voices were the only sounds to deepen the silence of the evening, unless the lap of water against the stems of the willows, a little intimate chuckle from the river now and again, could count as sound.

For an angler who professed some ardour for his sport Inspector Pardoe looked singularly uninterested. In matters piscatorial, that is. He was sitting on a steep point of the bank just before it dipped abruptly to a ditch of nettles and a stile at the side of the ditch. Rod, line and basket lay close beside him. At his back a small stream between deep banks thickly hung with alder and thorn and the foliage of last month's dog-roses bisected the meadow crookedly. In the twilight its tree-guarded curves seemed to embrace curious shadows. Pardoe's gaze was directed for the most part away from the river, though now and again he looked down at the gently flowing water below him, skimmed by the gnats that had been dancing deliriously since the sun set half an hour ago. He was hatless, his prematurely white hair caught by the sunless light that still lingered. There was something taut and expectant in the lines of his face, and at the same time a faintly deprecatory quirk at the corners of his lips as though he were secretly laughing at himself.

It grew damp as the last of the sun's warmth drained from the sky. A thin mist crept like a breath through the grass. A sudden nimble breeze set the water clapping dully against the willow roots. Pardoe got to his feet and took a step or two across the grass in the direction of the stream. Then turning he picked up his rod and again walked slowly towards the trees. The water they sheltered was invisible from the meadow. It ran in a deep channel and its course, until you were actually on the bank, looked merely like a crooked boundary of trees running the width of the meadow. On the other side, parallel to the river, a lane ran to join the highroad to Minsterbridge a quarter of a mile away.

Pardoe's step was noiseless on the moist grass. He kept his eyes on the trees as he strolled towards them. His mind reverted to Salt. He wondered where the sergeant was at that moment. Perhaps—

He did not stop in his tracks, though in that instant he could have sworn a face had appeared for the fragment of a minute between the boles of the trees. Immediately an unseen blackbird gave a loud mirthless chuckle and whirred among the branches. Pardoe pushed quietly between some bramble bushes, top-heavy with unripe berries, and found himself on a high bank of crumbling sand about four feet above the stream. Among the trees dusk turned suddenly to night. Here was no sound except the mysterious one of running water. He stood still, every sense alert, a frown between his brows. Something odd had happened. The face he was positive had looked at him for a fleeting moment had been the face of Carnowski.

He turned his head to the left where a few yards further on the stream curved boldly towards him. At the bend a two-plank foot-bridge spanned it. In a gap between thorn bushes he caught a glimpse of a gate in the hedge bordering the lane. He started to walk slowly towards it along the crown of the bank. Trees brushed him lingeringly, and twice he thought he heard a rustle to the right of him, but that was on the far side of the stream and he did not turn his head. Here it was quiet. Quiet as death.

Then everything seemed to happen at once. He noticed the gate into the lane standing half open; it had been closed just now. In the moment that he saw it his rod was almost snatched out of his hand.

He half-turned in a flash, to find it caught in a tangle of wild clematis. As he went to pull it free the very bushes seemed suddenly to close upon him. Simultaneously there were running feet, Salt's shout, a tearing and crackling of boughs, heavy breathing that seemed close against his ear, a figure that with raised arm assumed superhuman proportions, and at the side of his head a savage searing pain that slowly took possession of him. Then the loud voice of Dr. Faithful, and the sound of a desperate struggle abruptly silenced.

As the trees reeled languidly away from him, like those seen from a train window, and the sandy ground tilted upwards, his last memory before blackness whelmed his senses was of Carnowski's hands upon him and the actor's face, somehow larger than life, staring into his own.

Chapter XVIII

TRUE BILL

So then,—spight of my Care and Foresight,
I am caught, caught in my security.

Congreve: *The Double Dealer*

O ne evening, a fortnight later, Chief Inspector Pardoe, still on the sick list and to his disgust not yet fit to take his Cotswold holiday, was sufficiently recovered from Dr. Faithful's murderous attack on him to discuss the case with Sergeant Salt. He had not been out since what had almost proved his last adventure in Barr's Meadow at Minsterbridge, and this was the first protracted call Salt had made on him at his Knightsbridge flat.

At the moment Pardoe seemed inclined to accept without protest the sergeant's rebukes for his reticence in the closing stages of the case.

"And how was I to know," Salt grumbled, "just what you had up your sleeve? Lucky it was for you, an' me, you let me into it before the end, else sure enough I'd have nabbed the wrong 'un!"

"You mustn't blame me for that bit," Pardoe said quickly. "I couldn't have foreseen that Carnowski was going to assume the role of protector and attend my fishing party too, could I? I never knew all that he and Jenny suspected all along and unfortunately kept to themselves. I told you these family cases were the very devil. Nothing but misplaced loyalty to that murdering little cousin of hers kept her quiet on a good many points."

"Who'd 've thought," said Salt with heavy bitterness, "that that yellow-haired Quentin doll could be hand-in-glove with a devil like Faithful and keep us all guessing?"

"'Mm," Pardoe agreed. "I won't say she's worse than he is. She isn't. But she's more cold-blooded, and ultimately she can keep her head better. You've told me Faithful gave in directly when he thought she'd split on him, but when you told her the same story about him she wasn't having any, eh?"

"That's right. She wouldn't talk. There's nothing human about her, if you ask me."

"There isn't about a good many of the people in this story. Mind if I run through the evidence we've got against our man?"

"Mind?" Salt echoed. "I'm still playing blind man's buff."

Pardoe smiled. "Well, here's what happened. First, this case would have been over in half the time if two pieces of knowledge had come my way at the beginning instead of at the end. I mean the fact that Dr. Faithful was the son of Mrs. Lackland's old lover, and that he'd made a proposal of marriage to Jenny Hernshaw a year ago and been turned down.

"The first would have told me that there was every chance of his knowing from his father the financial situation at Lacklands, for we've the evidence of the letters Edith handed over that the old man knew what Mrs. Lackland was worth, and profited by the knowledge in his practice. And the second would have let me know that Dr. Faithful was anxious to marry an heiress. He wasn't in love with her. Jenny came to see me yesterday and brought Carnowski with her. She never liked the doctor, she says, and he knew it. He showed her no particular affection, paid her no little attentions, simply approached her with an offer of marriage, thinking no doubt she'd jump at it as a way out of her unhappy existence at Lacklands. Well, she had the wisdom to refuse him.

"Then he had to think of something else. He's a man of ambitions and arrogance amounting to megalomania. By hook or by crook he meant to have a picking of John Lackland's fortune, and the germ of that determination must have been planted by his knowledge of his father's relations with the family. His own constant connection with them, a sort of daily hobnobbing with wealth out of his grasp that he wanted to apply to his own advancement, only fostered the resolve. So when Jenny turned him down—she says he appeared to take it in good part—he gave his attention to Carol Quentin."

"Wonder why he didn't ask her first?" Salt remarked.

Pardoe shrugged. "I guess he knew her too well. She'd be an uneasy partner. Jenny's got a fine, staunch character. She's good through and through, and he knew sterling stuff. Carnowski's a lucky fellow."

He mused for a minute. "Well, you've examined those locked drawers in Carol's room and found some of the doctor's letters when he was away before. Cautious enough, and written long before murder was planned, but quite enough to show that the Quentin–Faithful alliance began months ago and that marriage was being planned back in the winter. I don't know how at first they proposed to get the old lady's blessing. Her consent was essential to Carol's inheritance. Faithful had a lot of influence with her and his overweening vanity may have led him to suppose that it would be an easy matter to get round her. I don't know. But what did happen in April was Mrs. Lackland's illness."

Pardoe paused. Salt looked at him with a puzzled expression.

"Why didn't he let her die? Easy enough then, I'd say."

"Because he was too clever," Pardoe said simply. "Early this summer he could have caused her death through neglect or even some more positive means very difficult to bring home to him so long as he gave a certificate of death. But that didn't suit his purpose. For one thing, Faithful's an extremely interesting case of dual personality. He's a murderer. He's also a gifted man of science with his heart in his job. Professional pride in restoring her to health was undoubtedly involved. Besides, I think he knew quite early that she proposed leaving him her money but hadn't made the will clinching it. Perhaps too with all his familiarity with the family's business he wasn't sure then what the actual amount was. Anyway at first it was wait and see.

"Then the whole brilliant scheme came to him. If she died during her illness and he married Carol afterwards, there *might*, who knows, have been insinuations later, unsupported by evidence, it's true, but damaging to an ambitious doctor. Why not nurse her back to health and then kill her by a means that any intelligent reasoning would say pointed to anybody rather than to her doctor as the murderer? So there wasn't to be the slightest attempt to make the death look either natural or suicidal. He would save—merely to destroy.

"Then several things intervened. And each one of them was seized by Faithful and made instrumental to his purpose. He's a supreme opportunist, Salt. A villain on the grand scale. Bold and subtle at the same time, with the gambler's instincts developed to the full. Carnowski was in love with Jenny? Very well, that romance should serve his turn. I've no doubt that he and Carol fostered it all they could. Carol would have welcomed Carnowski to the house, and the doctor would have dropped a word in the old woman's ear that a fast film actor was pursuing Jenny. Then quarrels, bad feeling, the chance to involve Carnowski in the final mess.

"The next thing was the anonymous letters. If the old lady's murder was ever in doubt before, Emily Bullen turned that doubt to certainty when she started her campaign. She muddled the issues tremendously, and was for a time the best ally the doctor had. Get this clear. She knew nothing about any intent to murder. Her intervention was purely fortuitous. She's a poor, repressed, unhealthy creature who was nourishing a secret and totally unrequited passion for the doctor. Somehow she got to know he had proposed to Jenny. Probably it was a mystery to her how any woman could refuse him. I expect she then made some timid advances herself which Faithful either ignored or more probably never recognized. It preyed on her mind, bullied as she was and starved of all affection. She started to hate Faithful, and thought she'd get a kick out of watching his reactions to a few anonymous letters. That's all there was to it. That's all there usually is to that form of sport. What was the date of the first letter?"

"June 12th," Salt replied.

"Yes. And five days before that the morphia was supposed to have been stolen. It never was, of course. I'll come to that in a minute. What I mean is, five days before he got her first letter the doctor was preparing for murder at some future date. That letter must have shaken him up a bit. Think of it, Salt, the confounded coincidence. She wrote that knowing nothing of the truth, yet to Faithful it must have seemed as if the first step he'd taken had been discovered. He held his hand for a bit then—and the letters went on coming. He got his brain to work on it, kept his head, and realized that nobody short of a mind-reader could possibly know anything of his intentions. So, as with everything else, he used those letters for his own profit. A weaker man would have cried the whole thing off. He took the inconceivably bold step of handing over to the police letters accusing him of a crime of which he was guilty! With the inevitable result: he was the last to be suspected."

"What about the morphia?" the sergeant asked.

"Let me come to that in a minute. It was partly the cause of Faithful's undoing. But first there's the other thing that happened in July. Mrs. Lackland told Rennie she meant to leave the doctor all her own money. She told Faithful too, and he knew the day the will would be drawn up, because it rested with him when she should see her lawyer.

"Now comes his master-stroke." Pardoe leaned forward eagerly. "It was brilliant. He decided to kill the old lady on the eve of the change of will which was to make him sole legatee of fifteen thousand! What could shout his innocence more loudly? He was willing to sacrifice a fortune because he was aiming at one a dozen times greater. That he would secure by marrying Carol. And if he could get the crime brought home to Jenny and Carnowski, so much the better—Carol would then inherit Jenny's share too."

"So what does he do? In a medicine bottle exactly similar to the one Mrs. Lackland was using, except that he forgot or never noticed

245 Postscript to Poison

hers had a conspicuously stained label, he prepared one dose heavily laced with morphia. Substitution of one bottle for the other would be an easy matter after he had given her a dose out of the harmless one. He was a conjurer anyway. He was freely using his handkerchief that hot afternoon. He was engaging the old lady in the deferential sort of conversation she loved. Hey presto, the thing was done. And for us, of course, there was a fine tangle. We were working all the time on the theory that the bottle we had was the bottle which had contained Mrs. Lackland's medicine the last few days. I told you that if we could find out why the morphine was in the bottle before it got into the glass we should be a fair way to solving the problem. And the answer was the simplest possible: a different bottle."

"And the prints were wiped off," Salt put in, "because it was Quentin who gave it her?"

"Exactly. They'd hoped it would be Jenny. But she refused to take it when Jenny went up, through sheer perversity of course because the girl was in her bad books. Carol *had* therefore to be the one to administer it. So she gave it her when she went upstairs later that evening. But the bottle probably wasn't wiped till Faithful came in the middle of the night and found the old lady dying. Then he used his handkerchief on it, was careful to leave his own prints clear as daylight, and so further confused the issue and strengthened the impression of his own innocence."

"And it was Hetty who saw Carol upstairs that night?" said the sergeant.

Pardoe's mouth hardened. "Yes, it was Hetty. The cook's told you since how the girl was up there at the linen cupboard just about that time. Remember it was at the corner of the passage leading to Mrs. Lackland's room. We shall never know, unless Quentin tells, exactly what happened. She must though have seen her coming from the room, perhaps with the devilish look on her face Jenny has told me she surprised there more than once when Carol was looking at her and thought she didn't know. There may even have been words

Hetty overheard. Anyway, she knew something that she interpreted rightly very soon afterwards and that she was afraid to put even in a letter to her mother.

"Now look at this, Salt. It's what first put me on to Carol Quentin. What does she do directly she comes downstairs from murdering her grandmother but tell Beadle Hetty Park's sacked? Sacked for eavesdropping was the explanation. Yet on Carol's own admission *only* Mrs. Lackland could dismiss a servant. If anybody else did such a thing it was tantamount to restoring that servant to the full favour of the old lady. So what? Carol, who had seen her in a place and at a time that might very well prove fatal, calmly dismissed Hetty *because she knew Mrs. Lackland would be dead before morning*."

"Why d'you think they waited till the Monday to kill the girl?" Salt asked.

"For two pretty good reasons at least. One inside murder was enough for the time being. They daren't risk a second they hadn't prepared. And there was Coster at Bullham. I think Quentin frightened the girl into silence here, partly by the bluff of half-accusing her of complicity in Mrs. Lackland's death by being upstairs just then, and making her think the police would be only too quick to jump on her for it. But they guessed her tongue would be loosened once she was home. Faithful had four or five days to plan the second crime. And there was Coster all ready and waiting to fix that murder on."

"And Mrs. Selby had never done any bandaging to him, she said," Salt interposed.

"No. That thumbstall evidence was a piece of dangerous over-elaboration on the doctor's part. His second worst mistake. But he was reckless by then. He couldn't endure suspense. He made the common and fatal error of decorating his crimes in the hope of bringing them home to other roosts. Of course Coster was wearing the stall when Faithful called on Monday. Not the bit of rag the doctor described. But when Coster saw that stall in our possession he wouldn't admit it for fear of incriminating himself. And the doctor *couldn't* admit the truth, of course, since Coster with a properly bandaged hand wouldn't have planted the stall there himself, and if it wasn't he then it left only the doctor who could have done it. So Faithful had to pretend that Coster had taken the dressing off again so as to commit the murder."

Pardoe paused before adding: "And it was Coster carrying on with Mrs. Selby that occasioned the quarrel between him and Hetty."

Salt nodded. "Ah. A fellow who had all the luck Faithful got didn't need to add bits of his own."

"They always do. And you've got to remember that what we're calling luck were the circumstances he had the brains to use. There wasn't a thing he hadn't the wits to make serve him. Look at the way he handled move after move so as to pile a whole lot of cumulative evidence in his favour. Mass-suggestion, so to speak, of his innocence. He engaged rooms right enough for that holiday in Scotland *and* got a locum, knowing all the time he wouldn't be leaving Minsterbridge. The patient whose recovery was such a credit to him dies during convalescence on the very eve of leaving him a fortune. He refuses a certificate and notifies the coroner. He gives the police the letters accusing him of killing Mrs. Lackland. In short, he establishes his innocence upon a rock—and then what does he do?"

"Writes a letter to himself," Salt replied promptly.

"Yes. He was worked up about Hetty's murder, he was very cocksure of himself by then, and at the same time he wanted to divert my attention from the girl's disappearance. So he wrote a letter to himself—and committed the minor mistake first of handing it to me unopened. Any man's natural curiosity in such a matter would have compelled him to read it at once. I'll go so far as to say that only a man who already knew the contents wouldn't have read it. There isn't anything gained by passing on an envelope unslit, but a murderer anxious to pile up evidence in his own favour might think there was.

"So he wrote his letter. And made his major mistake—by adding that postscript."

"That morphia business got me muddled," Salt admitted as Pardoe fell silent, a grim little smile on his lips.

"Yes. Well, it was a weak story he told in the first place—the theft of morphine tablets from his bag left in the car outside Lacklands. Its only strength—which is a weakness if you look at it one way—lay in the fact that it could hardly be refuted. But ask yourself, how could anybody else intent on killing Mrs. Lackland *know* that Dr. Faithful was carrying morphine round that day? They couldn't have spared time to rummage there and then, risking discovery any minute, *yet whoever took them didn't steal the case itself.* So the thief, besides being able to recognize the morphine as such, must have known the tablets were there. The only person to know this positively was Dr. Faithful.

"You see, it was the kind of preliminary step in the crime which committed him to nothing but might prove valuable. If for some reason or other Mrs. Lackland was not murdered after all, his report of loss of morphine back in June could do no possible harm. If, on the other hand, he carried out his intention, the very fact that he had brought the matter to the notice of the police, weeks before, told heavily in his favour. Pure fabrication that tale, and those tablets planted on Jenny, probably by Carol.

"Even then he couldn't let the thing alone. He must add to his faked anonymous message a P.S. referring to the theft. But he had already assured me that he had never mentioned the loss to anyone. The police—taking a hint from Faithful—had not given a specific name to what they inquired about. None of the previous anonymous letters had shown any knowledge of it. And what's more, I had Dr. Faithful's word that he would continue to keep the loss a secret. So, on his own admission, he alone had the knowledge that could have prompted that postscript."

"Unless somebody else had stole the stuff and done the murder," Salt said.

"And wrote the letters then," Pardoe countered. "We went through that before, that poison-pen wasn't the murderer. The doctor, on his principle of seizing every bull by the horns, obliged us by himself pointing out the weaknesses in any theory that identified murderer as poison-pen. It's right too. You'd find it much harder to account for a single perpetrator than for two. Apart from the utterly wrong psychology involved if one person only had been at the bottom of it, remember the wording of the last letter—the last genuine one, I mean—where 'slow poisoning' is mentioned. That came less than twelve hours before Mrs. Lackland was murdered. There is nothing in it to imply the writer knew the old lady's end was near. In fact, the inference to be drawn is an entirely different one. Emily Bullen expected to go on enjoying herself writing those letters for an indefinite time to come, and when Mrs. Lackland died the next morning and the police were called in, nobody in the case got a greater shock than she did."

"Why d'you think Quentin kept the doc's letters?" the sergeant asked with sudden irrelevance. "He wasn't such a catch, was he, that she'd have wanted him for breach?"

"No. He, not she, was the one who stood to gain by that match. But it was he who enlightened Carol as to her financial position, and long before he thought of murder, the girl's shrewd calculations probably warned her that the doctor was after the money more than he was after her. That being so, it wasn't likely he would want to wait for it indefinitely, and she at any rate couldn't visualize a marriage being brought about by any but crooked means. So she meant to keep whatever evidence she had involving him. Remember those letters were written last autumn when the doctor was enjoying his annual holiday, months before Mrs. Lackland's illness and in the first flush of the proposal when he supposed Carol thought him in love with her.

"No, if he'd planned murder then he'd have cut off his right hand rather than write her a line. But Carol must always have seen the necessity for dirty work—*otherwise she would never have accepted him.*"

"How d'you make that out?" Salt asked curiously.

"You said yourself he was no catch. Barring his sexual attraction, he wasn't, to an heiress. But Carol wanted the money, and her freedom, and she knew that marrying the doctor meant a speeding up of what she wanted. Why? Because he wanted it too, and he wouldn't wait. She knew him well enough for that. And the only logical answer to their joint impatience was—murder.

"When the old lady fell ill in the spring Carol must have thought the solution was at hand. But she went on keeping his letters. And she had locks put on the drawers containing them. They were pretty important to her, you see."

"Well, everything worked well for 'em until the end," Salt said.

"Yes. Even Hernshaw's uninvited entry. Jenny, of course, confided in Carol about her father, and Carol, with the doctor's approval, must have encouraged the secrecy for all she was worth. It would tell against Jenny in the end if suspicion, as they hoped, came to rest on her. And it was Carol, of course, who let Jenny in that night Mrs. Lackland heard them whispering and frightened Bullen with her inquiries."

"What about that other illness the old woman had one day the week before?"

Pardoe shrugged. "It could have been genuine, from over-indulgence, as Faithful described. But seeing it happened the day she quarrelled with Jenny I'd say it was worked to look black against the girl when murder was really done."

"I had to pretend to have a down on Jenny. I had to pretend to take Carol into my confidence and exclude her cousin. It was the surest way to keep Jenny safe. Else they wouldn't have scrupled to kill her and frame it as the suicide of the guilty party."

"The devils," Salt said softly.

"Edith Dawes was safe enough," Pardoe went on. "All she'd reported in the house was that she told the police there was something she couldn't remember. And she said that to Bullen who was in terror on her own account and so shut Edith up. She was afraid what she was trying to recall might be connected with her."

"Brassey says the letter with the postscript wasn't done by the same hand."

"I know. What's more, I have an idea Bullen sent the doctor at least one letter we never saw. He'd have kept it to copy her style of lettering."

"It was Faithful you thought was waiting for us at Littlejohn's office after we'd found Hetty Park's body, wasn't it?" the sergeant asked.

Pardoe smiled. "Yes, it was. I knew his methods by then. As a matter of fact it was no later than next morning he was trying to make capital out of his lack of alibi, which he argued to himself must be proof enough of innocence at that stage of the affair. Would a murderer dare commit his second murder with the police swarming round and no alibi? He did. Ergo, says Dr. Faithful, I'm innocent.

"And it was he who rang up Carnowski from a kiosk. Too much elaboration again. Jenny says it was Faithful advised her to drop a hint to Carnowski not to telephone because the police were keeping track of his calls."

"Why didn't Jenny Hernshaw let you on to what she guessed?"

"Fear, uncertainty, and loyalty to Carol. She sensed Carol wasn't feeling good towards her. Once she'd seen Bullen tracing out capital letters which she hid hurriedly. She thought about that. That was why she was odd when Littlejohn questioned her about the letters. But she didn't want to bring suspicion on either Carol or Bullen when she wasn't sure of anything. And at one time she was afraid for Carnowski when she thought he was trying to put us off the scent."

"Well," said Salt, "they all made some bloomers at last, thanks be."

"Yes, Carol too. Remember the morning before we found Hetty's body? She told me Dr. Faithful wanted to see me, and, 'he had another anonymous letter this morning,' she said. *Another anonymous letter*. And only the doctor and ourselves were supposed to know that he was the recipient. That slip told me she was in his confidence."

"All the way in," said Salt. "He's chucked in the sponge completely since we made him think she'd given him away."

252 Dorothy Bowers

Pardoe looked thoughtful. "'Mm. Good for us he has. It would still be an uphill fight if he'd kept his mouth shut. The business of the bottle, for instance. Evidence of that stain rests only on Edith's memory, and Jenny Hernshaw's now she's been reminded. The attack on me would take a bit of explaining, of course. But you'll see, Salt, Faithful will keep *nothing* back. He's an exhibitionist. Now he's found out he's proud of his guilt. And he'll have to boast about it."

He smiled suddenly. "D'you know what tripped him at last?"

Salt stared.

"Time," said Pardoe. "His cleverness asked for quick results— from us. The arrest of the wrong person and the closing of the case. He couldn't wait for anything. He had to relax. So he had to be still more clever, and still more clever, so as to be able to bear the suspense. Time doesn't necessarily tell against us. Ten to one it's the undoing of the other side."

THE END

*Also available from Moonstone Press
by Dorothy Bowers*

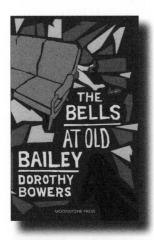

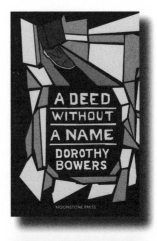

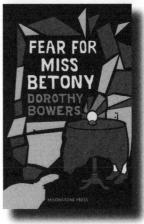